Becoming

SAM WYATT

Jeremy Greene

PRESS

Author Bio:

Jeremy Greene lives in Mission, BC with his wife and children.

Dedication:

This book is dedicated to Maureen Greene, my most cherished gift from God, my partner, and the entire reason anything I do goes anywhere

Author's Note:

This book is a work of fiction. All characters have been made up with two exceptions. There really is a Joshua House drug and alcohol recovery ministry for men which is run by Richard and Angie Korkowski, but it's not in Vancouver as the book suggests. It is in Abbotsford, BC, and I am sure they would welcome any donations one might be inspired to leave. You can find them at www.yahwehsavesrecovery.ca

The other real person is Angus, the 'giant of a man' who walked across Canada with an enormous cross. The story has always impressed me, and it just seemed too incredible to change the names or the facts, and I only hope my description of the event hit close to the actual facts.

Prologue

I looked at the clock. Then back to the exam. A lot of that went on during exams, it seemed. Clock watching. Time management. It was 2:30 and the exam would end at 3:00. I was done so I wasn't as concerned about the clock as I would be if I still had more to do. I was in the "review" stage of the test, but I wasn't really reviewing. I was just sitting there, thankful I was finished, even more thankful that I thought I had done okay, and still even more thankful that this was the last exam of my final year at the British Columbia Institute of Technology, or BCIT.

It had been a grueling two year program that had consumed me on every level. I struggled in school in general. Not for lack of brains, I think, but more from an interest level. School bored me. I was much more interested in real life experiences. Doing stuff. Not sitting around in classrooms and lecture halls learning about things I had little interest in and doubted very much I would ever use in real life. The net result was I wasn't a strong student. It was challenging for me to stay disciplined, get the work done, stay current with the information, and pass all the exams. My goal was certainly not to be any sort of star. Nope, my goal was just to finish. And there were times when I wasn't all that honest about how I did it. I did a little plagiarizing, a little copying of assignments, and a little looking over my neighbor's shoulder during exams. Not much, mind you. I did have a moral compass. But a little. I mean, it was a hard program! And it seemed as if everyone was compromising themselves just a little bit in order to get the workload done. Honestly, I just wanted to pass the courses and graduate.

Education had been strongly recommended in my family. So even though I didn't really know what I wanted to do with my life, didn't enjoy school and didn't want to do it, I did at least recognize I needed to have an education and I wanted to please my parents. I ended up in the Business Administration program because it seemed to me several career options would be available, and there seemed to be at least a number of "softer" courses involved compared to the more difficult courses like, say, Economics.

It was the Economics exam I had just finished. I knew I didn't ace it. I seldom aced exams. But I was pretty good at knowing if I landed just above the 50% mark or just below, and I was feeling good about this one. Plus, I now had two years of observing BCIT procedures, and felt like I knew that they didn't fail anyone who had already made it this far unless the wheels had come completely off. With the hardest exam for last, I now felt extremely confident I would soon be an official graduate of BCIT, diploma in hand and ready for the next chapter of life.

I wasn't sure what the next chapter of life held for me. One thing I felt pretty sure about: I was going to "sow a few wild oats" before looking for a career type job. This had been widely discussed with my parents and friends, and everyone seemed to agree that taking some time to wind down, do some travelling, take in an adventure or two, or just take a summer off wasn't a bad idea, which was great, because one, I wanted to wind down after doing this program, and two, there were definitely things I wanted to do before hunkering down into a serious career. Things like travelling. Maybe Europe. Maybe the Southern States which always fascinated me.

But I hadn't made any specific plans. Most of all thoughts had been focused on concentrating on school with any spare time spent trying to drink away the stress. And as I sat here in the lecture hall with the clock ticking on towards 3:00 P.M., I could feel the feelings of elation beginning to replace the feelings of stress and mental fatigue. I looked quickly around the hall and could see various members of my set among the hundred or so in the program and knew we were all more than ready to go celebrate as soon as this was done. The plan had been in place for the after final exam party for several weeks now. The first destination was The Villa Pub, a beer parlor in the Sheraton Hotel down the street a block or two, the destination of choice for all students who liked to party. And after a rather late start into the world of "tipping a few" I was now blossoming into a person who didn't mind a drink.

People started to head down the stairs, exams in hand, dropping them on the monitored table in the front. And I was beginning to hear some loud noises coming from outside the hall as people were letting out whoops of joy as soon as they got through the doors. A guy from my set came down the stairs on the aisle closest to me and gave me a knowing wink and smile and I returned the look. Yup, school was done, this chapter finished, and I felt awesome. My whole life was ahead of me and I couldn't wait to live it out to the max.

I got up and made my way down the stairs to the front of the room. BCIT had been one hard program. I was feeling both satisfaction at having done it, and exuberance at moving on. I had worked hard, harder than I had at anything in my entire life. And I definitely felt entitled and deserving of any rich rewards ahead. Okay life, what's in store now?

BECOMING SAM WYATT

PART ONE

IN

*"Having lost all sensitivity, they have given themselves over
to sensuality, so as to indulge in every kind of impurity,
and they are full of greed."*

Chapter 1

*C*rack pipes weren't indestructible, at least not the garden variety ones. Really, they were just glass stems with a small ball of stainless steel scrubber found around most kitchen sinks stuffed into one end. This would be referred to as "brillo" of which the crack is placed on and burned through as it turns to smoke and gets inhaled into one's lungs. After repeated uses, which happens when one smokes crack, and the constant picking it up and putting it down, and with all the changes in temperature, they tend to start to chip, crack, and generally break down.

Mine was now not more than three inches long, less than half the size of when it started its life. And the brillo was nothing more than a charred miniature ball of soot. Yet it didn't stop me from carefully pulling it out, placing it on a piece of paper and carefully trying to stretch it out and scrape any crack particles that may have somehow, beyond any law of science, not already been burned through the countless previous efforts to extract more crack.

I found a stick, small enough to go inside what was left of the pipe and firm enough to apply some pressure to it, and I tried to scrape off any residual crack that had built up on the inside of the pipe. The dust scrapings from both brillo and pipe were collected into the middle of the paper, and put to the side. I rolled the brillo back into a ball, stuffed it back into the end of the pipe, took the paper with the dust and sprinkled it carefully onto the brillo, careful to keep it in the middle and not lose it down the edges. Then, oh so carefully, I lifted the pipe up vertically and dropped my face underneath it and used my lighter to light the end and carefully tried to heat the end without frying it or having any of the dust drop out the end while I burned it. I drew air into my lungs slowly through the pipe and tried to talk myself into believing I could feel smoke fill my lungs. I was also cognizant of the fact that the flame from the lighter was starting to scorch my nose, a result from too short a pipe.

I held the air in my lungs for as long as I could, believing the longer I held it, the higher I might get. And then I blew the air out knowing the more smoke that came out the more successful the operation had been. But nothing came out. Absolutely nothing. It was pure cocaine induced insanity to believe any of that process would net any results whatsoever.

The theory behind the procedure was sound. Crack could build up in residue form and could be reused and smoked, netting the desired outcome. But only if there was lots of crack going through a proper pipe and brillo and allowed to build up over repeated uses. But I had gone through the same process not two hours ago. I had attempted to light every last particle of crack out of that pipe to the point that I had burned my lips from heat, refusing to move my mouth from a burning pipe in the insane belief I would get something from nothing.

There was no crack left in my pipe – not a morsel, not a hint, not a trace. Even the sharpest crack sniffing dog on any police force would find me 100% drug free. At least on the outside. On the inside they might have found I had consumed copious amounts of drugs over large periods of time on a twenty-four-hour-a-day, seven-day-a-week basis for quite some time now and would have deemed me a chronic street level homeless drug addict of the worst possible variety. Given who I was, and what I did, which was smoke crack, I would normally at this stage raise myself onto my ravaged street feet and begin the search to try and find more.

But I was exhausted, too exhausted to move. And all in all, this back alley wasn't a bad spot to just chill for a while. Exhaustion wasn't a bad state to be in. It was better than the beginning of the drug runs when the mind was demanding finding drugs at any cost, yet there was no money to do so. The panic, the anxiety, the fear that came with that was palpable. Yes, it was much better when the fatigue took over and the cravings subsided, even if it took a staggering three consecutive days without sleep to obtain. I had not been to sleep for three days. Most of that time was spent on my feet wandering the streets looking for means to satisfy my habit. I know I ate, but maybe no more than one or two times over those three days. Not sure as the time and memory is blurred and the mind does funny things when it's sleep deprived. One might think this impossible. But the drug is that powerful, that it can propel you forward with no sleep, no food, or water for incredible periods of time in utter desperation to keep using the drug.

But the fatigue of body combined with the length of time since my last hoot of actual real drugs, meant that finally, and I mean finally, I could consider myself in a state of relaxation. I was perched in the corner of a loading dock in a back alley. It was dusk and there was little in the way of alley traffic. Just the odd homeless guy passing through. That was about it. I put the crack pipe in my pocket and stretched out my feet. The concrete was slightly oily and slippery and the smell of the entire area was only marginally stronger than what seemed to be the perpetual smell of the entire area; it was a sort of a combination of low tide, garbage, industry, and traffic. But all in all, it was not a bad spot. I'd been in worse.

Finally able to see past my crack pipe, I now took in the area. There was an empty lot across from me that allowed me to see far into the distance, across Burrard Inlet and onto the slopes of North Vancouver, although I couldn't see the actual water from this angle. But lifting my eyes up the slope of North Vancouver and to what I knew was the east, I could see the "mountain."

Again.

I had this thing with this particular mountain. No matter how little thought I put into it, which was the rule over the exception, I seemed to end up in places that afforded me views of the mountain. Not just any mountain, as there were several on the North Shore of Vancouver which, I think, were part of the Coastal Mountain range, but one particular mountain that had a distinctive shaped top. It was like it had a missing chunk, or a bite taken out of the top. And as unlikely as it would seem given I was a hardened street level drug addict living, make that existing, in a small quadrant of the lower east side of Vancouver with the exclusive purpose of using drugs, I found myself looking at this mountain and contemplating life with growing frequency.

I don't know what it was. Psychologically, I suppose it could mean the mountain represented stability, which was a far cry from what I represented. Maybe it represented strength, dependability, consistency, or peace, all of which I craved. I don't know. All I know is my life existed in the craziness of inner city drug addiction, and I got peace from being able to see something other than the hell in front of me.

But it seemed more than that to me. It was almost like, call me crazy, but that the mountain was calling me. Calling me to come out of the hell that was my existence? Calling me to remember who I used to be, to do something about my life, to leave this place and find myself again. And as ridiculous as it may seem, that was what it seemed like. A mountain was talking to me and I was listening. Yup, that's where I am in life.

Sleep deprivation does funny things. It could certainly make you see things. In fact, that was one of the main symptoms. Usually I could determine in my mind that what I thought I was seeing wasn't reality, but sometimes I couldn't. Of course adding in all the drugs that had been consumed didn't help. So while it would be easy to dismiss many thoughts, including thoughts of mountains that spoke, as irrational, influenced by drugs, lifestyle, diminished capacity, and sleep deprivation, it could be countered with the argument that extreme conditions could give someone insight they would normally not experience. I'm pretty sure any reasonable person would suggest to me that history was full of examples of crazy people doing crazy things because of "voices" that told them to. Still, I thought I had things processed reasonably: at best I just found looking at the mountain calming. At worst I thought the mountain was somehow prompting me towards challenging my current lifestyle, provoking me towards thought. There was no real downside to either concept.

I stared at the mountain for a long time lost in thought. I knew I was going to fall asleep, a prospect I found both comforting and frightening at the same time. Sleep deprivation does funny things. The body does not always go gently into this good night. Sometimes I convulse when the sleep comes, or find myself somewhat delirious. And then there was the fact that I was in an alley. Going to sleep in public was unnerving. I had my shoes stolen on more than one occasion while sleeping in alleys, and one never knew what other indignity. But it was comforting as well as I so desperately needed the sleep. And there was a period of time, when the insanity of the addiction had subsided, when the sleep was coming and things felt, well, so cozy that I would forget where I was, forget how I was living, forget the things I had done. For a moment life would feel normal again. Often I would wake up, and in that nanosecond before reality would set in, it would feel like life was normal, that I was at home and looking forward to a new day. And in that nanosecond was the only true joy of this life that had gotten so badly away from me.

But then I would wake up and it would all start up again.

Chapter 2

"Feezy foe! Feezy foe! Feezy foe!"

I woke up to my own voice screaming out the words "feezy foe" over and over again at the top of my lungs. Huh? I wasn't comprehending. I was being kicked in my ribs and I was screaming feezy foe. What was happening? As I woke up I stopped screaming and slowly my surroundings were coming back to me. I looked up to see four or five guys in lab coats and hair nets staring at me with looks somewhere between shock and disgust. The one closest to me (the kicker I was assuming) was yelling something at me in broken English, "Go away, what feezy foe, wake up, you crazy, you go, you go now!"

I pulled myself into a sitting position. "I'm so sorry, forgive me, I fell asleep, just give me a sec and I'll get out of here."

I was back now fully comprehending, at least all of it but that crazy feezy foe stuff and the screaming while I slept. I was on the loading dock surrounded by factory workers, immigrants who came out for a smoke from inside. I must have slept all night and into the next business day and now these guys came out for a smoke, saw me on their loading dock screaming my head off, and apparently, wanted me out of there.

I pulled myself to my feet and with another lame apology, I beat it down the alley. I could hear one of them yelling at me still, "You go, you go away, you bad man."

Ah, the indignity. Not only had I regressed to "alley living," I was being yelled at in disgust by immigrant factory workers, many of whom were missing teeth and were probably working illegally. On society's pecking order, I was now residing at the bottom. And if that weren't bad enough, I had now apparently added mental insanity to my resume. Feezy foe? What the hell did that mean?

I did a quick inventory of myself. Clothes on? Check. Crack pipe in pocket? Check. Okay, I was good to go. But where? Where else but back into the war zone? At this stage of the game there just weren't any other options. The addiction ruled over everything to the point of being a necessity to the same degree as, say, breathing, and it prevented anything else from taking place. There was literally nowhere else to go and nothing else to do.

This was the Lower East Side. Hastings Street. And while I wasn't officially on Hastings Street right now (I was just coming out of an alley on the heels of a rather embarrassing incident with some immigrants in lab coats), I was in the periphery of Hastings, and was a Hastings drug addict. Hastings was the main drag that runs through the worst section in all of Canada. The poor, the addicts, the drunks, the prostitutes, the criminals, the drug dealers, the gang members, the broken, the destitute, and the insane that resided in and around these blocks were referred to as being on Hastings. I was on Hastings.

Hastings, at least the seedy part of it, was probably something close to rectangular in shape for where the most action is, running probably ten blocks in length east to west and maybe three blocks north and south. Within there is the epicenter, which is the corner of Main and Hastings. All of life's skid row can take place in this area. You can get your drugs, find a cheap room, reside in a slum drinking establishment, go to jail, go to detox, get your welfare check, get a free meal, stay at a shelter, or absolutely anything else needed for co-existing in a drug fuelled part of the world. Though it is an impoverished area, the trade is incredible, sustaining a lucrative underworld with tens of thousands of dollars trading hands each day.

I started walking towards the action. I had no money, but I seldom did, and something always happened to get the first hoot, and once the first hoot was done, well, look out, because addicts will find a way to get more one way or the other. I stayed off the main street. I didn't like walking down the main streets because I was cognizant of the fact that hundreds of cars were bustling along going towards wherever they were going and I always felt like they looked and stared at the broken people in disgust or pity. I hated this and I felt terribly self conscious. Just because I was broken and a detriment to society didn't mean I was beyond recognizing my state and feeling badly about it. And while it would be easy to suggest doing something about it, the reality is that it's harder to do than anyone would ever think. I had tried and failed many times over.

There were many areas of Hastings. I was going to Oppenheimer Park, one block north of Hastings Street between Princess Street and Gore and a major hub for street activity. As I entered the park, I couldn't help but notice again how eclectic the area was. There was a street nurse helping a man in the doorway to a clinic across the street not ten feet from a hooker hitchhiking on the street, a group of Asians practicing Tai Chi in the corner of the park, what looked like some demonstrators gathering in another area of the park getting ready for some sort of movement, some shirtless teens kicking a soccer ball but looking more like thugs than like athletes, various people sleeping on benches or under trees, some old men playing chess, and another group getting ready for what looked like another "help the needy" type barbeque. As I continued into the center of the park and towards the far side I could see the lineup of beer parlours and skid row hotels back-dropping the park along the far side, and the groups of thugs, addicts, hangers on, hookers, and dealers scurrying about back and forth doing their deals, trying to con one another and participating in the endless ritual of the buying, selling, and using of drugs. This area had been my hang out spot for the past number of weeks. As I ambled over in that general direction I caught myself muttering the words feezy foe a few times in my head thinking little of the craziness of this lifestyle.

I had no plan and only saw one person I recognized. Her name was Minnie and she was one of the few girls who didn't resort to selling her body for drugs. She was bright and energetic and somehow was able to steer enough people to the real dealers to make enough commissions for herself. But her real attribute was that she was relatively honest, generous, and likeable so people often found themselves wanting to share drugs with her. Not to say she wouldn't lie, cheat, or steal for drugs, as that was just a part of Hastings' life, but just that she seemed to do her acts of dishonesty in a way that wasn't so hard to take. Many others down here would steal from you while you were looking and then deny it right to your face. These people were much harder to like or trust.

Minnie and I had used a few times together and she was my current "street favorite." The street is different than real life. Amidst the horror of it were real people and relationships with people were easy to attain. There was a common denominator of the shared existence that made relationships seem more real. The flip side is no friendship or relationship ever lasted past a very short time frame because in a life where drugs take precedence over everything, everything else eventually gives way to those drugs.

"Hey Minnie, how are ya?" I said.

"Hey Sam, you look like crap," she said matter of fact.

"I slept in this morning and got a rude awakening," I replied with tongue firmly in cheek. "Anything happening? I could sure use something," I had already scanned what was going on. A guy was negotiating with another guy. Minnie had some part of a deal that was brewing, and my addict mind wanted in. For the millionth time I was aware I was about to grovel on some level and I hated it. But it was nearly impossible to be self supporting down here all the time, especially for someone like me who wasn't much of a criminal or a dealer.

"Hang on Sam, I might have something really good happening and, for sure, I'll hook ya up if it happens. Just stay close by for a bit," she said. "Okay?"

I'd heard this a hundred times before, the "just wait and I'll help you out" line, which was, of course bullshit ninety percent of the time. Even the good people, like Minnie, weren't immune to this behaviour. But I had no choice but to see how it all panned out. Slim prospects were better than no prospects.

So I just basically stood there trying to look both non-suspicious and tough at the same time, knowing full well I could never pull either look off. I think the look I portrayed was probably pretty close to my reality: I looked like a guy who just slept in an alley and who was hopelessly addicted to drugs. Not really the look I was striving for.

I guess I was so busy staring at nothing I didn't even notice Minnie waving madly at me. "Come on Sam, let's go man!" she said while waving me towards her. "We're going upstairs for a hoot!"

"Effing right on Minnie, that is so cool!" I replied scrambling after her. I couldn't believe my fortunes and immediately my body was starting to glow in anticipation. The power of the drug is hard to explain. Being on the street meant that at some stage drugs had come before family, friends, jobs, and virtually everything else the world offered that wasn't drugs or drug related. And now, at just the prospect of being offered drugs my body was reacting with a level of anxiety that was so strong I could easily have thrown up in nervous anticipation.

Minnie was following another guy and both were headed to The Sunshine Hotel. I would have followed her off a cliff, but the thought did cross my mind that I didn't like going into the hotels, and this one had a particularly bad reputation.

There were scads of dumpy skid row hotels. Many of them were barely decipherable with nondescript doorways that could easily be missed. Once inside, many of them had similar looks and designs. They were in general disrepair, were old, and had layouts that made little sense with hallways, staircases, and fire doors that changed from floor to floor making navigation somewhat confusing. Generally, they had a front desk area which was little more than a window with a grumpy or street tough, uncaring thug running the show. Often this person would charge non-residents just to go up the stairs, scam the welfare system by double renting rooms, sell contraband, or anything else to carve out his own endurance to this lifestyle. I should say too, that these hotels weren't hotels in the same fashion as, say, the Best Western, where they were rented by the night. These skid row hotels were almost always paid by the month and considered home by the tenants. Either that or they were rented by the hour for other types of "clients."

I didn't like going into these sorts of hotels because you never knew what sort of lunatic you could pass in the hallways. It felt like you were in enemy territory where help would never come, and it just felt kind of claustrophobic and threatening. On the street, there were witnesses that could sometimes sway acts of violence. It was in the back alleys and these hotels, away from watching eyes, where bad things could happen.

Minnie quickly introduced me to the guy we were walking with but who would remember? This guy was definitely familiar with the hotel and the street. He wasn't any kind of "chipper" who came in from the burbs to get high and then go home again once done.

The three of us climbed the first staircase, whipped past the guy at the desk who wasn't caring at this particular moment, went through one door, climbed another shorter staircase, went through another door, climbed about ten more stairs and emerged in an unlit hallway. We went down about four doors and stopped. Our tour guide, the guy with Minnie, did a quick look up and down the hall, sniffed onto his sleeve, did some sort of jerky street twitch, and knocked softly on the door.

"Who is it?" came the immediate response. This was standard operating procedure for any door in drug world. Kind of like customs where there are clearing stages to go through to try to protect against cops, bigger thugs, or whatever. It all seemed so lame to me because if we were cops we wouldn't say so, and who else but an addict would possibly be up here knocking on a crack shack door?

"Danny," came the reply from our guide. A pause, then a series of noises which were probably door locks of some sort, then the door swung open part way and a bulky, shady looking, dark figure peered through the opening.

"Who are these two?" the man inside asked Danny.

"Friends," said Danny. "Don't worry about them. They're okay." I appreciated the endorsement from Danny despite the fact I had never seen him before in my life.

The door swung fully open and we were allowed in. Obviously Danny was known and accepted. As we passed by the doorman (and that actually is his title being in charge of the crack shack door and general enforcement in exchange for some drugs at shift end) I could see the door arrangement where a two by four had been nailed into the floor of the room about 4 feet back from the door with another two-by-four braced against it that would lean against the door causing the door to be braced shut. Sort of like the old chair leaned against door trick from the movies but slightly more advanced and secure. Yet another two-by-four slid across the door through handles acting like an oversized deadbolt. It was a three two-by-four system which may have been considered advanced security. This was phase two of the customs clearing: getting through the security door. The theory was keeping people out who badly wanted to come in, like police or bigger thugs. The security door would keep them out or buy some time to get rid of incriminating things. I wondered for a brief moment if the landlord would have appreciated having two by fours nailed into his floors.

Phase three of security clearance was being initiated as we stood there being heavily scrutinized up and down by the doorman. Yes, we were at the mercy of this uneducated street tough who had to be accepting of our company or out the door we would go. Fortunately, it appeared we were in.

This was a crack shack. Before being a crack addict, I had wondered what they were like, having often heard reference to them in the news. I'm not sure what I actually thought they were like, but they were nothing more than a place where the addicted gathered to purchase and use drugs. The selling feature was you could use your drugs on site, as opposed to buying from a street or delivery dealer where you are left to find your own locale to use in. That's fine if you have a place where smoking crack is tolerated. But if you don't, then constantly ducking into doorways, behind bushes, or wherever to smoke gets old fast.

In this place, like most of them, the drugs were purchased through a "staff" member in the common area who would then take the cash to a back bedroom before reappearing moments later with the drugs. The back room was never seen by the commoners from the front. This way nobody actually sees the drugs and money exchange hands. I'm not really sure what the back room looks like. Sometimes I visualize a guy in a suit dispensing the drugs like at a pharmacy. But I doubt that is the case. More than likely, the guy in the back room is one level up on the drug chain from street, and as is often the case when in the drug world, the ones who are organized and making money aren't usually addicts. The addicts I could always understand stooping to drug dealer or low end criminal. But how someone who is not a drug addict could sit in a dingy skid row room selling drugs to helplessly addicted people on death's door as a way to make money was beyond what I could comprehend. These people I hated.

Once the drugs were in hand, the addict was free to smoke away in the front room with the only risks being, perhaps, getting raided by the cops, being surrounded by insane, unpredictable behaviours, being kicked out the second the money runs out, or the worst, running out of dope.

29

Minnie and I grabbed a seat on the couch. Danny was talking to the doorman who was also the runner of the drugs. Danny had cash in his hand and was counting out a few 20's.

"He's going to pay me back a 40 rock he owes me," Minnie whispered in my ear. "I just got lucky and saw him after he got some big payoff."

"Way to go Minnie!" I whispered back. Crack shacks were also a little like libraries in the sense that most people were very quiet for some reason.

"We'll do one quick hoot here then blast out of here back to the street and do some more outside," she said. "I don't like it up here. It gives me the creeps."

"Sounds good," I said. "I'm with you on that, I don't like this place either."

There was one other person in the living room sitting in a chair in the corner and rummaging through a giant purse. This was another common sight in drug land: watching someone looking endlessly for things lost or imagined. For some reason it was just a psychosis of the drug almost all of us were subject to. On some drug runs, I would search through my pockets scrutinizing every piece of lint in the insane belief I would find drugs in my pocket and I would do this over and over and over again. It wasn't uncommon to watch someone with their face inches from the rug scouring over every square inch of a room looking for drugs they believe might have fallen on the ground. This person we were sharing the room with right now was deep in a psychosis and oblivious to us being there. There were many forms of cocaine psychosis, but paranoia and "looking for things" appeared to be the most common. Although I must admit I had yet to hear of anyone else having psychosis that involved mountains or feezy foes.

Overstaying your welcome after the money was gone or creating a scene were grounds for eviction from crack shacks, usually with exclamation points, but quiet and insane rummaging was accepted and commonplace.

Danny had finished placing his order and handed over the cash. The doorman/first stage drug dealer took the cash and headed off to the back bedroom. The whole thing would normally take just seconds and he would be back with the drugs—money and drugs never being seen together. In the meantime, Danny joined us on the couch and we all sat there anxiously (massive understatement of the year) awaiting the arrival. Seconds ticked. In any other industry, the service level would not have been scrutinized, but in this world we need drugs NOW. If one calls a crack delivery line and they say thirty minutes, we would hang up and try the guy who said five minutes. I can't imagine faster service in any other industry.

And true enough, here came the doorman/drug dealer around the corner looking like he was carrying something small and precious. The nervous energy between the three of us could have lit up an entire city. But just then somebody else knocked on the door just as the doorman walked by it and he paused as if uncertain as to which task he should do first, be the doorman or be the dealer. This is why busy places have two people doing this work. And while the three of us were sending telepathic messages to him like mad to come to us first, he chose to stop at the door and grunt, "Who is it?"

The response was muffled. Could have been anyone. Male though. And again, you could see indecision with the doorman. As if he was debating being thorough and asking some questions through the door, or just rushing through one task so he could get to another. Sort of like he was at a real job. He decided on quick task completion and opened the door. The first two-by-four was taken from the leaning position and leaned against a wall. The second two-by-four was slid through the handles and leaned against the wall. The actual door lock was turned to the unlock position and he opened the door.

And then things went terribly wrong.

31

Chapter 3

*B*efore the door was fully open four men pushed the door the rest of the way in and came in fast all at once, pushing the doorman back a few steps. All four men were in the room and the door closed behind them before any of us knew what happened. The doorman was clearly shocked and had a look on his face somewhere between surprise and fear. All four men were white, ranged in age from early twenties to mid thirties, and also had two distinctive looks: they didn't look like drug addicts and they looked very, very bad.

All the glowing feelings of nervous anxiety for the drug were quickly replaced with fear. A different ballgame altogether. You can't co-habitat on Hastings without seeing your fair share of trauma, violence, and scary situations. No doubt about it, there were some very bad people on Hastings who didn't mind violence one bit. But it wasn't as common as many people might think. From my perspective, most addicts were decent people just pathetically addicted to drugs, and while they would lie, con, cheat, steal, etc., they wouldn't resort to violence. Debt collection though was a different business. The dealers had to establish themselves as people not to be messed with or taken advantage of and would resort to outlandish levels of violence over ridiculously small debts. The key was not to owe anyone, and if you did, then pay them back when you said you would. Unfortunately both of those things are virtually impossible for the hopeless addict who would take a loan from anyone for drugs no matter how impossible the paying back part, and who had a near impossible time of paying back debts because when they had money they had to buy drugs. It was a tough cycle. Fortunately not many people are stupid enough to give a loan to a drug addict. I had found myself in a couple of pretty scary situations over small debts, and was only able to get out of them because for whatever reason most people found me sort of harmless and honest. And if things got really scary I would find some way to pay back the debts.

One of the men, a thirtyish, clean cut guy with the hardened look of someone who has done some hard time leaned in close to the doorman and talked to him in a low voice. Now the doorman was no slouch. This wasn't a doorman like at the Carlton; this was a street tough thug who could only qualify for this position by being able to kick the crap out of most anyone. And he was big. But you could see the apprehension and fear in his eyes, subtle as it may have been, as he listened to the man speak to him. He knew these guys and he was scared. I quickly concluded that while this didn't seem to involve us, we had found ourselves in the middle of a very bad situation.

I assumed the position I had come to know for these sorts of tense situations that didn't involve me. I pretended I was invisible. I had found that by staying very still, non assertive and not making eye contact was a good way to slide through scary situations. It was the guys that watched like a spectator sport, or worse, those that chimed in with an opinion or stupid pleasantry that often found themselves being pummeled in the middle of the room.

The men were now starting to move into positions. Three of them flanked around the doorman, two to each side and one behind him and escorted him back towards the back bedroom. I could see from the corner of my eye that the one on the doorman's left side, the side closest to us, started to pull back his jacket and reach for a gun that was stuck in the left side of his pants. A GUN! This was Canada and guns were not an everyday sight. In fact, I had only ever seen one before in my life on the street and that was when some hapless addict I was with traded a gun he stole from his grandfather to a dealer for some dope.

The forth guy drew over towards us in the living room and sort of took up a position where he was close to the door but could watch us. He said, "You all just chill out here for a few minutes, okay? Nobody leave, just stay put, okay?"

It wasn't really a question, it was more of a statement delivered with more than a morsel of evil which suggested there should be no answer and none of us said a word, not even the street looking Danny who had brought us up here and who certainly looked stupid enough to say something. I could also sense that the "tweaker" who was going through her purse also understood the gravity of the situation and remained very still as well.

It wasn't a long wait. Almost immediately voices started to escalate from the back room. Lots of voices like there may have been more than just the doorman and the drug dispensing guy who were originally back there. There were at least five men back there and the noises started to include not only voices but banging, thrashing, and clanging. Things had erupted into violence and other than perhaps the sound of a bad car crash, there were no sounds scarier. Well, at least to me. The guy watching us just had an evil smirk like he was enjoying it. There were some seriously bad people on this earth.

All of a sudden, gun shots rang out. Pop, pop, pop, pop. Four or maybe five shots, screams, banging, yelling and then a massive crash of what appeared to be a moving brawl of fighting and shooting crashed through the bedroom doorway and into view. The doorman was covered in blood but had one of the visiting men in a headlock and was screaming like a lunatic. One of the other intruders was trying to shoot the doorman and everyone else was still blocked off from leaving the bedroom. Unless they were dead that is, in which case, they weren't trying to leave.

Someone yelled "We need to kill them all now. Shoot them all, shoot them all! Cody, blast those guys...no witnesses...no witnesses!"

Cody was the man guarding us. He was the guy with the evil smirk and he already had a gun in his hand. But the doorman was causing problems. He was going absolutely primal and was a shrieking, bleeding, raging unstoppable bull of craziness and he was going to overpower both men he was fighting. He had one pinned under him and the other pressed against the wall and was trying to pry the gun out of his hand. The forth intruder was blocked off from leaving the bedroom.

Evil Cody had to help with the doorman or the doorman was going to beat them all so he rushed away from the door towards the avalanche of bodies in the hallway and exposed the door by doing so.

Not one of us wasted any time. Danny, Minnie, and I all leapt off the couch as one and sprinted for the door without a word being spoken. No words were necessary or even thoughts for that matter. This was fight or flight in its most primal form, and each one of our minds chose flight. It was either get out now or die in this cesspool hotel room.

Danny made it to the door first, swung it open and was gone. Minnie hit the door second and I was last. I have no idea about the purse tweaker but for all I knew she was still sitting on the couch too stunned to move.

As Minnie was midway through the door, I could see that Evil Cody was swinging around with his gun and he started blasting for all he was worth. Wood splintered the doorframe on the left side. Minnie ducked and swung left down the hall. The next shot hit the doorframe immediately above my head and I instinctively ducked and reeled to the right, and I was in the hall and running. Three steps into my run my head came up and I could see that I had picked the wrong way down the hall. I was running down a dead end hallway with nothing at the end of the hall except a window. I was into a full sprint and had maybe twenty-five paces before I ran out of real estate.

I sensed more than felt that Evil Cody was now in the hallway and taking aim. Fifteen paces before the hallway ended I felt a bullet fly past my ear, so close that I could hear the whiz and feel the heat against my cheek. Ten paces to the end and another succession of pops. Pop, pop, and I could see the impacts in the wall surrounding the window frame in front of me. Five steps till the end and only one option existed. Another pop.

At three paces from the end I launched. It was a classic long jump move when hitting the board. Mid air, I raised my knees and brought my elbows and forearms in to protect my face and hit the centre of the window like a horizontal cannonball. I guess I can be thankful for the material used in skid row hotels, because the glass shattered without really even breaking any momentum and I was airborne immediately. If I could have processed a thought, this is when I might have wondered what floor I was on, but there had been no thoughts since leaving the couch, just instinct. And it was still this way as I fell two floors into the back alley below. I landed well, all things considered. I'll give credit to natural athleticism and my mother's enrolling me in gymnastics as a kid. Most of the impact was on my feet, but I was rolling as I landed so dispersed the impact over feet first, then side and shoulders. I immediately tried to get to my feet which I think was more like a staggering, falling forward sort of motion, shaky at best. I knew being under the window was not good. I had to keep moving.

I lurched around the corner of the alley and into the side street that the alley fed into without noticing any more bullets fly by. Right in front of me was one of those pickup trucks with extended wooden side panels making it look more like an open at the back panel truck. The makeshift truck box was paneled on all sides except the back which was paneled to a lesser degree, open from about one third up. The driver would not have any visibility behind him except through the side mirrors. The truck was at a red light waiting. I really didn't give it much thought. I needed to escape and be hidden, so I just took advantage of the opportunity and climbed up and into the back of the truck and quickly laid low between a few boxes and miscellaneous items. I thought for sure that a gunman was just going to walk up to the back of the truck and shoot me, or, equally bad, the driver of the truck would have seen me or felt the weight imbalance and come back and kick me out and back into hell. But neither happened. The truck just pulled forward, went through the light, went up a block, turned right onto Hastings Street and kept going.

Chapter 4

I didn't move a muscle. I felt completely paralyzed. I was lying on my back with my feet towards the back of the truck. The tailgate of the truck was just high enough that vehicles behind could not see me, and my view started only at the tops of buildings, street lights, and the sky. I was too afraid to move, too afraid they were still after me, and too afraid the driver would discover me. After a block or two of driving through heavy traffic, I started to breathe. But it was hiccupped breathing and I was hyperventilating. I was going through some shock when the adrenalin diminished. I took some deep breaths. "Breathe... breathe," I whispered to myself. "Breathe." Slowly I was coming back to my senses and I assessed the damage.

It appeared I hadn't been shot, although it wasn't a no-brainer to figure out. I literally ran my fingers over everywhere to make sure. I knew there was a chance I had been shot and didn't know it through the fall and adrenaline-filled stagger to escape. Plus, the guy had fired at least four shots at me so how could he have possibly missed?

I was cut though. I was bleeding from one forearm, one knee, and seemed to have some fairly serious road rash on one hip. But the bleeding was minimal, not stitches material. And nothing was broken. Final assessment: I was ok. But what of the others? Did people die? They must have. Did Minnie? Or that street thug Danny? I didn't think so. The gunman picked one direction to shoot just as I chose to run right instead of left. All the gun shots went my way I think. Still...

And what was happening now? Were police collapsing in on the situation? They would have to be. Not even the inside depths of a skid row hotel could hide multiple gunshots and murder. No, the police were surely there by now in force.

I could tell that the truck was heading west. I just knew from the buildings we were passing that we were now on Georgia heading westbound, towards Stanley Park and the causeway. I found myself transfixed, just staring into the open gap at the back of the truck, watching the sky glitter past between the tall buildings. It really was a spectacular day. Well, weather-wise that is. I had seen better days personally.

It did occur to me that I was driving away from where drugs were obtainable and debated jumping. But I dismissed the thought as irrational (really?), and once again recognized the power of the drug to keep its lure even in these circumstances. But common sense prevailed for once and I dismissed all notions of going anywhere. I was actually feeling incapable of moving and was being lulled by the movement and coming down from the adrenaline. Right then and there I could have driven forever and was actually getting a little drowsy. We were driving through the causeway and approaching the Lion's Gate Bridge. I would have known this even without being able to see anything, as there was a very familiar sound from the road through the causeway and over the bridge as the truck drove over the paving grooves and dividers. It was so familiar because I was heading over the bridge to where I had come from.

The Lion's Gate Bridge separated downtown Vancouver from the North Shore, which consisted of West Vancouver and North Vancouver. I came from West Vancouver. West Vancouver was one of the richest, if not the richest community in all of Canada. I was born at Lion's Gate Hospital in North Van twenty-eight years ago and raised in West Van in the same house all my life, at least until the drugs had made me unwelcome there.

My parents were fairly old when they had me; my father was in his early forties and my mom in her mid thirties. While West Van was filled with extremely rich people, the prices for real estate were at one time, many years ago, quite reasonable. My father had bought the property I grew up on when he was in his early twenties, the result of wise spending of an inheritance. He loved the area because he had spent a lot of time in the area as a bird watcher and found a modest house on a sizeable lot for about $30,000. This was deep West Van, at that time just a house in the wilderness close to the ocean. With heavy development over the years, the house now found itself sitting amongst some of the most expensive houses in the world in one of the most desirable areas of the world, and I dare say his $30,000 original investment was now worth decidedly more.

When my father bought the property, West Van was sparsely populated, and with the exception of the British Properties community within West Van which was always rich, the entire area could easily have been considered middle class. Even in the days of my own childhood West Van did not seem overly wealthy. In recent years, things changed and older houses were starting to get torn down to be replaced with massive monster homes and property values went through the roof. Vancouver was being recognized as a world class city and people from places like Hong Kong were flocking to buy in with money being no concern.

But there still remained some of the old culture and my family was one of them. Middle class income and values living amongst the rich. My dad was never wealthy. He was an IBM sales person who spent some forty years as a loyal salesman selling products that ranged from typewriters, to fax machines, to computers, depending on the decade.

My mother worked as a cleaner for the police department as well as private cleaning jobs for some houses through various contacts. She was of Scottish descent, was hard working, complained little, and was not much for emotional demonstrations of love.

They both did well. The house had been paid for up front on purchase. I was the only child to drum up expenses, they maintained the property well, got along, and lived quiet, modest lives. Since they were both now retired, they putzed around the garden, did a little travelling, and spent time together. Really quite a charmed existence. At least it would have been had they not had a cherished son lost and dying on the street.

So how did a West Van kid who grew up with two loving parents in a terrific environment end up on Hastings? You would think I was unique. And I was to some extent given that I not only grew up privileged, but I was also reasonably well educated and did not even try alcohol until I was nineteen. Most of those I met on Hastings did not grow up like I did. Many of the stories were what you might have expected: harrowing childhoods in terrible neighbourhoods filled with abuse, neglect, single parent (or no parent) homes where children never really had much chance at success. Winding up on Hastings could have been predicted.

But addiction did not discriminate. I met a doctor once who had lost his license and fell all the way to the street, and I went through a few week period of using with a former recognizable Hollywood actor who was one of the most pathetic drunks I had ever seen. There were others too, many others who came from the middle class, rich families, or just good homes with loved ones who cared and were devastated with the hopeless feeling of being powerless to help sons and daughters, brothers and sisters, friends or whoever they deeply cared about.

However, as hard as it was to figure out how I became who I did on a psychological level, it was easy to know where it started. I had never had a drink until the age of nineteen. I was in the midst of a challenging two year program in Business Admin at BCIT when, for no particularly good reason, just decided one Friday afternoon to join my classmates when they invited me out for a beer. I drank four pints of beer in that session, felt as if I had been introduced to a long lost friend, and fell in love. While I was able to keep it limited to "controlled" binging over the next 18 months or so until graduation, I did drink every Friday night and many Saturday nights, and always to excess. Always.

Within two weeks of graduation I was drinking by myself in dark lit beer parlours having the time of my life hanging out with fascinating story tellers of every walk of life. Some of these fascinating people also did drugs, and because I was apparently in some sort of "agree to anything with reckless abandon" phase of life, I tried some too. Within four months of graduating from BCIT, I tried crack for the first time. I spent $400 and partied for sixteen straight hours.

The next day I recognized that I was potentially in trouble and I suffered great guilt at having stooped so low as to try these sorts of drugs. I vowed I would never do that again. Alcohol was one thing, cocaine was clearly another, and I was deeply ashamed. Two weeks later I did it again and suffered all the same feelings. No way was I doing that again. But I did, and then I had a week when I did it twice in one week. And then I did it two consecutive nights. And after that? Well, I have been high every day since that I was not in rehab. Every day. All day every day.

The spiral to skid row did not take much time at all. I would say within three months I was unemployed, thrown out of the family home, and had burned all bridges. Crack was expensive and impossible to stop once you started. Any savings evaporated almost immediately, followed by borrowing, pawning, selling, trading, whatever. And from there the cycle of trying to get clean, going to rehab, doing well for a time, falling back into addiction, re-losing everything, slipping a little farther down, trying again and so on and so on has been going on for the past few years. The more my patterns emerged, the more people in my life learned about things like enabling, then the less people would put up with me. At a certain stage, I became very alone and even if my life depended upon it, there was nobody who would listen to my pleas for help. There were no more friends' couches to crash on. No more people who would lend me money. No more income coming in from any sources. No possibility of keeping a job. No success at trying to change. It had been six months since I attempted to get clean on any level, a lifetime in street drug addict terms, and I had arrived at a place of true hopelessness. Where for the longest time this felt like a bad dream, but certainly one that had an ending in sight. Where once I thought I certainly would move on from this chapter of life, I now sensed the very real possibility that this was not going to be won, that getting clean was not possible for me, and that this was it. There was not going to be any happy ending to this story.

As I lay in the back of the truck, lulled by its movement and the come down of adrenaline, and with thoughts of a previous life from a different world coming to mind as we drove past "memory lane," I just stopped caring. This truck was not taking me home, and this truck was not going to wipe out where I was coming from. I did not care if the truck stopped or drove forever. I didn't want to think of where I came from as a child, or where I came from just minutes ago. I did not care about drugs and I did not care if I lived or died. I just did not care anymore.

I don't think I fell asleep, but I was definitely in a trance of some sort. I know we had headed north or northeast after leaving the Lion's Gate Bridge. We did not come into West Van; we came into North Van and kept on going. I recognized where we were for a while, but at some stage stopped paying attention, and now I had no idea. We were climbing. That much was certain. So it meant away from the ocean. There were no more landmarks to tell by, only trees it seemed. This wasn't unusual for the area. It didn't take long to leave the city and enter wilderness. But we drove for a long time which did seem unusual and I began to wonder where this was going to end. It isn't like I couldn't have jumped out, because I could have. Heck, I had already done a free fall out of a second story on a building, so surely a slow moving truck would have been easy. But now speeds were up as we were away from traffic so it would have been harder and more painful.

It seemed pretty clear to me now that we were out in the middle of nowhere. I was braver in sitting up now and checking things out as there was no traffic behind us. All I could see was the winding yellow line in the middle of the road, trees blanketing both sides of the road, and that we were going uphill.

Suddenly the truck started to move to the right, and before I could prepare myself, the truck was pulling in hard and fast off the road onto a gravel opening and pulled into what seemed like a big open gravel parking lot. Within seconds the truck pulled into a line of other parked trucks and came to a dusty stop. Then the truck engine shut down and I could hear the truck door open. And all of a sudden I cared again.

I lay low, completely freaked out all over again about discovery. I knew we were on gravel and I knew I would immediately know if he was walking away from the truck or to the back of the truck. I heard the door open, heard the door close and heard the footsteps heading right back to where I was.

Chapter 5

There was nothing I could do. If he looked in the back of the truck he would see me and I was in a near state of panic. But he didn't actually look into the truck. No, he hit the side of the truck with something heavy and said, "Ok sonny, rides over. Jump on down nice and slow."

I paused for a second. Was it possible he could possibly be talking to someone else? That was highly unlikely and I only needed a couple of additional seconds to realize the gig was up. "Okay, I'm coming out. I don't mean any trouble," adding the last part to try and set a peaceable tone.

I climbed out of the truck slowly while he stood back about ten feet. He was an older guy, late fifties maybe, overweight but on a powerful frame, so the excess weight merely made him look stronger. He could kick my ass, that much I knew for sure. He had a big white beard and was wearing blue coveralls. I couldn't help but have the Dukes of Hazard flash through my brain for a second. I also noticed he was holding a crow bar in one hand, hanging down the side of his leg, not held in a threatening gesture, but in his hand nonetheless.

"What do you think you're doing?" he asked as I finished coming off the truck and stood in front of him.

"Hey, gosh, sorry about that," I said. "I, uh, I jumped in the back in the city because I was in some trouble and needed to get away. Really, I'm so sorry."

"Yeah, I kind of figured that's what was going down," he said.

"You mean you knew I got in the truck downtown?" I said.

"Of course I knew," he snapped. "Am I an idiot? This is only an F250 half-ton pickup son. Built in 1984 and crappy suspension two years after that. I would have known if a five year old got in the back. Course, you don't weigh much more than a five year old, so maybe it *was* pretty perceptive of me. Why didn't you jump out?"

I wasn't following. "What do you mean?"

"I mean why didn't you jump out after we got out of the downtown core? I stopped at enough lights. Was barely moving other times. I kept watching my mirrors convinced you were going to jump out. But you never did. And now here you are in the middle of nowhere. So why didn't you jump?"

"Well, I dunno really," I said. "I, uh, went through this pretty freaky scene back there and when I got in the truck I think I just got lulled and felt kind of safe, and well, I just didn't move. But I'll be on my way now, if you don't mind."

He didn't seem to hear the last part "You're all banged up. Leg bleeding through your jeans. You bleed in my truck?"

"Uh, no, I don't think so. They're more like road rash sorts of cuts as opposed to, like, bleeding gushing sorts of wounds. I think your truck is clean." I had a thought: "Why didn't you stop and kick me out then?"

"I almost did a few times. But I got nothing back there worth anything," he said as he pointed to the back of the truck. "And I figured maybe you was in trouble. So I just thought, well, what the heck...," and he sort of trailed off. "Drugs?" he said. "Its drugs, right?"

"You mean are my problems drug related?" He nodded. "You mean the issue I had in the city was because of drugs? That I'm a drug addict?" He kept nodding. "Well, yes to it all. Sadly, yes."

He just nodded his head slowly and after a pause said, "So you get yourself in some serious trouble and you're running from it, and you decide to just jump in the back of my truck and maybe bring all this trouble right to me? Is that what happened?"

He didn't really say it with menace. More like disdain, or sadness. I didn't really have a comeback for that. "It just all happened so fast. I'm really sorry about that."

He just looked at me for probably a minute straight. Then he walked towards me and raised the crow bar. I instinctively flinched, but he didn't hit me with it, just tossed it over my shoulder into the back of the truck. "I could tell right away I wouldn't need that with you even if it came to it," he said. "You're like a twig, son. You're in bad shape aren't you?" He paused again. "Come on, I'll buy you breakfast," and he walked by me towards the restaurant without looking back. I just stood there not sure what was happening.

He stopped about five paces away and looked over his shoulder. "Well come on son! I ain't asking again. Let's go for breakfast. Move it."

I followed him. I really didn't see a choice. Crossing the parking lot I was able to take in the surroundings. The truck I had stowed away in was among a line of a few other trucks parked in a semi organized fashion in a big, open, dusty gravel parking lot. The only building was a restaurant. It was a log cabin, well kept, with a big neon sign that said Momma's Country Cabin Restaurant.

Catchy name. There was actually a certain charm about it and perhaps it was one of those places that could exist all alone in the middle of nowhere because of good food and down home service. And that certainly seemed to be the case based on how many cars and trucks were in the lot.

So we went for breakfast. To Momma's Country Cabin. I just followed him in. He found himself a booth, sat down, and a waitress came over immediately with two coffees, two waters and one menu.

47

"Morning Danny," she said to my host.

"Morning Momma," he replied. "He don't need no menu neither Momma. Just bring him my usual as well."

"You got it Danny," she said and walked away.

He took a sip of coffee. Black. And said to me, "Do you sell drugs?"

I took a sip of coffee too. Cream and sugar. More sugar than necessary. "No, I don't deal. I'm strictly a consumer. I don't meet the criteria for being a dealer. As you say, I'm like a twig," and I smiled lamely.

"You got yourself a brain son," he asked, "or are you just hopeless?"

The entire scene seemed somewhat surreal to me, but I just went with it. Life as an addict was never normal. "Well, that's a tough one to answer. A bit of both. I am actually pretty well educated, and my childhood was normal. But I haven't been able to get clean, so, yeah, pretty hopeless as well."

He nodded then said nothing. Looked out the window for a few minutes and then breakfast came.

"Two Yukons now being served," said Momma and she dropped two enormous platters of eggs, pancakes, bacon, sausage, hash browns, and toast. And I mean enormous. I didn't know they even made plates that big.

"This is your regular breakfast?" I said to Danny. "Wow, it's the biggest plate of food I've ever seen."

"It's a good 'ol sized breakfast, that's for sure," he said. We ate for about five minutes straight and nobody said a word until finally he said, "I have a son down there you know." I didn't say anything, but I stopped shoveling food down my throat and waited on him to continue and he did.

"Yeah, his mother, my wife, got cancer and died when he was thirteen. We live in the back country. Middle of nowhere. I fix people's crap, car's, lawnmowers. I weld stuff, or whatever. He got a little lost after she died. Then, when he was like eighteen I started to lose him downtown. Took a while, but eventually I lost him completely to the drugs. I haven't heard from him in months. I take junk downtown sometimes. Stuff I fix up but don't want to sell and I take them downtown and give them to places like the Salvation Army. But really it's because I am looking for my son...," and he trailed off and started eating again.

"What's his name?" I said. Maybe I knew him.

"His name is Sheldon. He's a bit younger than you, maybe. He's twenty-two and the drugs done him too so he's pretty skinny. Not like you though. Got more meat on him."

"I don't think I know him, but yeah, the drugs can get a hold of you before you know it," I said. "That's too bad. I'm sure he'll surface in rehab one day, you know? And give you a call."

"Kid's a dumb ass," he said. "Like you by the sounds of it," and he took a huge bite of pancakes.

It wasn't one of those chat back and forth conversations with lots of dialogue. He was a man of few words. And big bites. But there was a kindness behind the gruffness, exhibited by the fact that he was eating breakfast with me. I could see he was assessing me as well. I don't think he was anyone's fool.

"Why don't ya just go home," he said, "you know, to your folks' house. I'm betting they're pretty worried all in all. Why don't ya just finish breakfast and go home? Like today. Right now."

I took my own huge bite of pancakes. I was keeping up with him on emptying the plate. Twig or no twig, I had the advantage of being severely malnourished and I was only keeping pace with him to be polite. Left to my own, my face never would have left six inches above the plate and it would have been finished by now.

"Well, for one, they wouldn't have me. They don't trust me, rightfully so. They're mad at me and they know not to enable me. I think I've figured out there are only ever two options for me: drugs on the street or getting clean in detox then rehab. I have actually been thinking a lot about rehab lately, so now that I'm out of the city maybe I'll go to North Van and make some calls."

"Well, I ain't driving you son. I head farther up and there's nothing left up there but wilderness and my land, so you're on your own now. But you should do something. What kind of a life is that you're living? A complete waste is what it is. Gonna kill ya."

We finished off. I drank the glass of water and he picked up the bill and paid at the front counter to a different lady wearing a nametag that said "Momma" and I wondered how many momma's *were* there here?

Once outside, we walked in the direction of his truck. Before he got in, he turned to me, "Listen son, if you do end up back on the street, even though you shouldn't, but if you do, and you happen to run into my son, well...," and he paused for second and looked up to the sky then back to me again, "...well, just tell him his old man said he should come home."

"Yeah Danny. For sure. I'll keep my eye out for him and I'll give him the message."

He started up the truck and drove it about ten feet, then stopped, rolled down the window and yelled over to me, "His name is Sheldon. Okay? Try to remember it. Sheldon." And before I could say anything, the window went up and he pulled away.

I stood there and watched his truck drive off and continued to just stand there watching the dust dissipate into the air. Now what?

I really had no idea as to where I was or how far I was away from any other civilization. I had no money and no prospects, so it seemed my only choice was to start walking back along the road towards civilization and maybe hitchhike. I moved over to where the parking lot met the road and just stood there for a minute. Was I really just going to head back into the city? Seriously. I should make some sort of change. Call detox. Something. Anything but go downtown. And I guess I was just sort of lost in thoughts, thinking through limited options when my eyes lifted up over the restaurant and towards the sky.

And that is when I realized that I was standing pretty much directly at the base of "my mountain" with its distinguishable missing chunk.

PART TWO

UP

*"You must no longer live as the Gentiles do,
in the futility of their thinking."*

Chapter 6

I decided I was going to climb the mountain right then and there. I guess you could say it was one of those "WTF" moments. In fact, what else could it be? Call it a hundred different things: playing a role, severe addiction affecting mental health, malnutrition as a result of the addiction, sleep deprivation (again, addiction), permanent psychosis of the drug, affections towards this mountain that were, well, unstable, trauma from the lifestyle and today's events, detachment from real relationships, seeing too many bad things, or just an uncanny series of events that led me here to this moment.

I was going to climb this mountain. Now.

From a practical perspective, if there was one available amongst this craziness, it was early in the morning, it was a decent enough day with variable sun and cloud, wasn't terribly cold and I didn't think the climb would be so bad. In my early BCIT days, a group (not the same group that introduced me to beer) of my classmates and I decided to hike the Grouse Grind, one of the most popular hiking trails in the world. It was virtually straight up on a well maintained trail that was sort of like a vertical staircase to about 3500 feet. That hike only took us an hour or two, and I couldn't see the elevation of "my mountain" being that much higher. Plus, you had to appreciate what these mountains were like. They weren't like the vertical cliffs, ropes and gear kind of mountains. Nope. These were more like giant hills. Sure they were steep, but I didn't think it would be too bad. And finally, I grew up in these parts. Before all the development the area I grew up in was surrounded by forest, ocean, and hills and I spent tons of time outside and loved it. No, I hadn't actually climbed any of the mountains, but it did have a familiar feeling about it all.

Of course, on the downside of the argument, I wasn't exactly in hiker shape, was malnourished from the drugs, at least thirty pounds under weight, probably only slept twenty hours the past week, had only the clothes on my back, no food, water, compass, map, or really, even a destination. And I couldn't even be sure that where I was standing actually was the base of the mountain I wanted to climb. It was hard to look up and have accurate depth perception. For all I really knew, "my mountain" was two mountains back from the base of where I was standing. But this wasn't a topic up for debate anyway. The circumstances were unusual. I was here now and I was going to climb the mountain. End of story.

And so I just walked back through the cars and trucks in the parking lot to the end of the lot where it seemed like the most logical place to start and started climbing. There was no subtle warm up phase. Nope, it was steep from the first step. I just looked up and assessed the most logical direction and took it. There were trees everywhere, dense forest growth but not to the extent that it impeded movement. The biggest obstacle was just that it was steep and footing was difficult amongst the dirt, rock, and forest floor.

As a kid I used to look out the window from the backseat of my father's car and stare at the mountains. Every one of them was covered completely by trees from top to bottom. I used to daydream about climbing the mountains and I believed every one of them would be climbable because all you would have to do was pull yourself up by tree bases and branches all the way to the top. In reality, it only looked that way as the trees were not close enough to each other to do that. Close, but not that close.

At about fifteen minutes in, my thighs started to burn. It was no wonder, really, given my condition entering the hike. Really it was surprising I wasn't down for the count inside five minutes. It's a funny thing what the body is capable of when the drug is still in the system. Not that I felt high, as I hadn't used since last night, but I guess there was still enough in my system to propel me forward. I think the body sort of acclimatizes itself to the toxicity of the drug, and is fooled into believing you could stay awake forever, walk insane distances for drugs, and get so high the heart beats off the chart. Sometimes people would just die on the street, and not like immediately after, say, shooting lots of heroin into their arm, which also happens. But just, like, be sitting there and then the head drops down like they are nodding off and they die. I was at a crack shack once and a guy was just sitting in the corner in a chair slumped over. Nobody thought anything of it and we used for hours. Later, after I left, I found out he had been dead the whole time and nobody even knew. Maybe from just too much of too much. I know I often wondered just how close to death I was during many nights where my heart was pounding madly and I was sweating profusely from too much drugs.

It was really when I stopped using that I felt mortal, and weak, and skinny, and disheveled, and unkempt, and malnourished, and desperately sick. But I wasn't quite there yet. I was still being propelled on, driven by irrational thoughts.

It was tiring. It was so steep! But I just stopped lots. I took ten steps, rested for one minute, took ten more steps, and so on. I was now at least two hours into the hike. It wasn't straight up and down like the Grouse Grind, nor was there any nicely marked trail with nicely maintained steps. I had to change direction frequently, having to go sideways between vertical bursts to pick routes that made sense. Some places were completely impenetrable, so I had to deviate from my course. I had long ago already realized I was probably close to being, or already was, lost. Not that I even really knew where the starting point was anyway, but I did know I would be safe if I could find the restaurant, and I was not convinced at this stage I could. But I wasn't unconvinced either, and I wasn't scared or distracted from my cause so I just kept climbing.

Again, if I considered two hours to climb the Grouse Grind, and I considered Grouse Mountain to have an elevation similar to my mountain, and then I added maybe another two hours to my time to compensate for no trail and a malnourished hiker, then I had to be over half way. Still plenty of light, so no worries. And besides, did I care? No. I did not care. Still, I really had no idea about where I was in proximity to the top, bottom, or middle. I couldn't see anywhere, except some sky through breaks in the trees, and maybe up a hundred yards and down a hundred yards. I was on the side of the mountain and that's all I knew.

Two hours later, I was definitely not at the top and little seemed to have changed. I was dirtier, drenched in sweat from the exertion, and was starting to wonder how much further I could go. And it had to be getting on late in the afternoon. Not only that, but it was cooler in the shade of the trees than it had been at sea level. It was early October after all, and I was climbing in elevation. I could sense the cool air even though I was gasping for breath and dripping in sweat. For the first time I asked myself whether or not this was a good idea and almost laughed out loud at the ridiculousness of the question. This was neither a good idea nor a bad idea. It was an insane idea.

I pulled myself up and over a steep outcrop of rocks and continued upward. There had been a continued slope on my left hand side that became more pronounced the further up I went to the point that going left in any way was out of the question. As I came around a large tree that opened up some visibility to the right, I could see that it was becoming an equally steep drop off to the right. My only real choice was to go straight up and things were starting to seem progressively dicey. I continued to climb in the hope that things would sort themselves out and easier routes would be revealed but the climbing was becoming seriously vertical and eventually I had to stop.

I stopped at the base of a tree breathing heavily. I assessed the situation left. No way. To the right looked downright scary and straight up impossible, at least to me.

I had reached a dead end.

Chapter 7

*O*kay, so I needed to think about this for a minute. I took a few tentative steps in all directions as a test to see if maybe it was easier than it looked. Nope. All I knew for sure was going left and up was out of the question. Going right looked daunting and frightening, but perhaps doable. And then of course, there was going down.

I thought about going down and broke it into two options. Going all the way down and aborting the climb, or going down far enough to find another route up. It seemed to me that finding another route up would be challenging and time consuming. My fear was that I was going to have to go a long way down and then over before really being able to find another route up that wasn't going to be affected by the steep ravines by which I was now trapped. Plus my legs were done. It was getting late and I just couldn't actually see pulling it all off.

So the options became turn around and go all the way down, or attempt the right side. It seemed to me I must be near the top. I had to be since I had been going all day at this. But so what? I reach the top and then what? I come down anyway. If I can that is, given the light left in the day, not getting lost, not finding myself in another impassable position, and once down being able to find civilization. I had to consider the possibility that there could be some dangerous and ugly outcomes to some of my decisions. It could well be that I was already in a grave situation. Still, I was this close and wanted to finish it.

Going right was scary. Very scary. There had been a ravine that had become steeper and closer to me as I climbed and I was now on the edge of its very steep wall. The ravine ended (or started) above me, so there was a route to the right where I would essentially have to scale against the rock wall on the side of a cliff and move laterally about thirty feet until I got to the other side, at which point there appeared to be good route options to continue on. The traverse itself seemed from this angle to have enough foot and hand holds. It wasn't completely sheer and it might have been relatively easy had it been, say, three feet off the ground. But it wasn't. It was steep. Not vertical, like if I fell I would scream for two minutes before I hit the ground. More like I would fall forty feet, hit the near vertical slope, and bounce off rocks and trees for another 200 feet or so. No doubt about it, if I slipped and fell, I would be dead.

About halfway across the distance I needed to traverse was a large tree that had grown out from an impossible position on the side of the cliff. It came out in sort of a "J" shape where its base grew out horizontally from between rocks and then headed straight up to the sky. Maybe fifteen feet of scariness to the tree, then another fifteen feet on the other side of the tree and then clear sailing.

Thirty feet of terror or go down.

It reminded me of when I was a kid again. There was a cliff called the Parthenon in Eagle Harbour in West Van. It was a vertical sheer cliff coming out of the ocean and was about fifty feet high. You would have to swim over from the Eagle Harbour Yacht Club to the base, then pull yourself up out of the water onto the rocks, then climb up a steep trail to the top. Then jump off back into the ocean. I remember the first time I jumped. I had never been so scared in my life and I was literally up there for hours building up the courage before I leapt. In the end, it just came down to a decision. I stood about four paces from the edge and just decided that I was now ready and that I was not going to overrule myself again. In a heartbeat, a second or faster, I just took the first, second, and third step and the forth step out and over the edge and did it. The jump itself was so scary, but I did it!

And then I did it again, and this time I only had to psych myself up for about twenty minutes. The third time I jumped I just launched myself off. But there was still some fear. And the fear was in itself sort of exciting.

I stood where I was for a long time looking at the rock face in front of me. I knew time was a real issue now and that if I was going to go forward I would have to do it now. So I made the decision and I moved into position. I reached up on the rock wall and felt for a handhold. Then I moved my right foot out and secured it on a foothold. When I released my left foot, I would be committed. I took a deep breath, made the final decision and allowed my left foot to leave the ground and join my right foot. I was now on the side of the cliff and scared shitless. Going back seemed as scary as going forward, so I felt as if I was the kid who had already jumped. No choice but to carry on.

I secured my right hand, then right foot, then moved my left hand and left foot and, inch by inch, went laterally across the face. Each foot and hand hold was dangerously small and precarious. It was probably elementary to a real rock climber, but to me I was severely out of my depth. But, doing it. Slowly but surely, I was making it across.

And then it started to rain.

British Columbia. Rain forest. October. I had lived here all my life and knew all about rain. There were different kinds of rain in varying degrees of raininess. This was real rain, real Vancouver style hard, wet, persistent, and sustained rain that went from no rain to hard rain immediately.

I froze on the wall. The rain came hard and fast and the rock wall was instantly wet and slippery. And it was decidedly more treacherous than it was a moment ago. I literally could not move and felt certain if I did I would surely fall. So I just froze against the wall. I could feel the rain washing over top of my hands. I could feel the slippery feeling on the rock and water was running down the neck of my shirt. The sweat generated from the climb up was gone and my body temperature was dropping quickly. I was wet, getting cold, and I was stuck against a rock face in the middle of Lord knows where.

The rain wasn't letting up. Chances are it wouldn't. I know Vancouver rain and how it works. It could rain all night and then some. Heck, it could rain all month. I had to make a move. I just had to go for it in some way or I would be stuck there until I fell. There was no choice. Waiting it out was not an option. I was barely hanging on as it was. There was too little strength left, diminishing daylight, my fingers were getting too cold to hang on, and I was starting to suffer the effects of being stuck in one position.

I had to move. No choice.

So I just carried on. No choices on strategy. I moved my right hand, found a handhold, moved my right foot and found a foothold. I moved my left foot out into the committed position. And then my right hand slipped off.

I started to fall. There was no saving it. When my hand slipped off, it slipped completely off and I started to fall backwards off the face. Things started to go into slow motion and I could see the rock face just getting inch by inch farther away from my face. My right foot was still on a pretty good foot hold, so I started to pivot away from the rock and turn my body to the right and I launched off the rock face by pushing off with my right leg. It was instinctive and I knew what I was trying to do, which was jump to the other side in a last ditch desperation. Only thing was, there was no way I would even come close.

But things were in slow motion. I noticed that the tree that came out from that weird angle in the side of the cliff was just below me, and that my angle of launch could land me on top of it. So I aimed for the base of the tree, the part that came out horizontally from the rock. While airborne I plotted my landing, by straddling the tree like I was one of those cowboys jumping onto the back of his horse from the saloon roof. I needed to land directly on and not roll off the side or that would be the end. I hit directly onto the base of the tree crotch first, one leg to each side, and wrapped my arms around it and hung on for dear life.

The momentum made me want to roll right off the side of it and keep going. But I hung on with everything I had left and was able to stop the motion and then pull myself back to the top so my weight was centered on the tree base. I was safe.

Once again I didn't move. The tree base was quite large. I was nestled in the base of the "J," on the horizontal part of the tree right where it changed directions and shot up vertically. My arms and legs were both wrapped around the tree and I was totally secure. I was, however, suspended on the side of a cliff in the pouring rain with no discernible way off my perch and no strength left even if there was.

I was done. Physically and mentally done. All those little chemicals in the brain that get you through things like getting shot at in crack shacks and instinctively saving your life while falling off mountains had apparently reached their maximums for one day and were shutting down. I could not move and didn't for a long time. I was done.

I just stayed there face down against the tree, arms and legs spread around it, and waited. I was in a state which felt like a semi-coma. I could not move, and thoughts were far off, dreamy sorts of thoughts. My face was pressed against the tree and I could smell the bark. Rain was beating against my back and dusk was settling in. There was not going to be any more effort to continue the climb.

The darkness came fast. Faster than expected, helped along by the grey weather, rain, and the tree cover allowing less light in. It took me by surprise, but ensured I was stuck here for the night. There was no choice now even if I had the strength. If you grew up in BC, you had heard stories every year of people getting lost in the back country. Skiers that go out of bounds and get lost, hikers that lose their way, partying kids who fall off cliffs or cliff jump with deadly endings. The back country took lives every year and the stories were always very similar in cases where people were lost in the woods around this time of year: they sometimes survived the first night and seldom survived the second. I had to believe there was a very short list of people who had come directly to these situations after a Hastings street lifestyle and a crack shack shootout. I was less prepared for this than even the most unbelievable stories of moronic unpreparedness that you would hear.

I was thinking about West Van, my parents, my childhood. Happy thoughts: the laughter and innocence of youth. It occurred to me that maybe these were the sorts of things people who were going to die think about in their final hours. Happy thoughts and thoughts of innocence. It was getting very cold and I was very tired. But there was something I still needed to do. I found the strength to push down on the tree so I could sit up a little so I was able to reach into my pants pocket. I pulled out my crack pipe. I looked at it for a moment, like recognition of its role in my life, and then threw it away where it fell with the rain to its final resting place. If I was going to die on this mountain, and if someone was going to actually find me, it was all of a sudden very important to me that they would not find my body with a crack pipe in my pocket. I realized, albeit late in the day given the circumstances, just how important it was for me to die as an addict. Bodies were always being taken off Hastings. Statistics. Not deemed as real people. And I had taken for granted my mortality and assumed I wasn't going to be one of them. And now that I was pretty sure I was going to die, I was actually very grateful that it was on a mountain and not on the street.

I thought about where things had gone wrong and about what I should have done with my life. I thought about what my life might have looked like had I not become addicted. Would I be married right now? A father? Would I have continued on playing sports? It was a sad reflection of what should have been a good life and it was surreal to think the reality was looking like there were not going to be any more chances. Too sad and too painful, the reality of the situation, the rain, and cold, dark and lonely mountain forced me to push these thoughts from my mind back to happy thoughts. I desperately sought comfort and found myself trying to come up with a song that included the words "feezy foe" when I drifted off into the night.

Chapter 8

I didn't die that night, but it was the longest, coldest night of my life, and I actually had some very cold and desperate nights on the streets that I could compare it to. Maybe I had in a way actually trained for this experience and it ultimately kept me alive. I fell asleep for short bursts throughout the night. I would wake up freezing, shivering uncontrollably, soaked to the bone, and then drift back off again. A couple of times I almost fell off the tree and jolted awake just in time to center myself correctly. But mostly, it was just an endless period of time for day to break and it seemed impossible that it was just one night.

At some stage it stopped raining. Who knew what the time was, but sometime in the middle of the night. And as it started to become light the temperature started to come up a little. I was still freezing cold and wet, but with the oncoming of actual light and no rain, there was an uplifting of spirit and rejuvenation. It didn't take long for it to become fully light, and with my renewed sense of life, I was ready to explore options.

The tree and rocks were still wet, but with the rain having stopped, and a new day on the horizon, everything seemed brighter. The base of the tree I was on was about six feet lower than where I was traversing across yesterday and I still had about fifteen more feet of dangerous traversing to try and navigate. But I was done with hanging out on this rock face and wanted off it now. The fear and trepidation was gone and I was left with a determined resiliency and bravery. I got to my feet, standing on the horizontal part of the tree base, careful not to slip off, and raised my hands to the rock face to find holds. I had to be very careful with the wet rock not to slip, but there were holds to grip and I immediately started the traverse without a moment's thought.

I made it to the other side successfully, but still had to pull myself over the other side edge as it was about eight feet above my head, so my lateral traverse turned into a vertical climb. But it wasn't challenging, just a tad scary knowing how high up I was. On the final leg I had to pull myself up and over the last four feet. I got two good hand holds, was able to pull my body up, threw one leg over the top and was able to pull the rest of my body up and over the edge. I made it! I just lay there on my back breathing heavily, staring at the sky through the trees. Now what?

I was feeling pretty good. I mean, I survived the night, the adrenaline from the mountain climbing was still in my system, I wasn't all that cold anymore, and I could see some patches of blue sky amongst the separating cloud cover through the trees. I had to be close to the top and the route options looked pretty doable. Should I just carry on? I couldn't think of a reason as to why not.

So up I went. Things seemed to go as I expected. The climb was hard, but the routes doable and I didn't come across any more roadblocks. The sun did come out and I was dry, and if anything, too warm now as a result of the exertion. The only thing that wasn't working out was finding the top and I wondered where in the world it could be.

Clearly my comparison to Grouse Mountain was unreasonable. If this were the Grouse Grind, I would have done it five times by now. Either I was on a mountain whose elevation was a lot higher, the trail conditions a lot more severe, or I was somehow lost. Well, I knew I was lost, but I mean somehow I was not on "my mountain" anymore and just in some perpetual climb into the back country of British Columbia. And I couldn't figure out how that could be as there were no peaks and valleys in this climb. Just straight up. Surely there had to be the top somewhere.

Finally I came into a large area void of trees where I could stop and get some bearings as to where I was. I could see what looked like the top. It was hard to tell, because of the angle, but it seemed as if it would fit for the "missing chunk" part of the mountain and it wasn't that much farther up. It was hard to tell how far, as I was seriously second guessing any opinions I might have on distance by this stage, but, gosh, it wasn't that much farther. I sat down on the bluff and rested. It was turning into an amazing morning and the view was nothing short of spectacular. I was surprised to notice I couldn't see the ocean. Surely I had started the climb on the side of the mountain closest to the ocean, so I must have gone so far laterally around the mountain finding accessible routes that I was now on the other side. In any event, I was now looking out over amazing valleys and could see other mountains in the range and it was amazing. And I was high up, no doubt about it. I had done some serious climbing and was at a pretty good elevation.

I rested for a while. It was so nice sitting in the sun and I was tired, so I wasn't in much of a hurry. But I wanted to make sure I left plenty of time to get down so I pulled myself up and headed up. The going was a bit easier and not quite as steep. I seemed to be going over some sort of valley before the final rise. But I was back in the trees again, so was once again without any sort of bearing.

The final push only took about thirty minutes. I came up over a rock, around a dense collection of trees, and came out into an opening that was clearly the top. I made it!

Chapter 9

The "top" was somewhat relative, as it was sort of a plateau spread out with varying high points. And this was only the top of this mountain which was still surrounded by an entire mountain range of valleys, higher and lower peaks, and a never ending view of mountains as far as the eye could see. But I had perspective from this angle and I could see the missing chunk part of the mountain. And even though the lines of where one mountain started and another ended were blurry, I could also tell that the top of the chunk was also the highest peak of this particular mountain and I made my way up to it.

When I reached the peak, the view opened up to a panoramic view of valley, ocean, and yes, city. I was a long way from civilization, that was for sure, but I could see where I was – somewhere north and east of Vancouver with a series of lower mountains and valleys between me and the coast.

The view was absolutely spectacular. I stared at it for a long time. I could pinpoint in the city where I had come from. Not exactly, because it was too far away, but I could see the landmarks, like the Lion's Gate Bridge, Stanley Park and where the highest buildings were of the financial district. A little east of that was where Hastings would be. I thought about where I had come from and thought about lying in that alley looking up to this point and now here I was looking back. Pretty trippy. I could easily have stared at the view forever, but with every passing second I was beginning to realize that my physical condition was rapidly decreasing.

⸻ ❦ ⸻

I wasn't a heroin addict. Many of the drug addicts on Hastings were. Some, because it was their drug of choice, preferring the "down" of heroin to the "up" of crack, and others became addicted to heroin because they over-used it as a tool to come down off of crack highs and eventually crossed the line into being "wired" or physically addicted. The big difference between crack and heroin is the physical dependency. Heroin is physically addicting and crack isn't. Use enough heroin and eventually your body needs it and will let you know when that time is.

I only used heroin maybe once a week in very small dosages. So while I didn't feel I was physically addicted, I had probably done enough over time to feel at least minor levels of physical dependency. It was sort of like having the early stages of the flu. Not fully wired but not free of it either.

However, while the experts say crack isn't physically addicting, it sure seemed like it. Severe fatigue, depression, scattered brain, inability to stay focused, restlessness, and fixation on drugs (severe cravings) were all legitimate symptoms and very difficult to cope with when detoxing. Plus, there was the physical toll the lifestyle took on hardcore addicts. There was not a Hastings Street crack addict that was anywhere near their legitimate body weight. The calories burned during a drug run combined with the difficulty in eating while high created an environment for severe weight loss. Add in nonexistent diets, staying awake for days on end, miles upon miles upon miles of endless wandering through city streets in the crazy quest for more drugs, alley, floor or slum sleeping environments, lungs strained by cigarette smoke, crack smoke, heart rates that can climb to severe heights when doing the drug, and mental lapses into sleep deprivation, paranoia, and psychosis, these all combine for one sick individual, both mentally, physically, emotionally, and spiritually.

———— ⛬ ————

Upon arriving at this moment I had six months of severe drug addiction under my belt, was sleep deprived, unhealthy, had rotten "street feet" and had not changed my clothes in a week. Then I went through the hotel shooting, had the surreal drive to the base of the mountain I was strangely drawn to, had a harrowing night alone on the side of the mountain where I thought for sure I would die, only to further push my ill equipped body the rest of the way up the mountain.

And now I was into my second day without drugs which was the longest period of time without drugs since my last stay in rehab, over six months ago. With the summit reached, I was now falling into full-on detox withdrawals and I was feeling every bit of it. The adrenaline, or feelings of being driven to get to the top had now subsided. My feet were completely done, raw from having worn the same shoes and socks for weeks, and from climbing a mountain in them. And I was chilled, achy, and tired. Beyond tired. I was at a level where if my life depended upon it, and surely it did, I would not be able to move. I had a moment of clarity where I knew for a fact that getting myself off this mountain was going to be improbable if not impossible and that same knowledge of local mountains crept back into my head: people sometimes survived the first night, but seldom the second.

I hadn't completely given up. These weren't the same sets of circumstances as last night. Last night when I had resigned myself to death, I was perched on the base of a tree on the side of a cliff at dusk in a driving rain storm. Right now, it was the middle of the afternoon on a moderately nice weather day, and I was on the summit of a mountain with stunning views that included a world class city. But I knew the situation was dire should I not make it to the bottom before nightfall, and I knew I was incapable of moving until I had at least rested for a bit, as I was seemingly unable to move. So I rested and stared at the view.

It really was an amazing view. It seemed surreal to me that I was actually here and the circumstances that led me here. Had it all really happened? And I couldn't quite grasp the fact I could see the city yet was powerless to draw any attention to myself. I was alone in every way. Yet I had been alone for a very long time now, hadn't I? Ever since the drug addiction entered my life. Street relationships aren't real; everything is influenced and dictated by the drugs. Life has been the addiction, nothing more, nothing less, and it has been a very lonely and pathetic existence.

It hit me how badly I had ruined my life. I guess there had always been a sense of immortality. And because I had essentially come from a good home, and was educated, I sort of always felt I would return to normalcy one day because I knew what normal life looked like. Sure, things would feel hopeless, and sure, my actions might have suggested defeatism, that I had given up, but at my core, I think I really still believed I would one day resume my life where it left off before drugs.

But the shooting, followed immediately by a near death experience on the mountain showed me my mortality. And the very real revelation kicked in that I could in no way count on anything working itself out in time to change the legacy I would leave. And this realization made me very sad that my life had gone this way. That it was actually way more important to me than I ever would have admitted to have lived my life in an honorable way and be considered a decent guy. That the prospect of dying in active addiction before I was able to change the resume of life was not how I wanted to go. I did not want to be known as: "Samuel James Wyatt, dead at twenty-eight years old; a chronic drug addict and great failure to all." All of a sudden it felt very real, very important, and very far away from what I would have wanted.

73

Looking west of the city and the Lion's Gate Bridge, I could see up the coastline of West Van. The farthest point of land that I could see was Point Atkinson, and while I couldn't quite see it, I knew that the Lighthouse was on that point. Lighthouse Park. I knew that the coastline cut in a bit past that point, then went around another point farther up the coastline a couple of kilometers or so, then wound around Whytecliff Park and into Horseshoe Bay where the British Columbia ferries went up coast or to Vancouver Island. But the last piece of land I could see from where I sat was Point Atkinson and I knew that about one kilometer beyond where I could see was my parent's house.

I wondered what they were doing right then. Were they home? Were they puttering around in the garden, perhaps raking up the fall leaves? Were they having coffee in the living room talking about me? Were my mom's hands wringing together in her lap, as she did when she was concerned about me and my slide into addiction? I could picture the house, the yard, the street, the elementary school where so much of the innocence of youth occurred. And I longed for it and mourned the loss of it and I determined that when or if I ever got off this mountain that I would reclaim my life, that I would do whatever was necessary to get off drugs and stay off, and that I would find myself again. I wanted me back. I wanted the carefree, good at sports, lover of family and other people, interested in the world, fascinated by living *me* back. I wanted to live!

And with that determination I slowly rose to my feet. I wondered what time it was. It was probably light out at about 7:00 AM, and I was moving at the first hint of dawn from the tree base. Call it maybe four more hours of hiking with about another full hour of rests, and I had been at the top resting for another hour, all ballpark times. But given that, it was maybe 1:00 in the afternoon. It would be dark by maybe 6:00, or perhaps even earlier as day just seemed to fall away without warning on the side of the mountain. So, I had perhaps four hours to go down a mountain that had taken a day and a half to climb and I had to do it without a trail to go down, no idea of the best route, and in a state of full on detox. Okay then.

One thing I knew for sure was I wasn't going down the way I came up. I was pretty convinced that it was the lateral traversing and route changes that cost me so much time coming up to the extent that I started on the ocean side of the mountain and finished on the complete other side by the time I got to the top. I theorized that if I kept the ocean in view on the way down, and lucked out with decent paths down, not only could I get down fast, I would probably not have to worry about getting lost at the bottom. There would be roads between the mountain and ocean for sure. The big advantage from being on the top and looking down was the perspective of the way was clearer. Of course this was all theory. I didn't want to think about the fact I had intended to hike straight up and somehow got so lost I practically circled the mountain. One thing was certain: if darkness fell before I made it to the bottom, I would not make it through another night.

I got to my feet, barely able to stand. I fought off a chill and instinctively hugged my arms around my body. My legs felt like they couldn't support my body and every step felt shaky, slow, and agonizing. Though an athlete in my youth, and still young, I desperately needed my body to respond, but I was helpless to make it comply. I was in rough, rough shape. The easy thing would have been to just sit back down again, but there was no part of me at this point that was just going to roll over and wait on death. No way. But the feeling of powerlessness was overwhelming.

I walked the plateau area while keeping the ocean in view. I was looking for a starting point for the downward trajectory but it was all so steep or impenetrable, or both and I realized that all good planning and strategies would go out the window in lieu of what the mountain would allow. I was a good distance from where I had been perched on the summit now and the ocean was gone from view (already) as I continued to look for a good access down. Finally I spotted something that looked promising. An open area fed into a tree line with only a moderate slope and it seemed as good a place as any. Actually, it felt more like it was the only place available and I left the openness of the plateau and went into the tree line for the start of the descent.

It was in fact only a moderate slope. For the first forty feet, it was like walking an easy forest trail but I could see where it started an immediate drop off. Now it was just a matter of walking around a few trees to find the next most logical path down the steepness.

I walked around the base of one massive tree with the intention of starting down on the other side of it. My foot landed on top of one of the roots at the base and slipped off. Perhaps the athletic "me" of my youth may have saved me from falling. But the addict "me", the one in full detox, didn't stand a chance. My foot slipped off and I fell face forward over the edge and went into a free fall tumble. The fall had propelled me forward into a somersault so the back of my neck and shoulder hit the ground first on a steep incline and the momentum put me into the full on snowball effect. I was semi conscious as to what was going on, and was aware that my ass and feet were the next body parts to connect with the earth but as my chest came up for its second rotation I slammed into something that stopped me dead in my tracks. The impact against my chest knocked me flat on my back on the side of the mountain with the wind severely knocked out of me.

I gasped for breath and tried to keep myself from doing something stupid like rolling into an angle that would again get me rolling down the slope. My eyes were closed and I mentally calmed myself and told myself my breathing would come back. Slowly it did, and I was able to draw some oxygen into my lungs and breathe out; in and out, slowly while I did a slow inventory of broken parts. My ribs were sore, but probably not broken. My shin was sore, but probably just bruised and scraped. So, okay, I opened my eyes.

At first I didn't quite grasp what I was seeing. I was staring straight up at something big and metal. Metal? It was lying on a horizontal manner suspended on both sides by tree bases with its middle suspended right above my head, maybe three feet off the ground. I couldn't make out what in the world I was seeing. I pulled myself up so that I was now standing over it and I could now see its full length, overall shape, and design and I figured out what I was looking at.

It was a float from a float plane.

Chapter 10

No doubt about it, that's what it was. The shape was unmistakable and obvious. And the way it was positioned just saved me from my free fall down the mountain. Okay, so as unusual as it all seemed, could it be that a plane had crashed close by? I mean, wouldn't that be the obvious explanation? It seemed unlikely that hikers decided one day to bring one up the mountain with them just for fun. So how else could it have gotten here? It didn't appear to be some ancient relic. But it didn't seem like it just arrived either. There was some moss growing on it and it looked pretty weathered. But at the same time there was still some pin striping that had color in it and the design looked modern enough. So, what? Maybe it's been here a few years?

The next logical question (because this was a mission of logic, right?) was to wonder where the rest of the plane was. I had fallen about fifteen feet down from the tree root I slipped on and I thought if I could get back up to that point I might afford myself a better view around. I knew time was of the essence, but the prospect of something man made up here gave me a sense of hope that I felt needed investigating.

So I climbed back up to the tree I fell from and took a look around. I looked back down at the float, and tried to picture how it could have arrived at its current position and every scenario seemed impossible. I suppose the plane could have clipped a tree, lost a float which in turn fell from the sky. That seemed feasible. And maybe the plane didn't even crash. Maybe the only casualty was the actual float. Although I would guess the pilot would have had trouble landing later. Still, chances were the plane was here somewhere.

There really weren't many long views, just too many trees for that to be possible, so finding anything would be difficult and it was beginning to seem like a hopeless cause. Just as I was about to give up and hobble off towards my impending doom I thought I saw something just a little farther up towards the top. I was back on the moderate slope area again, and what I thought I saw came into view and I could see it clearly. It was the plane!

The nose of the plane was sticking through two trees, still intact and with the propeller mangled but still partially attached. As I came up alongside the plane I could see it was amazingly intact. It was missing a float (which made sense) and it was badly caved in on the opposite side to which I was standing, near the cockpit, but the body in general was in pretty good condition although it was missing both wings entirely. One was severed completely from the plane but in one piece, badly damaged, and at a distorted angle about twenty feet from the main body of the plane. I could see another piece of wing about forty yards farther along the forest floor but it was by no means the entire wing. The remaining float was still attached to the plane and was supporting that side of the plane, with the trees holding up the other side. All in all, it looked, well, sort of parked appropriately.

It was in surprisingly good shape, all things considered. It was consistent with the assessment of the float a few minutes earlier in that it looked modern enough to not be that old, but weathered enough to have been here at least a certain amount of time. But I didn't care about that, or the fact that there could very well be some dead people inside. I was going to try and get the door open and I was going to do it right now.

I tried the handle and gave it a tentative pull. It didn't budge, so I gave it a good pull and felt some give, but it still didn't open up. I stepped back and assessed the situation. I walked around the plane in its entirety. There were two doors, one on either side. And that was it. So if I was going to get in, it was going to be through one of those two doors. But the pilot side was badly mangled with a severe trauma starting on the front left nose and caving in the body all the way to the door. The door looked impossible to open. So it was back to the side I already tried, and this time I was going to make it open come hell or high water.

I climbed up on the float for better leverage and grabbed hold of the handle and then braced my foot against a bar that jutted out from the body, no doubt a support for the missing wing. The bar only protruded about a foot at which point, it was mangled off. It was no longer useful to hold up a wing, but was serving my purpose of leverage.

So one foot was levered against the bar, and both hands were on the handle, and I brought my body weight in, took a breath, and leaned back with all the force I could muster. Naturally the door came open quite easily and the momentum propelled me backwards through the air and I once again landed hard on the ground flat on my back. But the door had come open and that's all I cared about.

I got back to my feet, wondered for just a second how much one body could take, and approached the open door and peered inside. The first thing I noticed was that there was a body inside, presumably the pilot. He was sitting in the pilot's seat, which was intact for the most part but had been impacted by the indentation I had seen on the other side of the plane. Actually, he was a skeleton, more so than a body if that made a difference. If it weren't for the fact that he was on a slightly awkward angle as a result of how the body of the plane had indented inwards, pushing him off centre, then he may have looked exactly as he would have had he been flying the plane right now.

In any event, he was there, but he appeared to be the only body. The passenger seat was empty, and there were no more seats in the plane, just storage behind the front seats. Perhaps there was another row at some stage that was taken out for increased storage as it sort of looked that way. And I could see items back there that were stored.

It smelled pretty bad in the plane. There was no mistaking that. Sort of a combination of must, rot, forest, with a trace of dead body. But it wasn't overpoweringly bad. Honestly, I smelled worse on an almost daily basis on Hastings. I had spotted one item in the back of the plane that made all further decisions completely irrelevant. I saw a sleeping bag and knew I was going in and camping out for the night, no more questions asked or answered. Done deal.

Speaking of done, I was also a done deal. I had nothing left on any level. And knowing it was into the afternoon and I was still on the top of the mountain, and that I barely had the strength to lift myself into the plane made me realize that getting to the bottom never would have happened and that this plane was saving my life. For today anyway.

I pulled myself past the passenger seat and headed straight into the storage area to where the sleeping back was on top of a pile of other stuff rolled up in classic sleeping bag fashion. I undid the strings holding it in place, rolled it out, and climbed in. A quick look around and I could see there were other things stored here that could potentially be helpful, but at the moment I didn't really care. Space was an issue for my height, but if anyone thought I cared, they would be far from right. I curled into a ball and went straight to sleep in the plane on the mountain.

Chapter 11

I pretty much slept right through into the next day. I woke a few times disoriented in the total blackness until I realized where I was, then promptly went back to sleep again. The sleeping bag was amazingly comfortable and warm. At some stage of the night I stripped out of my shirt and socks which made me feel even better to be free of the disgust of those clothes. Just because someone was a drug addict didn't mean they *liked* the feeling of being in the same clothes for days on end.

The sleep was deep and blissful. And while I forgot where I was every time I stirred, when I remembered I was actually more comforted by being there than I was when I would wake on the street. I was safe, warm, and there was no check out time. While a normal person would never be able to understand what it would be like to stay up for four consecutive days without sleep, they would be equally unknowledgeable about what the fatigue was like when the drugs were gone.

I awoke again well into the next morning. I know it hadn't been light that long, maybe a few hours. And I could easily have rolled right over but I was cognizant of the fact that I needed some food and water so I took a moment to sit up and for the first time take a look around at what else was here. What I found was a virtual bonanza of items someone in my predicament would need.

On cursory glance, it looked as if this pilot was going on some sort of camping or fishing trip when he crashed, as there were supplies stored all around where I was sleeping. There were fishing rods, a tackle box, a duffel bag of clothes and toiletries, camping gear, a cooler with bottled water, food, canned goods, and probably more. This was like hitting the jackpot! Of course only the non-perishables were any good, but the water bottle still was good and so were the canned goods and I couldn't think what more I would need at the moment so stopped there.

I selected a can of Hungry Man Stew (because I was a hungry man) and a bottle of water. The stew had a pull tab on the top, so I didn't even have to find a can opener, even though I would bet money at this stage that there would be one here somewhere, and I pulled back the lid and dug in.

I was famished and more thirsty than I even knew. It actually made me wonder for a moment how I made it as far as I did with no water. The Yukon breakfast at Momma's had been the single biggest meal I had ever eaten, but in my malnourished state, I had burned through those calories long ago. I dug my fingers into the soup and shoveled it into my mouth and gulped down water like a man who just crossed a dessert. I polished both off in less than a minute, climbed out of the plane for a leak, crawled back in, and promptly went back to sleep.

I repeated the process again after it was dark on my next rotation of wake ups, this time with a can of spaghetti which was simply delicious. I went back to sleep again and did not wake up until it was light the following day. I sat up and took stock.

This was the beginning of my fourth day on the mountain. The first night was on the base of the tree on the cliff, the next two in the plane. And now here I was on day four and still on the top of the mountain. I was still not right, not by a long shot, but having detoxed many times in the past, I was familiar with the process. It wasn't about being physically sick, it was more about being physically weak and mentally unstable. Maybe not so much unstable, as much as say, having difficulty of the mind. It was like the mind was firing away as if expecting drugs, the pleasure centers, neutrons and endorphins having been badly abused over long periods of time. Net result: no peace of mind. And no strength. The thought of attempting the descent seemed ridiculous now that I was truly free of the drugs. At least not today.

But there did seem to be one bonus and that was I really hadn't craved using drugs since I left the city. In fact during this entire ordeal, I can't recall having one serious craving which I attested to the fact that I knew without a shadow of doubt that the possibility of getting drugs up here was nil. Out of sight, out of mind I guess. Of course I would check out the plane in its entirety in the off chance the fishing expedition was just a cover for a cocaine drug runner! One can dream.

I thought about the fact that I had been "missing" for four days and wondered if anyone would have noticed. I highly doubted it. The only possible scenario would have been that the police would be looking for me as a result of somehow placing me at the scene of the shooting. It seemed possible given that I was pretty sure at least one person had died that day in the hotel. But then again, maybe not. Maybe it was just a lot of shooting and violence but with no death.

Aside from that scenario, nobody would have known I was missing. And that was the sad state of affairs with people in addiction. The people who care for us have long gotten used to the fact that they would not hear from us for extended periods of time, and the people we used with were used to seeing someone one day and then never again. Who the heck knew where they would go? Maybe they died in an alley, went to detox, went to another skid row in another province. Who knew?

There was no job not to show up to, no family obligations, no concerned friends or neighbours, no clubs where people would begin to worry. Nope. The only people who I ever encountered were so busy fueling their own addictions they had no idea I wasn't there with them.

Maybe at some stage my parents would realize something was wrong. Well more wrong than what was already wrong. And maybe they would start a search of some sort downtown. But that wouldn't be in a few days. A few months maybe, but not a few days. So nobody knew I was here and nobody knew I was missing.

I got out of the plane, relieved myself, and for the first time since seeing the plane, took a look around. I took a stroll away from the plane and back to the opening of the plateau. It wasn't far at all, maybe about five rows of tress back from where the plane was. The plane was impossible to see from the opening and with the denseness of the tree line, I would imagine the plane could not be spotted from the air either.

Standing in the openness of the plateau I tried to picture what might have happened to the plane. I looked to the sky, to the opposite direction I knew the plane was pointing, and pictured the plane perhaps in trouble coming over the peak of the next mountain back. This opening I was standing in certainly didn't look possible to land a plane on, but given the trees and cliffs all around had to look like the best of many poor options. Maybe he was trying to limp back to the coast, which would have been one more peak (the peak I was on) and then a coast down to the ocean. Or maybe he was forced down by weather. Maybe he came in over the second to last peak and knew he had to put it down and this plateau was the only option. I could picture him coming in fast, desperate and fighting for control, and overshooting the landing by just a bit. Maybe he clips one of the floats against a rock outcrop breaking it free from the plane and sending it careening into the forest where it ends up perched between two trees. Then the plane goes into the forest fast and out of control, hitting one tree hard on the pilot side, and coming to a stop some five rows into the forest. Maybe something like that happened.

I tried to picture what happened in my mind and walked back into the forest along the line I thought it might have crashed. It all seemed to make sense. Doubtless, there was a search, but for whatever reason, nobody ever found the wreckage.

When I came back to the plane I opened the co-pilot door and looked into the cockpit seriously for the first time. It looked amazingly like all those movies where they come across plane crashes and find the WWII pilot still sitting in the cockpit, a uniformed skeleton at the controls. This pilot wasn't uniformed but he did have on a leather jacket, pants, and shoes. And he had something else I was entirely unprepared for.

Chapter 12

In his lap was a book held open to a page by one of his skeletal hands. I had been in enough hotel rooms to know it was a Bible. I could now also see that the damage to his side of the plane had caved in so far as to trap him in his seat. His left hip and arm appeared to be completely pinned by the plane. The seat belt had been stretched by the impact and was pinning him in the seat. Again, trying to picture what happened, it seemed as if he survived the impact. That part seemed obvious as it seemed impossible to think he had busted into a book during the crash landing. So he had survived the impact but was hurt and trapped in his seat. But he was alive enough to have somehow dug out his Bible, propped it into his lap, and read it up until he died.

I imagine there had to have been a period of time where he tried in vain to extricate himself, and that upon exhausting all means available had ultimately resigned himself to acceptance and just waited on death. I wondered how long it took and I wondered how much pain he was in. Must have been a lot.

And I thought about how frightening and lonely it must have been. Having myself just a few nights ago been perched on the side of a mountain sure that I would die, I could strangely relate. He had been alone, hurt, scared, and resigned to death. And he somehow is able to reach for his Bible, which had to be close at hand already, and decides that his last moments on earth would be spent reading this book. It must have been of terrific importance and brought him great comfort.

I wondered what he thought about in those last moments (days, hours, minutes?). Probably about life, family, and concern over who knew he was there. The usual end of life thoughts. Regrets though? Could his life's resume have been as appalling as mine I wondered. Doubt it. And clearly he was thinking about God. And it made me interested in what he was reading, so I leaned into the cockpit, and slowly and carefully pulled the book out from under his hand and brought it back towards me.

The book was leather bound, well made and had those beeswax type pages. Probably how it lasted so well after this long. It was a big book, with easy to read print. Maybe my friend here had been old with poor eyesight. Hard to tell by the skeleton, but maybe I should have a look for his ID and flight logs as well. But one thing at a time....

The book was open to a chapter titled Ephesians 4. I read the first line: *"As a prisoner of the Lord, then, I urge you to live a life worthy of the calling you have received."*

I stopped there. I felt something a little like being short of breath as if I just read something of tremendous importance. *The life worthy of the calling you have received?* Did I receive a calling for my life? If I did, I certainly hadn't lived a life worthy of it.

I slid the Bible carefully into the back area. I made two decisions right then and there. One, I was not going to be in a hurry to leave this mountain, and two, I was going to read more of what I just read. Well, maybe three decisions with the third being it was time to go back to sleep.

I woke up a few hours later. There was still some daylight left, but not much. I went outside for a minute for relief and then settled back inside. I propped myself up and went over a few things in my mind. I was approaching the end of day four on the mountain, and was four days clean. As far as detoxing was concerned I had already come through the worst and was rounding the corner into getting better. I was feeling ready to take a few things on. I was beginning to see some benefits to being up here. With four days clean under my belt, unheard of numbers of success for me as of late, and some harrowing, life-changing experiences now under my belt, I was now thinking about staying clean. If that were the goal, then what better place to build a foundation of sobriety than up here where even the most insane cravings for drugs could not be satisfied. All the best treatment centers in the world shared this one common trait: keep the addict away from drugs. And while, sure, they also have counseling, offer coping skills, do group processing, and serve food, I have learned that the "not using" part was the most critical. An addict will slowly gain strength with every passing sober day.

But the bottom line was, if I was going to try and stay sober, my only two current options were to stay up here or attempt to get back to civilization. And if I made it back into town, and wanted to stay clean, I would have to get on a waiting list for detox or treatment and drift around the city staying in shelters until something came up. I rated the odds of me pulling this off without falling back into addiction at a hair above zero. And that was being generous.

If the plan was to stay up here for a while, then I needed to preserve the food and water better, take stock of what I could use, formulate a plan of sorts for mountain survival, and put it into action. I determined to take a complete inventory once morning came and put some plans into place. I knew there were supplies for at least a few days more, so I wasn't overly worried about the short term. I had a warm place to sleep, food, water, and, apparently, a good book.

I have to admit I actually found the prospect of camping up here quite exciting. I felt safe, comfortable and was grateful for the reprieve of the grind of the street. I really didn't feel any sense of urgency to leave at all. For what? More misery?

With decisions made and a plan for morning, I relaxed and opened the Bible back up to Ephesians 4 and read the entire chapter, which was no real feat, only about a page long, which was about right given my fried out brain. I laid back and propped my hands behind my head and thought about what I had just read. Then I fell asleep as the darkness came.

Chapter 13

ay five. Definitely on the mend. In fact, I was feeling much better than I would have expected. Almost normal. Perhaps the environment was contributing to my accelerated good health. Normally on day five, I would still be shuffling up and down detox corridors waiting for snack time and wondering when I would be discharged to another recovery facility. Up here, with plenty of fresh air, no constant visual reminders that I was in a sick ward, and the unique conditions were apparently good for my health. I was up at a reasonable time too. I considered it day one of a life lived under normal timelines.

Okay, time to get to work. I got busy seeing what exactly I had here with me. The first thing I did was empty everything out of all bags, storage areas, coolers, and anything else I could find and sort into categorized piles: food, clothing, gear, etc. Apparently my friend in the pilot's seat enjoyed canned foods, because there was still about six days worth of food in cans. Plus there was a full box of powdered instant soup, a box of granola bars, a tin of coffee, a jar of peanut butter and a fairly good sized package of hardened candies. There was fishing gear, rod and tackle box, hip waders, gum boots, fresh clothes for a few days, a toiletries bag, a first aid kit, a lighter, a heavy rain jacket, and a flashlight.

So it seemed pretty clear my friend had been going on a fishing trip but crashed before he got there. Maybe he started somewhere up north and was coming to Vancouver, or maybe he left Vancouver for a lake somewhere when he got into trouble and didn't quite make it back. Or maybe he was just going to drop some supplies off somewhere. Or maybe he was going to visit a friend who had a cabin on a lake somewhere. After all, there was no tent, cooking stove, or anything. Who knew exactly? But the general theme seemed to be fishing. And then of course, things went very wrong for him.

I debated going through the cockpit. I was quite sure I would find some identification, perhaps a flight log, and more evidence as to what had happened, but for some reason I just felt his space should be left alone for now. It just seemed, well, sacred, I guess to leave his immediate area untouched, and I couldn't think of anything more I might need anyway.

Except water, which I was out of. I was aware the water bottles were being consumed quickly, but I didn't care all that much. I was in a British Columbia rain forest. In fact, it was raining outside right now. If I couldn't find water pretty quickly up here, then what kind of survivalist was I anyway?

But it did take over as my number one priority and so I prepared myself for my first venture away from "home." I changed out of my clothes into some of his. Not a bad fit. I was used to scrounging clothes from street life anyway and generally found most average men's clothes fit me more or less. These clothes really weren't a bad fit at all, and his wardrobe was much better suited for these sorts of conditions than mine was. Besides, mine were disgusting and I was all too glad to be rid of them. To me they represented the old and I was now interested only in the new. I tried on his gum boots and rain jacket and found them a pretty good fit as well. Great! I put together some water bottles and ventured out.

Once in the plateau area I only really had one option which was to head in a general direction north or northeast away from the ocean and farther back into the mountains. I made sure I marked my direction carefully. The last thing I wanted to do now was get lost. The hiking was easy, without any serious elevation changes and it allowed my mind to wander.

I was thinking about Ephesians 4. In fact I couldn't seem to stop thinking about it. In one chapter it seemed to cover so much to think about. It was the line about living a life worthy of the calling that I have been given that I couldn't shake from my mind. Maybe because of these recent life experiences where my thinking invariably ended up in the knowledge that first, I was not immortal, and second, my life to date really sucked.

This book seemed to suggest that I was given a calling by God and that I had an obligation to live up to it. If this were true, then I wondered what my calling might have been, and whether or not it was still valid or not after the butchery I made of my existence.

I wasn't religious. I was never taken to church as a child, and in fact, had never been inside of a church except for one wedding I went to with my parents when I was about eighteen. Perhaps I shouldn't say I wasn't religious. I did think about things like God, but mainly in the context of looking towards the skies and wondering how the whole thing worked. I could certainly say I wasn't an atheist. I wouldn't have been so bold as to suggest I knew for sure there was *no* god. I was more a middle of the road guy. One of those "I don't know but please don't preach to me" guys.

But I was open-minded enough. If there was a divine influence on things, and I was being included in it, then I wasn't going to dismiss it as impossible. It was just me here now and I was walking around on the top of a mountain wearing a dead pilot's clothes and living in the back of a plane, and this after arriving here straight from skid row. So if there was a message from God somewhere here, then I was prepared to run with it. And if there was a calling for my life I wanted to give it thought.

But there was more to Ephesians 4 too, including a segment within the chapter that said, "Instructions for Christian Living" which I also found fascinating. If I interpreted it correctly it was essentially suggesting that my ignorance has darkened my understanding of God, that my thinking has been futile, and that I lost all sensitivity and had been operating with a hardened heart.

This all seemed to resonate such truth in me. I had been living on skid row, the gutter of all existence, and despite all my best efforts I had been unable to do anything about it. By living a life of making my own decisions and by abiding by my own concept of what rules were, my life had been an unmitigated disaster. If there had been a purpose for my life, I had certainly fallen well short of fulfilling it. I did not think about God, seemed to have entirely lost any moral compass I may have once had, was not honorable on any level. I was desensitized to just about everything and was a denizen of society. I was reading about myself in Ephesians 4 being described as the exact *opposite* of how they were describing a man of God. And that realization was hitting home right about now.

I had been wandering for a while. I did a couple of peaks and valleys and was getting tired. I had found a few areas with some dribbles of water runoff that would have sufficed but not the type of stream I was looking for where filling water bottles would have been easier. I was just about to settle for the dribble and turn around when I saw one more peak of sorts that might open up some views and decided to end the trek after I had checked it out. I climbed up to it and found there was in fact a pretty good view offered up of mountains, valley, and say what? A lake!

Yes, there was a small mountain lake just down and over a bit from where I was. Not far really. I decided I would venture down and fill up the water bottles, but about halfway there, I found a stream heading for the lake, so I filled up the water bottles there and had had enough for the day. I was still struggling with weakness and fatigue and wanted to head home for a nap.

I marked where the lake was and headed back. I wanted to make sure I knew how to find it again as a plan was formulating in my mind. Tomorrow, I would try my hand at a little fishing!

I made it back easily. My sense of direction was pretty good and I had been very careful about making sure I knew where I was. I had another cold Hungry Man Stew for lunch with a granola bar and washed it down with some very refreshing cold water. I settled into the sleeping bag, propped up against the back wall of the plane, grabbed the Bible and popped a candy in my mouth. I re-read Ephesians 4 again. Then I read the entire book of Ephesians which had a total of six chapters. Then I fell asleep.

I dreamt something about Ephesians 4 and in my dream I was saying it out loud. But it didn't sound quite right. Not so much Ephesians 4. More like Epheezee Four. Pheezee Fo. Feezy Foe? I was dreaming about Ephesians 4 and I was yelling Feezy Foe.

Then I woke up and completely freaked out.

Chapter 14

The next day I went fishing. I packed the rod, the entire tackle box, and a snack and headed off into the back country. I had fished before as a kid in West Van. Tiddlycove had a small marina as did Eagle Harbor and then there was the West Van Yacht Club and Thunderbird Marina where masses of boats were. I enjoyed going to all the marinas as a kid and wandering up and down the piers. There always seemed to be something going on: boats coming and going, people needing help mooring boats by throwing a line, people coming and going up and down the piers for various reasons, often with wheelbarrows full of items needing transport to and from their boats, and of course, people who were into fishing.

Fishing was a big topic around the marinas. Maybe not like at a marina where commercial fishing took place. That wasn't happening in West Van. No, West Van was all about pleasure boats and people with money enjoying an expensive hobby. But within that, many of them were into fishing. So people came and went with fishing rods, or bought bait from the live bait holds, or just dropped a line right there in the marina and fished off the wharf.

The first time I fished my father took me down to Thunderbird Marina with a cheap rod and some worms for bait and we fished right off the wharf at the end of one of the piers. I caught a Bullhead. It was a catch and release type thing, with the fish only being about four inches long. But I liked it. And I liked the culture around fishing. People were interesting and were always friendly. "Catch anything?" they would ask. Or, "Ya doing okay there young fella?" Things like that.

And other people would fish nearby and we would be always aware as to who was catching what. And people coming back to the harbor in their boats would often clean their catches on the wharf after tying up. And I would watch how they did it.

So, while I wasn't any kind of pro, I wasn't a total novice either. But there were certain things that concerned me as I made my way to the lake, like what kind of fly to use as all my experience was on the ocean. Or whether or not there actually were any fish in the lake. That seemed relevant. But I wasn't deterred. It was raining again, but my gear was good, it wasn't overly cold, and I had all day anyway. So, let's fish, was my thought.

It was about thirty minutes to the lake, now that I knew the way and wasn't stopping frequently. The lake wasn't big. I don't know at what size a pond becomes a lake, but I'm calling this a small lake. I could swim across it probably, but only barely. That big. I found a spot where a tree had fallen partially into the water. From there I would be able to cast from the shore, or even a few steps down the tree to get over the water a bit more.

The tackle box was full of stuff. All kinds of flies, lures, weights, floaters, extra line, and hooks. Plus, tools like pliers, a knife, a club and ruler for, I guess, measuring how big the catch is. One thing I knew about fresh water fishing is that you cast as opposed to dropping your line straight down. So I only wanted enough weight to keep the line firm but not enough weight to sink the line like a rock. I selected a very small weight and attached it to the line a couple of feet from the end. This should enable me to cast into the air while keeping the integrity of the line together but would still be able to slowly draw the line back to shore without it sinking too much. It wasn't the weight I was as worried about as much as the lure.

I had several options to choose from. There was a fake worm, several colored lures that I knew would reflect in the water, and flies. I stayed safe and went with the fake worm, given the one thing I knew for sure: fish like worms.

The rod already had a hook on it, so I attached the worm, spent a few minutes trying to figure out the spool and then did a few tentative casts. It wasn't that hard. I had seen enough rods in my youth to understand the concept. One button locks the line in the rod, another button releases it. So, throw the line behind you locked in place, throw the line forward, and then at just the right moment, release the lock, and send the weighted line far into the lake with the spool letting off line. Cast out as far as possible and then slowly reel the line back in. The reeling in keeps the line from sinking to the bottom, as well as keeping the lure like a moving target that the fish like. Easy. Except it wasn't. It took timing, skill, and patience. Most of my first throws were not good and I'm glad nobody was watching. It must have looked pretty uncoordinated as I was dropping the line way short of the water every time. Once I came very close to hooking my own head with the throw.

But slowly I was getting the hang of it and I was getting the line out into the lake a little farther every throw. I got off a couple real solid casts and was able to leisurely bring the line back in. If I was going to snag a fish, it would be on one of these good casts. Patience was the name of the game. Of course doubt crept in with every passing cast. Did I have the right bait? Was I throwing to the right area of the lake? Was I reeling in too fast? Was the line too close to the surface? And the biggest question of all: were there any fish in this lake?

But I settled into a routine and told myself not to doubt anything. The worst case scenario was not bad. So I don't catch a fish? So what? I wasn't going to starve. Not today anyway. So I cast and reeled and changed the landing spot a few times and tried a few different angles and waited. And I thought about Feezy Foe.

Funny things about dreams, how you felt about it upon immediately waking up, compared to what you feel about it later on. The more time that passed the less sure I was of what was reality and what wasn't. Did I really dream about "feezy foe" in the night? Or did I just *think* I did? Dreams are weird.

Of course having that dream, or the thinking that I had that dream made me think back to waking up in the alley screaming "feezy foe" out loud. That episode was verified by the factory worker in his lab coat. He was yelling at me, "What feezy foe you bad man," or something like that. That was definitely reality and he definitely confirmed that I was screaming those words.

And then I got shot at, climbed a mountain, found a plane with a dead man inside who was reading the Bible turned to Ephesians 4. Crazy as it may seem all that stuff happened for sure. So I guess the only real question was could there possibly be some sort of link between the "feezy foe" of the alley and the Ephesians 4 of the plane? Was God speaking to me? When I was on Hastings Street and staring up at this mountain, was He calling to me? Saying, hey, climb this mountain, find the plane, read the book and change your life. I giggled a little. I don't know why, it just all seemed so, well, strange.

I was second guessing myself from start to finish. Did I really stare at this particular mountain from the street or was I just staring at mountains in general? Did I scream "feezy foe" in the alley, or was it maybe, oh I don't know, "I'm Freezing Joe." Or how about "Sleazy Hoe?" I mean that would have been more relative to the street surroundings I was in at the time.

And was it a coincidence I landed at the base of this mountain, or was it just how the circumstances played themselves out? And does the fact that the pilot was reading Ephesians 4 have anything to do with "feezy foe?" It seemed much more realistic to think I was yelling at a sleazy hoe on the street in my dream in the alley, went through a series of events that, albeit unusual, were just a series of events where I ended up in the plane reading the guy's book which was having a legitimate affect on me that caused me to dream about it. "Sleazy Hoe" one dream and Ephesians Four the second. Random events. Both sounding like "feezy foe." Total coincidence.

Still, as much as I was second guessing myself away from believing the unbelievable, the unbelievable seemed real and more than that, it *felt* like it was real. And really, what did I care if I chose to interpret it all as real. I'll tell you what else was real: that my life was completely messed up. And if this chapter of my life could net me a real change by believing that I was being intervened with by God, then I was going to roll with it no matter who said what.

There, I said it. I now believe in God.

I had been fishing for two hours when I snagged my line. At first I actually thought I caught something. But eventually I realized that the pull I thought I was feeling was actually a snag, and a bad one at that. Ultimately I had to cut the line and start over. I selected a weight that was slightly heavier, and then once again guessed at a lure. I found one in a package called the Rebel Tracedown Minnow. Rebel seemed appropriate, so I went with it. It was a lure and hook combination, so I attached it to the end of the line and was good to go again.

I changed sides of the log for no other reason than to change things up and threw my first cast. With the added weight and a few hours of practice under my belt I moved it out there to record distance. And I was no sooner than a few rotations of the reel in when I got my first legitimate nibble. There was no mistaking it. It was like three of four fast tugs and a slight change of direction and then nothing. Not a snag. A fish.

I reeled all the way in, then cast again. Another beauty. And another bite. This time the fish stayed on. It was more violent than I would have expected and there was some serious action on the end of the line. I reeled in when the line went slack and was careful not pull too hard when the fish was fighting. I didn't want to break the line. But I did give a couple good tugs to try and make sure the hook was going to take.

I slowly reeled it towards shore. I didn't want to lose it at this stage. I could see the fish now as it surfaced a few times. I had it into shallow water and the fish was starting to give in. I reeled it in the last few feet but wasn't sure what to do. There was a net attached to the outside of the tackle box but I hadn't prepared it and I didn't want to let go of the rod to get it, or attempt to get it one handed. So when the fish was about a foot from shore, I just yanked it up and out of the water and it landed right by my feet. I grabbed the line about a foot from the fish, and walked it over the few feet to the tackle box and got the club and whacked it in the head a few times till I was pretty sure it was dead. Phew.

I will probably stop short of calling it an epic battle for a mighty catch, but it was thrilling none the less. In fact, I think I could say it was one of the most thrilling experiences of my life. I actually caught a fish on the top of a mountain! And at this very moment I was feeling very, very good about a lot of things in life.

The fish itself was about fourteen inches long. I measured it with the ruler, and it was about two inches longer than the ruler was. I'm going to say it was a trout, because that's the only fresh water fish I know of in BC and from what I could recall about trout, I think it looked like one. Okay then, so now what?

Well, I was going to eat it, that's what. I decided taking it back to camp was the best option. I would clean it, try to start a fire, and cook it up. So I packed up and headed back to the plane. While I was walking I thought about bears. I mean, here I was walking around in the mountains carrying a fish. I wondered when exactly bears started hibernating. I hoped it had already happened. But fortunately, I didn't run into any bears that day and made it back to camp safely.

I spent the next hour making a fire. I had the lighter from the plane and enough paper but the wood was all so wet. I ended up finding all kinds of sticks and twigs and used the knife to shave down far enough to get some semi dry shavings which I put into the base of the fire. I put more effort into preparation than I did the actual lighting as I wanted to try and preserve paper. But the task was almost as challenging as the fishing and I started to become skeptical I would be able to light one at all when finally some of the shavings caught and I was able to blow into it enough to generate some heat. I did nothing but monitor and feed the fire for another thirty minutes until it was good and hot and able to take wet wood easily. Then I moved on to cleaning the fish.

I had seen this done before but had never done it. I had never done it primarily because I was uneasy with the whole blood and guts thing. I didn't like touching fishy things and was never that kind of kid. I was going to have to tap into that "I don't care" mode in order to do this.

I knew I had to remove the head, spine, and organs and I knew there was a quick and easy way to do this, leaving prime fillets at the end. But it didn't exactly go that way. I cut the head off and sliced the fish right down the middle from top to bottom. Perhaps rip and slash might describe it better than cut. The entrails were easy enough to pull out. But I was still left with the entire spine. I wasn't sure what to do so I sort of improvised and tore and cut at the fillets where I could.

The end result was a rather messy assortment of various sized fillets that was probably half the size it could have been with proper cleaning. I washed them off with water and laid them down on the biggest, flattest rock I could find that would serve as a frying pan, and placed the rock onto the side of the fire where I thought it would heat up quickly.

While waiting for it to cook, I took one of the empty cans and added a soup mix and water and placed it near the heat as well. Then I did the same thing with another empty can with water and coffee added to it. I used the knife as the all purpose cooking utensil, switching between stirring, flipping, or moving. It was a messy, unorganized, fly-by-the-seat-of-the-pants butchery of a meal from start to finish. But I was quite pleased. By the end, I had something that loosely resembled a meal of freshly caught seasonal trout, soup, and coffee.

I had just enough light left to make sure I disposed of the fish guts well away from camp, cleaned up the messes, made sure the fire was contained, stored all the fishing gear, and clothing away into the plane, and tidied the camp. I climbed up into the plane, stripped down, jumped in the sleeping bag, and picked up the Bible.

I re-read Ephesians 4 again. It seemed a never ending source of inspiration and direction. Then I sort of flipped around the book to see what else there was and came upon the first page of the New Testament, the book of Matthew. I knew just enough about the Bible to know the story of Jesus was in the New Testament so it seemed a logical place to start if I wanted to actually try and read in any sort of order. So I started in the Book of Matthew and read until I couldn't see. Then I used the flashlight for a little while longer and then went to sleep.

Chapter 15

I settled into a routine of sorts and the days started to drift by. I would wake up at first light and prepare the wood for the fire I would light later in the day. I developed a system of collecting wood in varying degrees of wetness from the forest to keep under the plane for storage and ease of access. Kindling and shavings I would prepare and leave inside the plane to try and help with dryness, and I would try to preserve as much burnt wood from the night before to use again.

With that done I would prepare a lunch and hike down to the lake to fish. I was becoming a better fisherman with every passing day. I began to understand lures, improved my casting abilities, and learned where the fish were. I had success in catching fish every day I was there and would generally catch between one and three. I would then clean the fish right there at the side of the lake finding it easier with lake water to help with the cleaning. I got better at this too, although was quite certain I never did figure out the best possible way. But the fillet sizes seemed adequate and I didn't have too much trouble with bones, so it was good enough.

With the fishing and cleaning done I would head back to camp. I would light the fire, cook the fish, and eat to my heart's content. I tried to use the fish as the bulk of any meal with small amounts of the other stuff. For instance, one meal might be a third of a can of say, canned spaghetti, fish, and coffee. Another meal, half a package of soup, fish, and coffee and perhaps half a granola bar. A snack might be a scoop of peanut butter and a candy. I also had to maintain my water supply which I generally did on the fishing runs. In the in-between time I would read the Bible or hike up to the summit to look at the city or clean up the camp area.

My days felt full and satisfying. There was essentially twelve hours of light in the day, so I had to stay busy and semi-organized to keep things going. Between the wood gathering, hiking to the lake, the fishing, the fire starting and cooking, maintaining the camp and supply rationing and storage, it felt like a full time job. If I slacked off, darkness would come before tasks got done. But if the fishing and fire building went well, then there was generally lots of time to read, hike, and think.

Incredibly I was gaining weight and strength during this time, even with rationed food and this survivalist lifestyle. I had been so malnourished before that any food and rest would have netted weight gain, and I was grateful for it. It was embarrassing being such a skinny druggie, and now I was transforming into a healthy mountain man of sorts.

The improvement wasn't just slowly coming back to my normal body weight, it was also my strength. In the detox period I could barely climb in and out of the plane and the first hike to the lake felt like it was going to kill me. Now I was doing that hike without any issue at all, and I could feel the strength in my thighs as I went up the hills and felt the stamina grow with every passing day. I was getting stronger and stronger! Now I could hike to the lake in the morning and up to the summit late in the afternoon.

But it wasn't just physical. I was coming back on every level. My energy was better and naps were no longer necessary. My reading retention was getting better as well and I could read the Bible for long periods of time and feel like I was retaining everything. I didn't feel restless or scattered with jumbled thoughts either. I was not completely restored yet, but well on my way.

I enjoyed the evenings too. After a day of building fires and catching fish and eating what I caught and organizing a home of sorts, I felt rewarded. I was pleased with my day and would try to settle into the plane before dark so I could get comfortable, read some more of the Bible, and drift off to sleep. I slept great.

There were lonely moments certainly, but nothing overpoweringly so. I knew I was gaining strength in every way and knew that this experience was saving my life so I had little problem in trying to preserve it. Why try and stop a good thing?

I also knew that the day was coming when I would have to leave. I had been up here twenty-six days now and it was into November. The snow would come one day soon and I would have to attempt the descent before then. I was also just about out of all the rations even with using increasingly smaller amounts as I saw the levels drop. I could maybe stretch it out another four days before I would be left to a diet of fish and water only.

As I increased in strength I would hike to the summit on an increasing basis. I liked it up there, sitting on the peak and looking down on the city. It was there that I would do the most thinking about my life, what had happened, and where I was going. Looking at the view was like seeing my life from start to finish. I could see to West Van, where I was born, grew up, and went to high school. I could see Burnaby were I went to BCIT and the area I had my first beer. And I could see the city and where I ended up in the very worst part of. And I could see the curvature of the earth, the vastness of the ocean, the majesty of the mountains, and the incredibleness of the Creation that would symbolize where I was now in life – as a believer of God.

To say that I dove into the Bible would be an understatement. It seemed to me that the entire business depended on whether or not you believed God was real. I had had enough evidence delivered at the right time of my life to believe it without a shadow of doubt. And because I believed it, the Bible was true. And because I believed it to be true, the reading of it became fascinating. But not just fascinating, but of critical importance. To believe that this book was written by God for us makes it the most important thing in the world.

That is, if you believed it to be true. And I did.

I read the entire New Testament. On virtually every page something jumped out at me that seemed relevant, inspiring, or worthy of thought. It was almost as if the words were alive, jumping off the page. And while lots of stuff was confusing to me because of my ignorance, plenty of it was easy to understand and applicable to me. I was surprised to know just how ignorant I had been. I saw plenty of things in the Bible that I had heard before, but had no idea they were Biblical. Even the story of Jesus, that one might think everyone would know, I didn't. Sure, I had a vague idea, but reading the whole story of the gospels left me feeling like I really knew nothing about it before. It made me feel really ignorant of the truth while out there living life, casting opinions, making judgments, and living by my own rules. Because I believed it to be the truth, I was able to see how far from the truth I had been living.

But for every part I read where I saw myself as having lived my life as an ungodly fool, there were a hundred times more parts that offered me hope, love, and forgiveness. I found the story of Jesus to be, well, beyond my means of understanding. His capacity for love, his relentless teaching on how to live, the rebelliousness of going against the teachings of his time, the forgiveness, the faith, and above all, the courage to sacrifice himself on the cross. It is an incredible testimony of self sacrifice for the benefit of others – for the benefit of me.

And it was all so applicable. I read countless stories of how we have gone off the rails of life, drawn by the sins of the world, and fallen from grace. This was so me. But the Bible showed me there was hope for me, that there were answers to my problems, that I could be forgiven for the things I had done wrong, that there are instructions for how to live in this world, and that there was power to do these things through Jesus, who was God.

And if I believed this to be the truth (and I did) then that meant that the God who created the Universe also planned me, cares about me, and wants me to follow Him.

And if I believed this was true (and I did) then it became critically important. What could possibly be of greater importance?

I also went into the Old Testament but only read it in spots. I read the book of Genesis, because, well, it was the beginning. Then I jumped around. I found the Proverbs and read those, and they gave all these points of wisdom on how to live. And also about how not to live, where, sadly, I saw myself again. And then I came across various stories which I had heard of in the past but I am not even sure I knew they were in the Bible, like Samson and Delilah, and Moses and the parting of the Red Sea. How could I have not known that was biblical? Really?

But the greatest story I came on was the story of King David in the Books of Samuel. Wow. It was like reading an action adventure and I found I would think of David often throughout the day and marvel at the kind of man he was, his deep faith, relentless pursuit of following God, and his remarkable achievements and bravery. Again, I am not sure I knew anything about David besides the fact I was pretty sure there was a famous statute in Italy somewhere of him. And I didn't know the story of David fighting Goliath was biblical either.

It made me stop and really consider my ignorance. How could something like this, of such incredible importance, escape me to such a degree for all of my life until now having grown up in a modern culture and gone to good schools? Even if I chose not to believe in it as a youth, how did I go through life without having any exposure to it whatsoever?

I thought about my upbringing. What world concept was I exposed to if not the concept of Creation and God? Not an easy question to answer, but I am pretty sure I learned about evolution in school, and it seemed to me much of my formidable years were influenced by things like TV shows, fiction novels, academic courses in school, famous people, or sporting idols. And of course there were my parents and the things I was exposed to. Lots of healthy things, but some not so much so.

But essentially I felt as if I was a product of the rules of the world which seemed to me, perhaps cynically so, to have a lot looser moral compass than the Godly principles I was reading about now. The world seemed to promote things like sexual liberation, money as power, power as success, survival of the fittest, the importance of how we look, media driven belief systems, live to excess, an eye for an eye. The list could go on forever.

While I could certainly not profess that I was any sort of biblical scholar or expert on anything, I did know that from my perspective I did not do well in the world. Ending up on skid row will change one's perspective. So at this stage I was open to new ways of looking at things and the Bible was suggesting that if I accepted Jesus into my life, not only could I be forgiven for what I have done, that through the strength of Jesus I could actually stay away from drugs, live in freedom from the bondage, and live a pleasing life by a different set of guidelines.

And because I believed it to be true, I found this a very exciting prospect.

Chapter 16

On day thirty-one two things of note happened: I ran out of food and ran into a bear. Running out of food had been no big surprise, as it had been long expected. For days now I had thought that the official day of being out of food would be the day I should start the journey down. But the weather on that day was flawless, without a cloud in the sky. Though cold during the night and in the morning, when the sun hit it was a glorious day, and I couldn't bring myself to do anything but go fish. What was one day living exclusively on a fish diet? I mean my diet had been 90% fish for days now anyway, so who cared?

I caught three fish that morning and had cleaned them and was heading back before the midday sun even hit. After so many dreary, grey, rainy days, the sun coming out made all the difference. The scenery was simply spectacular. The cool fresh November air with a little heat from the sun, and panoramic mountain views in every direction was nothing short of stunning. Walking back along my now familiar route I couldn't remember a time I felt so good.

I wasn't far from the plane now, just on the other side of the plateau edging close by a small ravine before heading in a lateral direction across the plateau when up over the rise on the other side of the ravine came a bear.

And really, it wasn't just a bear. It was a BEAR! The thing was absolutely massive, and had to be a grizzly. I'm no expert on bears, and had only ever seen a couple of small black bears in my days, but this thing shouldn't even have been in the same category.

We were approximately a hundred meters away from each other, but, thankfully, there was a ravine in between us, and while not deep or even steep, I figured that I could run to the plane faster than he could go down and then up the other side of the ravine no matter how fast he was.

We seemed to see each other at the same time, me coming down one side of the ridge and him heading up the other side. We both stopped and sort of stared at each other. I became acutely aware of the fact I was carrying three fish. And as if on cue, his nose started to twitch as if he smelled them. And then he rose up into the air standing straight up in all of his magnificent glory and just stared straight at me.

I was in one part just in awe, and another part worried. I mean, I was *pretty* sure I could make it to the plane, but how fast were these bears anyway? After what seemed an eternity, he dropped back onto all fours, took a final look at me, and just ambled back on up the trail.

I didn't move for several minutes, and then hurried back to the plane. I have to admit I was constantly looking over my shoulder the rest of the day especially when I was cooking the fish. But the wonder of the sight, along with the stunning day, had an impact on me and I no longer felt I wanted to leave. Man can survive on fish alone, right?

It remained sunny for the next few days. Cold at night, sunny during the day. I considered myself quite the avid outdoorsman by this stage – a master fisherman, fire maker, hiker, and camp steward. A confidence was being instilled in me and I felt at ease with myself and my surroundings. I knew the day was soon coming when I would have to make a change, but in the meantime, I was becoming more and more at ease with myself, my direction, and who I was becoming.

I was spending more and more time at the summit overlooking the city. With the sunny skies the views were world class and the afternoons were warm enough to just sit back and enjoy the view. I would bring my Bible up there and read and stare until the sunset kicked in which had to be the nicest view on earth. Just before dark I would hightail it back to the plane before the darkness kicked in.

I was living on fish and water. There was wildlife around – squirrels, birds, raccoons, probably deer, and a bunch of things I would hear in the night but I had no idea as to what they were. But my survivalist skills only went so far. It seemed futile to even attempt hunting, and if anyone thought I was going to get the flashlight and start poking around in the night with the knife they were crazy. But even with only fish, I felt alive, healthy, and satisfied. Although, I wouldn't be ordering fish in any restaurant down the road.

During the time I spent on the summit, I decided to try prayer. It was clearly stated throughout the Bible that this was a necessary thing to do and that God would listen to the prayers. It felt awkward and unnatural and I actually felt embarrassed despite the fact that I was completely alone. But despite not knowing what I was doing, I launched in anyway. I started out with confessions. Given my lifestyle, I just thought it best to admit to God where I had been wrong. I did it out loud and just rattled off everything I could think of. I told Him how selfish I had been, putting my addiction before everything. I told Him how sorry I was for all the pain I caused my family and friends, and I confessed all the criminal things I did in my addiction, how self absorbed I was in taking from people, putting me first in everything, and all the hurt and pain that was caused by me. I confessed it all; from the first Playboy I looked at as a thirteen-year-old, to the first cigarette smoked, all of the lies I could remember, the classes I skipped out of, the sexual sins, the drunk driving, the so many lies along the way into the addiction. I went on and on and the more I confessed the more I remembered. It was a cleansing experience, made more powerful by speaking it out loud. I asked God to forgive me, and I asked for mercy, and I thanked Him for putting up with me and guiding me to this place.

I had a lot of gratitude for where I was right then, and knew the credit did not belong to me, so I thanked God for this journey. I found this confessional prayer of sorts to be an emotional process. It was way more so than I would have expected. But there was something healing about it, like a cleansing of the soul, and when I was (finally) done I was exhausted and near tears.

I continued on with my fish diet for several more days. I was aware I was day to day towards leaving and had formulated something of a plan towards the descent and what I would do once I got down. But there was reluctance every day to actually pull the trigger on the operation.

———— ❦ ————

Ephesians 4 held a lot of information. An amazing amount considering it was literally only one chapter of six in the Book of Ephesians and Ephesians was only one book of twenty-seven and that was just the New Testament which was nowhere near as big as the Old Testament. Ephesians 4 was literally one page.

But it was my one page. It was now the theme of my life, or at least that's how I interpreted it. God had clearly wanted this one particular chapter to be what I focused on and I read it virtually every day I was up here. And while there was more to it than I think I understood, the message I saw seemed fairly clear. It was calling for me to live up to the calling that God selected for me. It was saying that I had fallen into a darkened world of ignorance due to a hardened heart and as a result had lost all sensitivity and was living a life of reckless indulgence. Read lost.

So it was a challenge to throw off the old ways, to grow up, and live up to the calling God had given me. And while the "calling" part was unclear, the changing of direction wasn't. I needed to cast off the world's point of view and get on board with Jesus. Ephesians 4 went on with clear instructions as to how to do this. Live gently and humbly, be patient, and bear with one another in love. Speak in truth and put off false things. Do not let the sun go down before anger is resolved. Do not succumb to the devil and his plans (read don't fall back into drugs!). Get rid of bitterness, rage, anger, and lying. Be kind and compassionate, and forgiving of one another.

It also listed off some callings that God wanted. Things like pastors, teachers, evangelists (not really sure what they did), and apostles (not sure what they did either). But it seemed like the essence of what God wanted was to equip me for works of service. I guess it could be summed up that I was being called to switch teams – to drop out of Satan's team and join up with Christ.

But the key to it, which was not only supported by this one chapter, but also seemed to sort of be a running theme throughout the entire Bible, was that I did not have to do any of this by my strength alone. This was key for me as I had proven over and over through my failings that I was woefully incapable of any real change left to my own devices. I had experienced some of God's plan just by being on this mountain, so I did not dispute that I could conquer anything as long as He was with me. Including drugs. And I was more than happy to be guided towards whatever He wanted me to do in gratitude for saving my life. If I only knew what exactly that was.

So with the confessions done, I moved my summit prayer sessions towards a general theme: I thanked God for saving my life, for bringing me to this mountain and revealing Himself to me. I thanked God for Jesus who resided in me now that I accepted Him, and I thanked Jesus for guiding me in how to live, by giving me such mercy and forgiveness and grace, and delivering me from bondage. And then I asked Him what he wanted me to do? It was a now what plea: "Dear God: now what, exactly?"

I repeated this for about three days in increasing increments. Like I became a better fisherman and fire maker with practice, I was becoming a better man of prayer with the amount of time I was doing it. My general theme: "Thank you for what you have done." That was followed by, "Now, what do You want me to do?" Over and over. Repeat.

The good weather had ended after about four days. Then it clouded over and the rains came. It rained hard for about three days in a row, and I mean hard! A typical November storm system. I continued to go to the summit every day, sitting on the top in the rain gear, praying to God. It just felt like my time on the mountain was just not complete somehow so I just stayed. I stayed and prayed. In the driving rain.

I arrived early to the summit on what would turn out to be my last night on the mountain. It was maybe two o'clock and the rains had stopped early in the morning. It felt cooler and the cloud cover looked more white than dark and grey. I prayed earnestly while looking over the city. I felt almost trancelike and lost track of time. Perhaps I fell asleep, as later I would have trouble remembering how exactly it all played out. My eyes were closed and I was deep in prayer and I found my thoughts dancing around in a frantic series of images: childhood, parents, the bullets flying in the crack shack, school, my first car, thinking I was going to die on the mountain, Hastings Street, crack pipes, sore feet, movie theatres, sporting events, my father reading stories to me, swimming lessons, high school graduation, the bear. I was here and there and couldn't keep up to the images nor seemed to be controlling them. Then whiteness. Bright light into the back of my eyelids, like I was being blinded followed by a quietness that felt nothing like the quietness I thought I knew, then nothing. And then a voice. Calming. But not a voice. A voice combined with images of things I didn't know. Familiar, yet different. The voice and images were one. A combination of one thing, something new, and I didn't know what it was. But it was a message. It was a picture. It was a script of things to come and for a moment I had the entire picture. I knew the plan. God had spoken to me and I knew what He wanted me to do. I knew all of His majestic glory and it had a vastness I couldn't comprehend. I had had a glimpse of something simply beautiful, Holy beyond measure. Pure and divine. God had spoken and I knew the plan He had for me. I now knew what my calling was and what I was supposed to do back in the city.

It was too great for me to understand. The love was unparallel. It was bigger than love. It was love times infinity and I couldn't handle it and I broke down and wept like I had never wept before. I was bawling like a baby completely engulfed and powerless over feelings of love and it was beyond anything I ever experienced.

And then I opened my eyes and it was snowing.

And I knew I was leaving the mountain the next morning.

PART THREE

DOWN

"Instead, speaking the truth in love, we will grow to become in every respect the mature body of him who is the head."

Chapter 17

*I*t took me seven hours to get down the mountain and another two hours of hitchhiking and walking down a relatively desolate road where someone stopped to pick me up before I was back in civilization. Going down had been decidedly different than going up. There had only been a light dusting of snow that was nonexistent 1000 feet down. Perhaps I didn't quite "bound" down, but I felt strong, familiar with the mountain, healthy and alive with the task. It was decidedly different than going up. I won't say it wasn't fraught with some concern, as I was still navigating by feel, ran into a few very difficult patches, felt relatively lost on a few occasions, and started to seriously doubt whether or not I would make it during daylight. But I also felt strong and I had spent so much time on the mountain that I felt I could tell direction and distance fairly well, so I never really felt I was in serious trouble.

I had packed the sleeping bag and some leftover fish with me, in the event that I did get lost and needed to spend a night on the side of the mountain. As for the rest of the camp, I cleaned it up as best I could it and tried to return it back to how I found it. I put the Bible back in his lap, opened to Ephesians 4 and gently placed his hand back on the page. It seemed important and respectful to my friend the pilot to leave his ending place as in tact as possible. And then I started down.

I found the road and started walking the direction I felt sure was west, back towards the city. I must have looked pretty rough despite the fact I had attempted a couple of baths of sorts over the forty nights I spent on the mountain. I had not shaved and the clothes I was wearing were, well, looking like I had lived on a mountain for a month or so. But after living a life shuffling around looking like a skid row drug addict, I actually preferred my current look.

There hadn't been lots of traffic. A few cars and trucks had driven right by my outstretched thumb while attempting to avoid eye contact at any cost. I couldn't blame them given the fact I looked as I did. I was in the middle of nowhere, walking down the road carrying a sleeping bag.

But finally an old pickup pulled over and I climbed in beside a guy who I thought looked a lot like I did. Long beard, dirty clothes, and pretty rough all over. But friendly as all get out and seemingly uncaring as to what my story was. He just told me where he was going, said to tell him when I wanted out, then proceeded to talk about his truck.

He was heading into the Lower Lonsdale area of North Van, which suited me just fine. He ended up dropping me at the foot of Lonsdale, which was at the ocean's edge, the lowest point of North Vancouver and directly across Burrard Inlet from the city of Vancouver. Lonsdale is a street that runs North/South and ends at the foot, where I was now standing with my sleeping bag.

The foot of Lonsdale, at one point all industrial, had redeveloped itself into an attractive waterfront area with the arrival of the Seabus sometime in the 1970s I think. The Seabus was just that. A bus on the sea. It was a passenger only ferry that ran between North Vancouver and Vancouver city, about a fifteen or twenty minute run that went back and forth all day. In fact there were two Seabus's that passed each other in the middle running during peak hours. There were only two bridges connecting the North Shore (West Van and North Van) and Vancouver: the Lion's Gate that I crossed over in the back of the truck, and The Second Narrows (or Iron Workers Memorial depending on who you talked to). The Lion's Gate crossed from the west side of

Vancouver to the western side of the North Shore. The Second Narrows crossed from the eastern side of the city to the east side of North Van. The Seabus crossed pretty much in the middle of them both, from the heart of North Van, to the heart of the city and the transportation hub, where Seabus, Skytrain, Westcoast Express (train), and busses all met. And only a few blocks from the skid row area of Hastings.

On the North Van side the Seabus terminal was nestled beside Lonsdale Quay which was a modern shopping area, market, hotel, restaurants, and food court that was right on the water. Nice pier, stunning city views, lots of boats and water traffic to check out, and often cruise ships docked on the other side as well. It was a bit of an artsy area too, with lots of tourists, people hanging out outside, some painters, jugglers, and the like.

My problem was that I had no money. Not a cent. It was a problem that I had hoped to rectify at the Welfare Office tomorrow. But it was pushing 6:00 p.m. now, so it would be closed, leaving me with no money and nowhere to stay. I knew there were shelters downtown off Hastings, but I was aware now that I was back in civilization that I had to be careful with all the inner strength I gained on the mountain or it could come crashing down the minute I was triggered by environment. I decided staying well away from skid row was the wise decision.

Most of the shops were starting to close, not staying open late like they do in tourist season. The food court was still open and there was still a lot of foot traffic coming off the Seabus's, and there were people generally milling about waiting for busses or going to restaurants or whatever. I decided I was just going to hang out and crash out somewhere and wait until morning, so I just laid out the sleeping bag and sort of hung out in a covered area near some closed shops. My life on the street had prepared me well for sucking it up to some of life's indignities, so I wasn't overly bothered by people's looks. I wasn't feeling like a drug addict, so I was far less self conscious as to how people were looking at me.

And I guess people didn't see me as a drug addict either, because before long these three guys, all sort of dreadlocked young white guys with skateboards just sort of planted themselves down beside me to hang out. I'm assuming they must have thought I was one of those travelling, grunge loving, granola, hillbillies or something, because they seemed completely unaffected by me.

They turned out to be Swedish travelers soaking up the Canadian experience and had been killing some time before heading back to the youth hostel they were staying at nearby. They had just bought a whole bunch of deli food from inside and busted it out, picnic style right in front of me, outside, in Vancouver in November. They told me to just help myself, and after a polite thirty seconds while I watched them make sandwiches, I dug in! I made myself this French bread, Swiss cheese, and ham sandwich that was simply the best thing I ever ate.

We all sat around in a circle sitting on my sleeping bag which I had opened up blanket style and swapped stories. They told me about their travels, the places they had seen, the sorts of places they had stayed at, and the people they had met. I told them I grew up not thirty minutes from where we were, but had just camped out on the top of one of the local mountains for the past forty days. I hadn't been prepared to share my story so I omitted most of it, like the drug addiction, the shooting, the plane, and meeting God. I don't think I actually lied but I just sort of painted a picture of a back country sort of survivalist test, so I talked about the fishing, the camping, and told the bear story. We went back and forth talking about travel, Sweden, Canada, the back country and the future. I told them I was heading back into Vancouver the next day to re-start life. They told me they were going to Whistler to look for work for the winter at the ski resort and they gave me their left over bus pass. Sweet! I had been worried about sneaking onto the Seabus. Not because I was worried about how, I was worried about being dishonest with my new belief system.

They left around 9:00, all of us stuffed and having enjoyed the experience. They genuinely seemed grateful for all that I had shared with them and it struck me that I had not enriched anyone's life in years. And it made me very grateful. I crashed in the doorway, sort of half slumped into the doorway wrapped up snug in the sleeping bag. It wasn't the worst night I had ever had. Not by a long shot.

The next morning, I was up with the first commuter traffic, used the pass I was given and jumped onto a Seabus and made the crossing. I exited the main terminal and made my way to the street to catch a bus up to Broadway. Busses pulled in one after the other to various destinations and I just jumped on one that said Broadway on the top sign. It made its way south along Granville St, through the city core, over the Granville St. Bridge and then turned right on Broadway. I wanted left on Broadway so I got off crossed the street and used my pass to get on another bus heading east along Broadway until I crossed the border at Main Street which separates Vancouver west from Vancouver east. A few more blocks and I got off and walked a short distance to the welfare office.

Welfare. There was a system in place in British Columbia and nearly all Hastings Street addicts were on it. It was a system designed to help people who were out of work for long periods of time, incapable of work, in dire straits, or had issues, but it was also heavily abused. Sadly (or gladly if you were a drug addict) getting on welfare in BC wasn't that difficult for those who really just wanted to use the money to get high. It was a flawed system but one could appreciate how difficult it would be to monitor, sift through the lies, and deliberate on who got money and who didn't.

Virtually every person on drugs on Hastings was on welfare, and for the most part, virtually every single drug addict on Hastings spent their entire welfare cheque in between one and three days. It was called Welfare Wednesday, and it was usually the last Wednesday of the month. On Hastings it was also called Mardi Gras because it was generally quite the party. The drunks were drinking up a storm, back slapping, buying rounds, then later fighting, yelling down the street, or stabbing each other. The druggies were buying drugs with reckless abandon with grand allusions of selling, making profits, keeping cash flow and drug flow going, and sustaining themselves and a habit, only to just end up smoking all of it until nothing was left, neither money nor drugs.

I did not receive the rent component of the welfare cheque as I did not have a residence. So I only collected the comfort money which was only about $170 a month. This was a figure which was determined enough for all non-rent related expenses a person could live on for a month. Hard to imagine, even without a drug habit. With a drug habit? Well I generally blew through my months income in one day.

Welfare cheques were, for the most part, mailed out, unless of course you had no mailing address like me. For me, I would pick up my cheque here at this office, lining up before it even opened with the rest of the people eagerly waiting on the party to be able to start. Except last month, as on the last Wednesday in October I was on top of the mountain. So I wasn't here and I didn't get my cheque. It would be unusual in the world of welfare employees to see someone not come in for their cheque, and they might do any number of things, like flag my account as inactive, send the cheque back to the head Government office, or Lord knew what else. I only knew that things rarely went smoothly at the welfare office and was in no way certain I would walk out with any money at all.

I was early. It didn't open until 9:00 and it was only a little past 8:00. I didn't mind and just used my sleeping bag to stay warm by wrapping it around me sort of like a shawl. While I waited I thought about the sleeping bag and all of the various functions it seemed to give to me since I found it.

I wasn't the first in line though when the door opened. These places were busy with people needing things. Like money. And business was always brisk. Even getting there an hour early on a non-welfare day, I was still fourth in line, with one non-caring tired and unenthusiastic employee slowly reviewing each person's needs.

When it was my turn I sat down at the cubicle in front of her and explained that I wanted to pick up last month's welfare cheque. She opened a drawer in front of her, asked my name, and then just flipped through the folder until the "W's" and pulled out an envelope.

She asked me my code, for those of us without identification, and she checked it against her computer along with an image she had of me and, seemingly satisfied, passed the envelope over to me.

"Little late, aren't you?" she asked, without even looking at me. "What happened?"

"I was up on top of a mountain," I said. "I found the Lord my God up there and He spoke to me and gave me a plan for my life. I am giving up drugs. I'm going to use this money respectfully and discriminately towards moral purposes and I'm going to get a job and get off welfare permanently."

She stopped her shuffling of papers and looked up at me. "Well, okay then Sam. I happen to believe in the Lord your God and I wish you all the best in making that happen. On behalf of the welfare system of Canada, we will say goodbye forever then." She smiled and I smiled back.

"You know it. Thanks for everything. Sorry I abused the system for so long. I don't feel good about it anymore," I said.

"No, I would imagine you wouldn't if God did get a hold on you. But it's okay, as long as you go on and do what you say."

I left the welfare office with a cheque for $170 in hand and a smile on my face. So far things were going quite well. Next, I went to the same place I always went immediately after good news at the welfare office: the cheque cashing place.

This was another trait common amongst us skid row people: nobody had a bank account or ID. I never really knew why. For me, I "deposited" an empty envelope into an ATM after punching in a bogus $200 deposit. I then immediately withdrew the $200 which I had fooled the bank into believing was in my account. I got the money but a day or two later I got threats from the bank threatening legal action and all of my banking privileges were immediately suspended. Permanently. For my ID, I gave it to a dealer to hold for drugs until I came back with payment, which I never did. Wallet with drug dealer. At one stage I went to rehab, got a new ID, relapsed back into my addiction, and repeated the same thing with my new ID with a new dealer. I wondered how many wallets drug dealers had. Or other objects of collateral like wedding rings, family heirlooms, electronics, and whatever else we could exchange for drugs. People would sell anything that netted money or drugs. Anything.

The people with no ID and no bank accounts had to cash cheques somewhere, and this is why there is such a glut of cheque cashing centres everywhere you look. I personally couldn't stand these places. They charged enormous percentages to cash cheques, or offered easy to get pay day loans with high interest that people struggling to stay afloat should never agree to. But they preyed on people desperate for cash. Plain and simple. No different than a pawn shop in my mind.

But I had no choice but to use them to cash my cheque, and did just that. I allowed them to take their 7% for the privilege and walked out with $158.10 cash in my pocket. And then I had problems.

Money and drugs were really the same thing. For the hardened drug addict, all money turned into drugs. All of it. So money was a trigger. In many ways it was just like having someone place the drugs directly in your palm. The only difference was that if it was placed in your palm in cash form, one more step was required before the smoking began. And when the money was counted out and placed on the counter I immediately went into some intense cravings. My mind raced through the scenario. I was on Broadway. I could call one of the Chink dial-a-dope numbers and meet him up here in five minutes, then scramble over to one of the shady corner stores a few blocks down and buy a "glass stem" and some brillo. Buy a lighter as well and good to go. Or I could head down to Hastings and buy down there and get everything else I needed to.

Before I knew what had hit me, I had run through all the various scenarios and plans and was feeling my stomach start to turn in the nervous energy one feels when on the verge of being able to get high. The last time I felt this I had been sitting on the couch at the crack shack before things had turned ugly.

I was sitting on forty-one days clean. Not a bad foundation, but still nothing really in the grand scheme of things towards any real and sustained sobriety. But it was enough to give me a moment to stand back and assess the situation. With one day clean, or one week clean, or even thirty days clean, my feet would already have been walking to either a phone booth or Hastings Street already without really even being able to control it. From a mental perspective, the relapse would have occurred the minute the money hit the hand.

But with forty-one days clean and having gone through circumstance that were, well, new and unusual, I was able to stand back and think about how far I had come, and the plan God had for my life.

I also learned something about how God was working. It felt like I had been given absolute freedom from this bondage while living on the mountain. I had started to re-think that as I came into civilization yesterday, and now I downright dismissed it. I felt now that I had to nurture breath into my freedom to sustain it. That it was entirely possible that if I did nothing, I could easily fall and eventually forget I ever was given the freedom. So right there on the sidewalk I knelt down on one knee and bowed my head.

"God, thank you for giving me the freedom from my addiction and planting in me a purpose greater than my wildest imagination. Lord, thank you for the mountain and for saving my life. But God, I don't have the strength to exist down here in this world without You giving me guidance and taking the strength of the addiction away from me. Please help me by guiding me and showing me the way and please help me overcome these cravings."

Immediately I felt better. The cravings were diminishing and I felt I could control how my next moves went. But I had been given a real look into how easy it would be for me to fall back into my old ways, and thought, if I were wise, I should get this money out of my hands sooner than later. So I carried on with my plan.

Chapter 18

There was no shortage of stores downtown for what I was looking for. Pick a street, really. I walked west until I hit a bus stop, then jumped on a bus and got off once again at Granville Street. I walked down Granville northbound in the direction of the downtown core until I saw the stores I wanted. The first was a dollar store and I bought toiletries: toothbrush, toothpaste, deodorant, shampoo, razor, comb, scissors, gel, and a toiletry bag. I was quite pleased with myself for buying things that were not drugs. It felt very good, as if I was rebelling against the nature of addiction. I couldn't remember the last time I had spent money on something that wasn't drugs.

Next I went directly across the street to a Value Village and bought myself two complete sets of clothes and one pair of running shoes. Shirts, pants, underwear, socks, the lot. Plus a heavy jacket. And then I went over to the books section and found quite a selection of Bibles. One looked exactly like the one I had read on the mountain with a nice leather cover, big print, and in the NIV translation and I bought it immediately. The total, including the stuff from the dollar store: $38.00.

My next stop, again without leaving the block, was to Starbucks. I figured I deserved a latte after over a month on a mountain, a couple of near death experiences, and nothing but fish the past couple of weeks (except for that oh so delicious ham and cheese sandwich last night with my Swedish friends). I ordered up a Vanilla Latte, Vente size, and an oat fudge bar, the latter being an impulse buy. It just seemed so good looking at it behind the counter. I caught a few people staring at me inside Starbucks, perhaps not approving of my mountain man look. But I actually liked the looks better than the "I'm staring at a junkie who I am afraid is going to rob the place" looks I used to get. People were just glancing and looking away unconcerned. It was downtown after all and people were accustomed to strange people.

From there I walked over the Granville Street Bridge back into the downtown core. It wasn't a bad day and I wasn't in any hurry, so why not? Once over the bridge, I hung a left on Davie and walked a few blocks west to Burrard. The YMCA was down Burrard a block or so on my left. The YMCA in Vancouver doubled as a cheap traveler's hotel. Oh, it had the gym, programs and the like that I gathered most YMCA's had, but it had rooms upstairs, and this is where I was headed.

I knew that I could have perhaps gotten more out of Welfare. I could have explained my situation, that I was a drug addict with over a month clean and I could have tapped into their resources and maybe had some options. They may have referred me to a residential recovery house, or to a drug and alcohol counselor who could have made the referral. Or if I didn't want to take that route, I could have maybe gotten the forms to give to a potential landlord and have them filled out to maybe get a rental unit. Or at the very least I might have gotten a bus pass, or clothing allowance if I explained myself well enough.

But I couldn't stand the welfare office. I never could. To me, being an educated, healthy (well, healthy when not a drug addict) man who grew up in a functional house had no right being in a welfare office and the fact that I was on welfare was one of the most shameful indications to me that I had fallen too far. I'm not saying Welfare isn't critical to a society filled with people with legitimate reasons. I'm just saying a young man who grew up soundly should not be one of them.

I had given it a great deal of thought on the mountain. Having spent the better part of seven years as a full on druggie in and out of treatment facilities, on and off probation for minor criminal offences, applying and reapplying for welfare, constantly going through forms, changes of addresses, moving from place to place, couch to couch, centre to centre, I had had enough. I knew I needed to collect the cheque because I needed something to help me get off the ground, and I knew the cheque was not going to be for much. I wasn't going to live in a rundown flea bag skid row hotel as I would have never had a chance at sobriety so the only cheap place left I knew of that was not on skid row, was the YMCA.

I had made the conscious decision to go it alone, free from government help, referral programs, assessments, and the various indignant probing and therapies that come from being in the system. I had money for maybe three days, and that's only if I didn't eat probably! But I had a plan I had thought through and if it didn't work, then I would fall back on government assistance. At any and all costs, I told myself, a relapse back into the drugs couldn't happen.

I had been to enough treatment centres to have learned quite a bit about addiction and the tools needed to attain real sobriety so I wasn't naïve about having a plan of recovery and knew that I wouldn't stand a chance of doing this alone. A part of my plan was to immediately get myself involved in recovery minded groups and make sobriety my first and foremost priority. Without staying clean, nothing else was relevant. No life means no purpose.

And my purpose was to fulfill the plan that God had spoken into me on my last night on the mountain. I had not gone one minute without reliving the experience in my mind, even though it was impossible to recreate or even remember the vividness and detail of the experience. It was truly just too remarkable to describe or repeat in my mind.

The plan was too great to even talk about. It seemed completely unrealistic on every level that His plan for me could be attained. Too farfetched to mention and the only reason I didn't dismiss it is because I was there, and the moment with God was real, and who was I to dispute what He told me? So I believed it, but I couldn't for the life of me see how it would come to pass. I wasn't given instructions on how to pull it off. I was only given a vision of the finished product. So the only thing I truly knew for sure was that this vision for my life was not going to be done today. Or tomorrow, or anytime soon. And I had to get from today to the end result somehow.

God certainly didn't tell me not to go to rehab. He didn't seem to have an opinion on that one. It was me who wanted to try to do this on my own. But it was based on the experience I had with God on the mountain and from what I read in the Bible. My interpretation was that I had freedom through Christ. That by accepting Him as my savior I now had strength through Him. This changed my viewpoint on how to get clean. Before, it was all about "how *not* to do drugs." And now, it was about living out my rightful freedom through Jesus. And while I had already learned that this didn't mean it was all going to be easy, I did believe that if I leaned on Christ at all times, that He would take the burden of the addiction from me. Besides, I figured forty days on the mountain was about the equivalent to a round of detox plus treatment.

It worked out that four nights at the YMCA came to $100.00, tax in. Twenty five bucks a night. More in high season, but November was a slow tourist month. Good thing for me. Having the money out of my pocket and spent towards something worthwhile really helped with the cravings and bad thoughts. I got my own room, with a shared shower and bathroom down the hall. It was like a dormitory, or at least what I thought a dorm might look like. It was clean and appealing and had a gym and meeting rooms and stuff like that downstairs. Maybe they had AA meetings here. That would be nice.

The first thing I did was hit the shower. I cleaned myself up from top to bottom. I gave myself a clean shave, freshened up across the board and felt like a million bucks. Back in my room I put away my few things. The clothes I had been wearing went into the trash. They were just not salvageable in my opinion. I couldn't bear to part with the sleeping bag though, nor could I think about using it until it had been laundered, so I put it in the closet to deal with later. Done sorting, I laid back on the bed, hands behind my head, my Bible lying on my chest and I stared at the ceiling. Here I was, with my sleeping bag, dollar store bag of toiletries, my bag from Value Village with two sets of clothes and a Bible, and $12.10 in my pocket and I was ready to start living my new life.

Chapter 19

*D*uring my time at the YMCA, I rose early every day and went to Labor Unlimited, an agency that put people to work every day and paid them at the end. It was generally tough work nobody else wanted, but the upside is you didn't have to show up if you didn't want to, and you got paid at the end of every day. It was first come first serve, but as the city was booming in construction it wasn't terribly difficult to land a day's work if you got there early enough.

So by day I would go to Labor Unlimited and when I got paid I would immediately pay off another night or two at the Y and then go and eat. There was never much more left over as the wage was crap and the agency took their cut. But again, money wasn't the best thing in my hands right now anyway. By night I looked for a real job. I wasn't picky. In fact it was quite the opposite. I was purposefully looking for easy to get low paid positions, particularly in the hotel/restaurant industry. I wasn't being proud. My education seemed very far away from me, and I was in no position to look for a quality job for good pay. Not even close. But I was good at finding jobs. Street life does have some transferrable skills and getting what you want is one of them.

Vancouver had lots of restaurants and I had worked at a few when I was going through BCIT, so I felt this was the best place to start. Plus, I could look in the evenings while keeping cash flow going during the day.

Eventually, I landed a job as a full time dishwasher at one of Robson Street's trendy new restaurants. Robson Street was the premier shopping and restaurant stroll in the heart of the city.

The restaurant was called *Trattoria* and was owned by a well known restaurateur named Torsi (one of those guys who people just refer to by one name, like Pele) who owned about five restaurants throughout the city, all popular and trendy.

I walked right past the hostess table, right into the back kitchen and straight towards the man who was obviously the chef and told him I would reliably show up for work every night and wash his dishes if he would just give me a chance. He looked at me blankly for a moment and said: "As luck would have it, my dishwasher just quit. And in all my years of being an executive chef, I cannot recall a single white English speaking male who came in directly looking to wash dishes. So why not? The job is yours."

I started the next night. For two weeks I did both jobs as I needed to keep cash flow going until I got my first pay cheque at the restaurant. This was an exhausting period of time, but after I got the first cheque from the restaurant for a full two week pay period I was able to relax a little on cash flow. Next I started looking for a place to live.

In the in-between times of working two jobs and trying to sustain myself I went to both AA meetings and church services. I had never been to church before and it was like a different world in so many ways, one of which was the sorts of things their bulletin boards advertised. It seemed people were being overly generous in offering up rooms in their houses for travelling Christians, missionaries, and students and I saw one that advertised a room and board situation in a house in the West End of Vancouver for $650 a month. A phone call and an hour later I found myself sitting in the kitchen of one Mrs. Byrnes, a kindly Scottish woman who had been recently widowed and whose children were grown. She lived in one of the last actual houses that occupied the West End of Vancouver, the most heavily populated area of downtown Vancouver and predominately high rise apartments. Her house was old but well kept, and nestled between two high rises on each side and a small park opposite. It wasn't three blocks from English Bay and about a twenty minute walk to my job.

She was easy to talk to and we chatted about the fact my mother is Scottish, about what I knew of Scotland, where I worked, some of our backgrounds, etc. I even told her about my attempt at "recovery" despite the fact that every morsel of my being told me not to. In the name of new ways, I decided on honesty. Well, she didn't bat an eye and just told me a story of one of her sons dabbling a bit too much in Canadian beer. As it turned out, she came from the same area of Glasgow as my mother. And she and her late husband used to frequent the restaurant I now work at. The deal for the place was $650 per month, which included a furnished room, complete with a TV, all utilities, and dinner for the nights I requested it. For the other meals I was on my own, but she didn't mind if I put stuff in her fridge or used the kitchen to prepare food. I got my own key and there was a side entrance in which I could come and go. In short, it was perfect and I moved right in!

I was now off and running with a full time job and a place to live and things settled into something of a routine. Most of my shifts at work were in the evening, starting at about 4:30 and going until just past midnight. On those nights, I would eat at the restaurant, basically either just making myself something or having one of the cooks rustle me something up. That was just one of the perks of working in a kitchen which was good, because there weren't many other perks in the life of the dishwasher.

With my days at Labour Unlimited over, I was able to utilize my free time in the daytimes towards other ventures, like mainly my recovery. A typical day would see me rising around 9:00 a.m., having something to eat, spending some time journaling and reading the Bible, going for a walk, taking in a "nooner" AA meeting, going home to relax a little, going to work, and getting home around 1:00 a.m. The routine was important towards the recovery process and I was starting to feel a little more stable as days turned into weeks and my foundation of recovery was growing.

Chapter 20

The job sucked. There was no doubt about it. It generally started out fairly easy but got busier as the shift progressed and ended with a finale of greasy pots and pans from the kitchen as the closing down period commenced. When everyone else, both from the front of the house to the kitchen staff left to go home or out on the town, the lonely dishwasher was left with scrubbing the worst pots of the night, final cleanup and lastly, the mopping of the floor. With the exception of the manager who essentially got drunk while waiting for me to finish, I was the last to leave every night.

To add insult to injury, it was also the lowest paying position, and the least respected. The wait staff in the front of the house was all young, attractive, hip, and social and many of them would not even stoop to talking to a lowly dishwasher. In fact, on occasion someone who would have to speak to me would do so in a very slow, loud, and enunciated voice since they assumed I did not speak English. It was fairly ironic seeing as how I was probably more educated than most of them. There was the odd one who was friendly and non-judgmental, but it seemed like, for the most part, dishwashers were not in the social loop at trendy restaurants. The kitchen workers were a lot friendlier and treated me as an equal except, of course, when it came to the actual tasks. A chef wouldn't wash a pot and very seldom did anyone help out in the "dish pit." Just the way it was.

But there was one guy who seemed to grasp the position of the dishwasher and it was Torsi himself. He wasn't around often, as he had many restaurants, but when he was he would often come and stand in the dishwashing area and chat with me. It was always fairly idle conversation, not like we were becoming friends or anything. In fact, it often seemed as if he was just hiding from the front of the room, as if the social pressures of being "on" and in the spotlight were all too much for him and he just wanted to hide out where nobody could judge him. Often he would just stand back there and sort of watch the dishes come out of the machine to be put away, sort of deep in thought and transfixed by the never ending rotation of dishes going in dirty and coming out clean.

Dishwashing wasn't easy. It was a thankless position and it was easy to see why most people passed on the position. When the kitchen was closing and the front end staff was getting all excited to hit the town and the kitchen staff was starting to unwind and relax, the dishwasher was heading into the most difficult part of his shift.

The older version of me would have had troubles with this. It would have been easy to resent the task and envy the others. But things had changed for me. With my new found faith, I would start each shift off in prayer and carry a constant dialogue with myself throughout my shift:

"Lord, thank you for my life. Thank you for what happened on the mountain. Thank you for speaking to me on the mountain and telling me my calling in life. Lord, thank you for my sobriety and giving me the strength to abstain from drugs. Thank you for this job, for selecting this for me to do. May I wash dishes to Your glory. May I see this job as glorifying Your name by doing it properly, with a good attitude, and may I take this opportunity to look for ways to show people what You have done for me."

The more I read the Bible, and the more I learned about the life and teachings of Jesus, the more convinced I was that He was telling us that the key to life was to give of ourselves and not take. And the more I thought about it the easier it was to recognize that my life, and my life as an addict, was exactly the opposite: a life of selfish indulgence to please only myself. I had been delving into a pretty honest inventory of my entire life. I had been raised as a single child, and while no, I wouldn't have said I was spoiled, I was certainly more privileged than many. And a life of self sacrifice it wasn't. It was all pretty easy growing up in West Van, with little need for anything. A philosophy of sorts had been established, that it was okay to get what I wanted and please myself. To me, that seemed to be the name of society's game. So by the time drugs had found themselves in front of me, the pattern to want to feel good was well ingrained. So, I tried them and went on to get my Ph.D. in selfish desire. I don't think there can be another world more selfish and self centered than the world of the drug addict where self gratification is the only purpose for living. Drug addicts go to extreme levels of selfishness, throwing family, careers, homes, assets, items of personal value, and money under the bus in order to sustain the addiction. And while sure, the addiction is so powerful we may have had little say in it, it is still easy to recognize just how selfish we had been.

So while washing dishes wasn't easy, it was made tolerable through being able to make a contribution to society as opposed to taking from it. And if Jesus so wanted to save me, and He found it okay for me to humble myself to the confines of the dish pit, then who was I to argue? In fact, I would consider it a great honor, and I would wash those dishes to the glory of God and thank Him while I did it. And that was what made washing dishes a good job for me.

Of course I wasn't perfect. I aspired to wash dishes for the glory of God but I didn't always pull it off. On a bad day I was just a resentful grumpy late twenties guy doing a job I hated and thinking about how the grass had to be greener just about anywhere. On one really, really bad day I told this arrogant, minstrel of a waiter I was going to shove a carving fork up his ass because he was just so nauseatingly arrogant and stuck up.

But I aspired to wash dishes to the glory of God, and when I did, it was a glorious thing. Life just seemed "to work" giving of myself so much better than taking for myself and I was beginning to see it as the key to all my successes.

Chapter 21

ot long after I got back from the mountain I went to the downtown library and did some research on the mountain. I discovered that the name of it was Crown Mountain, which I found interesting seeing as how I met the King on it. There were various facts and figures about it which, while interesting, was not why I was there. I wanted the name and a picture both of which I found easily enough given the distinctive shape at the top. Once I had the picture I wrote out the following letter on one of the library computers:

> Crown Mountain in North Vancouver has a very distinctive top. If one were standing on the top of the mountain there would be an obvious spot which would be described as the peak, or the highest point from where you could look back over the city. Consider that the starting point, and walk away from the city in a Northerly direction following the edge of the natural plateau along the eastern tree line, and walk for about five minutes. From there, go into the forest about twenty yards, or the equivalent of about five rows of trees and search. You should find a plane crash with the body of the pilot still in the pilot's seat. Good luck with the search.

I did not sign the letter or offer up any other information. I just didn't really see the need to volunteer my story or involve myself. And I didn't really see how it was relevant. It just seemed important to report it at the earliest possible time so people would get the answers I am sure they sought.

I attached the letter along with the picture of the mountain with the map and put a little X on the summit indicating the starting point of the search, made a copy and mailed one to each the police and the North Shore Search and Rescue. Anyone who grew up on the North Shore was familiar with the North Shore Search and Rescue. They seemed to have the market covered on all issues mountain related. And then I waited.

I waited about five days until the news broke. I was just beginning to wonder if they either didn't find it or didn't take the letter seriously as I was pretty sure finding a lost plane on a North Shore mountain would have been newsworthy. After scouring the local papers every day I finally saw it easily on page one of *The Vancouver Sun* with the headline and story:

Missing Plane Found

Missing pilot Gordon Harley of Richmond was finally found yesterday after his plane went missing over 7 years ago. The plane, a 1976 Cessna 180 float plane was discovered through an anonymous tip on top of Crown Mountain in North Vancouver. The body of Gordon Harley, 51, of Richmond was found deceased in the wreckage. Harley's plane had gone missing over 7 years ago when he failed to arrive at a fishing lodge in northern BC. A major weather system was always believed to have contributed to the plane going missing but an exhaustive search had never turned up the plane.

According to Steve Jones of the North Shore Search and Rescue, "We believe he may have encountered bad weather, tried to turn around and come home when the plane went down. From the angle of the plane, we can surmise he was heading in a southern direction and would have been in site of the city had he cleared just one more peak."

Jones was a part of the search 7 years ago, "I remember it well. The search area was more than 200 km away from where the plane ended up being based on the last known contact from the plane. We searched for over a week with air, and ground techniques to no avail. It was just one of those mysteries that we had no answer for until today."

Harley, an avid outdoorsman, was the owner of the plane and had thousands of miles flying time under his belt. His disappearance had hit hard among many people in Richmond as he was active in community affairs and within his church. Pastor Dan Richards made a brief statement for the family when contacted. "We are so thankful to have Gordon back after he had been missing so long. His discovery helps put closure to this ordeal and we can now bring him back here to the church he so loved and send him away properly to the Lord."

Harley, a business owner, is survived by his wife Amy and two grown children. It is believed a hiker found the plane and anonymously called in the discovery.

I found more articles from different papers saying mostly the same thing. I found it all quite emotional. I felt, I don't know, bonded to him? Maybe the reason I never pursued finding details about him in the plane was a psychological attempt to not get close. Just hangin' out with a dead guy on a plane on a mountain. But now that I knew his name, where he was from, and about his family, I found myself almost feeling like I knew him. There was no mistaking the fact that I had been deeply impacted by him in a roundabout way and was now feeling more connected to him by knowing a part of his story. I was glad to have been able to have helped the family with answers.

Chapter 22

I was ninety days clean when I called home. I knew I had called them too many times in the past with news of newfound sobriety only to have disappointed them shortly after with relapses back into drugs. It had been a long time since I had given them any real hope and they received any information from me with skepticism and a guarded heart. And I knew this, and could hardly blame them.

And even though I wasn't expecting much to be different this time, ninety days clean, self supporting, and a job was new territory, and, well, it was just time to make contact. My mom answered the phone and we chatted for a long time. I told her the entire story by phone and it was the first time I told the story from start to finish. I started the story in the crack shack before the shooting and finished it with where I was then. It took a long time and when I was done I heard her cry for the first time in my life.

I found myself spending the rest of the time reassuring her that I was doing everything I could to stay clean. I told her I wasn't taking anything for granted, that I wanted to be clean, that I wanted to be restored as a son, that I was willing to do the work, that I knew it would take time to heal, that I knew I couldn't do it alone. But little did I even realize until she told me later that it wasn't so much what I was saying but also the fact that I wasn't asking for anything from her. She knew I was sincere because I wasn't setting things up for the "ask." And really, knowing that just made me all that much more determined to live in freedom from addiction.

But the other interesting bit of information I got out of my mom was that she knew a lot about the Bible. I had no idea. "Oh yes," she said, "we went to church all the time in Scotland and my parents were deeply devoted. I enjoyed it as a school girl, but then came to Canada, met your father, and well, just stopped thinking about it. I would still pray to Jesus, but just wouldn't talk about it." I wanted to know why she didn't talk about it and she didn't really have an answer.

When I got off the phone I felt better than I could ever remember. Even though I could sense the trepidation in her voice, I knew she was guardedly hopeful for my restoration and happy that I phoned. I promised that I would come out to the house on the next weekend as I generally had Sundays off. It seemed like things were really coming along.

I went out there the following Sunday. I enjoyed the bus ride out to West Van. Back over the Lion's Gate Bridge, west along Marine Drive all the way out and a five minute walk from the bus stop. My dad was there and we talked as well. They had lots of questions about the plane crash having seen the news coverage. I'm not sure if they didn't find the entire story pretty out there, but I could see it in their eyes that they believed me and that this was different than other times. Not to say there wasn't skepticism in the air, a guard against believing their son had been restored to health, and residual anger from all the things I had done. I'm just saying that all levels were a little better this time than past attempts.

We talked for hours, with me filling in lots of details. They seemed proud of the fact that I had been working full time and didn't care one bit that I was a dishwasher. Showing up for a full time job had been a feat I hadn't been capable of for a long time. I guess having a son as a dishwasher was a lot better than a drug addict. I only asked for one thing, that they keep the details of my involvement with the plane crash private. I just didn't feel comfortable in telling the story yet, but if anyone deserved the whole truth, it was them.

When I left, I told my dad we should think about going fishing one day. To my mom I said maybe we could go to church together one day. It was a more emotional goodbye than I was prepared for and I told them I would like to come out again soon.

And I did go back out again the following Sunday after a church service, and the weekend after, and most Sundays from there on. I didn't need to or necessarily want to. In fact it was another new territory for me that was a direct result of my new-found belief system. I wasn't necessarily going out there for me, but because I knew my parents would feel reassured that I was okay if I showed up consistently and reliably. But I also enjoyed many of the visits. With the old man getting old, I helped out in the yard, cleaned out gutters, and putzed about helping out wherever I could. And I just loved being back in the old neighbourhood. I would go for walks, remember being a kid, go down to the wharfs and watch people fish or check out the boats. My mom would cook Sunday dinners and I would head back to the city on one of the evening buses.

Chapter 23

*T*ime moved along at a snail's pace at first as I gutted out every new day to keep clean, then with a faster pace the stronger I got. Mrs. Byrnes, my landlady, and I became quite good friends often having morning coffees together and she would tell me about her Christian experiences and love of Jesus. She had an amazing faith and had a wealth of information for someone like me who knew nothing about anything. She would tell me about different denominations, where groups met, missionaries (wow, what a concept!), Bible studies, Bible interpretations, etc. It seemed that every day I would have new questions for her and she would gladly answer them for me.

In turn she seemed completely fascinated by my journey and how God seemed to have chosen me for a specific calling. I ended up sharing most of my story with her over time, and actually told her that God spoke to me on the mountain and exactly what I heard Him say to me. She looked at me with unwavering faith, not for a second doubting what I had said, and immediately started to praise God for such a mighty calling on my life.

"But don't you think it's a little farfetched?" I asked her. "I mean, how in the world would it seem possible for it to happen? Seems more than impossible."

And her response was, "Sam, the Bible is full of stories of people who were told by God what would happen and then had to wait on that promise for many years. This is not unlike God, to plant the vision that would make no sense or seem impossible by any worldly standard. And it will only come to be if you maintain your faith in what He said. God gives us the ability to choose and if you choose to believe in what He said and continue to walk towards that vision, then it will happen. I just hope I will still be around to witness it!"

So I made sure that I kept God's calling for me at the forefront of my mind. I made a conscious effort to not allow doubt to creep in. And why did it seem so easy for that to happen? I found I could so easily second guess what I already knew to be the truth. I could doubt that God had actually spoken, chalk up the entire mountain experience to coincidence or random events if I wanted. It would have been easy to do. And even though I knew in my heart what the truth was, I felt like I had to deliberately sustain that truth within me. So that's what I did.

It was all part and parcel anyway. I knew my recovery depended on my relationship with Jesus. The evidence of that was indisputable, especially when compared with years of failing without Jesus. If I didn't put my relationship with Jesus in the front and centre of my life, I would not stay clean. If I didn't stay clean, well, I would be back on Hastings. Then I could forget about any plans God had for my life anyway. So if I wanted to stay clean, then I needed to follow Jesus, and if I followed Jesus then the calling on my life would be fulfilled. At least that's the way I broke it down.

And so far it was working. I wasn't overwhelmed on any level. I paid one bill every month to Mrs. Byrnes and didn't have to worry about shopping for food, organizing utilities, establishing credit, cooking, my job was brainless and lacked any real stress. I didn't have or need a car and I had the time to concentrate on my recovery. If God was orchestrating my steps, He was only putting one very small thing on my plate at a time which was good because, I would have to admit, I was a frail and damaged person, more so than I would have liked to have admitted as a result of my severe addiction and it was a long and slow process to anything resembling real wellness. With every passing day I was able to see more clearly just how sick I had been.

I continued to work at *Trattoria*. Again, I wasn't about to mess with a recipe that seemed to be working. One night the chef came into the dish pit and told me the head chef of one of Torsi's other restaurants was in desperate need of a lunchtime dishwasher the following day and asked me if I would mind doing a shift over there. I said sure, why not? So the next day I worked at this other restaurant and learned that the dishwasher there had quit the night before in the middle of his shift, apparently threatened the chef in a foreign language, and stomped out.

Apparently, by doing this I had set some sort of precedence, and found myself on some sort of call out list because it became something of a fairly regular occurrence to be asked on an emergency basis to fill in on a shift at one of the other establishments. Torsi had five restaurants and I had worked at least one shift at all of them inside of two months of that first call out.

One day, when I was doing an emergency lunch shift at Torsi's original restaurant in Gastown, appropriately named Torsi's. The man himself wandered into the dish pit area in similar fashion that I had seen him do many times at my "home" restaurant on Robson. He did a double take and sort of pointed a finger at me and said, "Hey, what are you doing here?"

I explained I had been farmed out for an emergency and he just stared at me thinking and blinking. Finally he said, "Dishwashers. Man oh man. You know what Sam? I'll tell you, I never would have thought my biggest concern over owning lots of restaurants would have been keeping the dishes clean. Tell me something; how long have you worked for me now?"

"Uh, I think about nine months," I said.

"Okay then, you're probably one of the longest serving dishwashers in the history of my company. You tell me, why do they leave, and how should I keep them?"

"Well, the reason they leave is easy," I said and then paused wondering how politically correct I should be. Then, in customary fashion, I threw that out the window. "They leave because it's a crappy job. It gets progressively harder the longer into the shift you go. You have to finish the night with the worst, most grimed on pots in the kitchen at the same moment of the evening when everyone else is kicking back and doing nothing. It's the worst paying position in the company and everyone basically treats you like you are a second class citizen, almost as if the dishwasher isn't of equal importance to any other position or person. Not everyone is willing to work in a dish pit. Here is your breakdown: you got your immigrants who can't speak English. They leave when they learn the language or when something, *anything*, else comes up. You got your under achievers who settle on the position because they fail at every job they take on and they leave because they fail at every job they take on. You got your kids and they leave because kids always leave because their lives are always changing. And that's about it. Why they leave is easy. How to keep them would take some more thought."

He stared at me again and looked at me like he was seeing me for the first time. "Okay then, who are you and why are you still here?"

"Well, I'm different," I said. "I'm here because I became a Christian and am making some significant life changes and this is, apparently, where God wants me to be while I go through this."

"A wise man will listen to his God," he said. It amazed me just how many people didn't bat an eye when I tell them I am on a mission from God. I just don't think I ever realized before just how many people believed and thought this perfectly reasonable.

"This is what I have been learning," I said. "Listen, Torsi, I like my job and I like my bosses, but I do think if you wanted to keep your dishwashers there might be some strategies you could consider. Would you mind if I gave it some thought?"

"Yes Sam. You give it some thought, and maybe ask your God at the same time. Let's see what comes of it."

And I did give it some thought. And I did ask God. And I found I could draw on some of the information I learned at

BCIT at my business administration program and I came up with a few ideas. I wasn't going to try tracking him down mainly because he was a very busy and successful man and I thought he probably had forgotten about even talking to me. But if the opportunity presented itself, I would say something.

Chapter 24

A week or two later he came into my dish pit area for his semi-regular escape from his obligations. He stared at the dishes coming out clean for a few minutes then looked over some papers he was carrying. Then he finally looked in my direction and said, "Well Sam, did you come up with any ideas as to how to keep a good dishwasher?"

"Here's the thing as I see it, Torsi," I said. "Dishwashers are under the control of the chef and in the hierarchy of the restaurant, they are on the bottom rung. And while the chef controls them, they really have nothing to do with the cooking of the food. So I would separate the dishwashers away from the chef's control and create their own category. Currently you have kitchen staff, bar staff, wait staff, and the hostesses, and all these stations have their own manager. I suggest adding dishwashers to the mix. This way, dishwashers are instantly more recognized as their own department and can have a voice in the big picture of the how the restaurant is run. Having a voice will give them a sense of involvement and, in theory, will build the general esteem." I stopped for a moment to open the machine, pull out the hot, finished rack, and load in the next dirty rack. I waved some steam out of the air and carried on.

"Further, you have five restaurants and dishwashing is the kind of job where one person can step in seamlessly to fill in for another. In the current system you have five head chefs all in charge of hiring, firing, and dealing with all the no-shows or ineptitude. Why not put one person in charge of this new department and that person can set the schedules, do all the hiring, and take the burden away from the chef's so they can concentrate on the food. Yes? So one person in charge of ALL your dishwashers, and this person would be the head of this new department we could call, what, 'Dish Department'? The person in charge can have a pool of staff from which to draw. If one quits, he can draw from a pool of many to dam the leak quickly instead of having the head chef having to find a replacement from outside resources.

"Next, I would start a campaign of 'dishwashers are people too.' Lame, I know, but these restaurants only operate if all spokes in the wheel are operating. By that notion, dishwashers are just as important as bartenders, or cooks, or the dimwitted hostesses and with a little education the dishwashers might be treated with more equality. God loves the dishwasher you know Torsi.

"And finally, I would take all those horrendous insert pots that had stored baked on food in them up until the kitchen closed and instead of piling them up in the dish area, I would fill them with hot water and soap and store them for the day-time dishwasher to clean. The night dishwasher does all the pots and mops the entire floor, while the morning dishwasher sips coffee until the dirty plates start coming in, and doesn't have any closing responsibilities. It's simply better distribution of duties and evens out the work load. I guarantee these ideas will keep your dishwashers longer, eliminate dishwasher down time, frees up time for your head chefs to concentrate on what they need to be doing, and you won't be incurring any additional expenses."

I had his attention; that much was pretty clear. He had a finger on his lips, like he was thinking hard. "One question: How do you figure I won't be incurring any additional expenses if you are suggesting incorporating a department head?"

"Well, I think someone could act as department head and be a dishwasher. I mean, your head bartender still bartends, doesn't he? Okay, so maybe that person makes a little more than the rest.

Maybe your expenses go up by a couple bucks an hour, but you wouldn't have to incur a brand new salary."

"Where did you come from Sam and how do you know so much about business?"

"I'm a BCIT graduate in business administration. Then I got in trouble with drugs," I replied. "I'm rebuilding myself. Foundational work." I smiled and added, "With God."

Torsi smiled. "You're a piece of work, Sam. I'll think about what you said, okay? Sounds like you're looking for a promotion."

"Au contraire, Torsi. I'm just a humble dishwasher, more than happy to stay at my position for my current wage."

In the end he did promote me and put me in charge of all the dishwashers throughout his company and gave me an extra $2.00 an hour. I bought a bike so I could get from restaurant to restaurant quickly, dropped one shift a week of washing dishes to organize and communicate and coordinate all the obligations and put together a pretty well orchestrated show, if I do say so myself. I went and spoke to each dishwasher personally, made them understand they had a voice that would be heard if they had a concern. I re-organized and re-delegated responsibilities, found a system of scheduling, and dealt with each crisis as it came up.

Most of the dishwashers were foreigners. In fact, only one wasn't and he was another young drug addict in recovery who I got the job for, and I was fully expecting him to not show up one day. The rest of them, about fifteen in all, were of various ages and from all over the globe.

I "interviewed" one person a week, wrote it up and then hung "their story" on a wall near the dirty dish drop off areas at the various restaurants where the wait staff would have no choice but to notice. It was my intention for it to give all the English speaking staff an idea as to who they were sharing work space with. It was an eye-opening experience for me as the stories behind how they arrived at this position were intriguing, fascinating, and sometimes harrowing. Here is an example of one of the write ups I posted:

Sulyman

Meet Sulyman: He is in charge of the dish department tonight.

Sulyman is a 28 year old Tamil from Sri Lanka. Sri Lanka has been in a dire situation with civil war for a long time. After an armed conflict that saw his father die and his only sister taken away by armed men, Sulyman and his mother fled and joined up with a smuggler who promised them escape. The smuggler robbed them of all they had after sending them off in an overcrowded boat to cross the Pacific. The boat was eventually boarded by the Canadian Coast Guard and, after a period of detention, Sulyman and his mom were given refugee status. Sulyman is now working here, with us, to help provide for himself and his mother while he tries to make a life in Canada. Before the conflict in Sri Lanka, Sulyman was a student and farmer, who loved animals and spending time with his family. Sulyman believes all people are essentially good, and prays to God daily for everyone he comes in contact with.

His story was sadly not uncommon amongst those I interviewed. The interview process, often done with interpreters I had to find, were powerful sessions, with one unmistakable common denominator: they were grateful to share their stories, grateful that people cared, and grateful for the opportunities they received in Canada. It also bonded them to me and established trust. In the end, very few dishwashers left.

And changes happened to the staff; not with all, but with some who would stop and read the stories about the people who they worked alongside but rarely spoke to. And they would invariably say, "I had no idea," and then make more of an effort to say hello, be friendly, and to generally make life easier for them.

In any event, the plan worked and dishwashers turned over less, felt more important, had their tasks better distributed, and were generally more respected. For me, I didn't have to wash as many dishes, got to organize and delegate more, which I liked, got to meet many very cool people I would not have had any idea about, and was considered management, for whatever that was worth. Torsi got more mileage out of dishwashers, freed up his chef's to do chef stuff, and didn't have to worry so much about the "Dish Dept."

So, all in all, a win-win.

Chapter 25

I passed the first year sobriety mark for the first time in my life. Despite all previous efforts I had never made it past seven and a half months. And I knew the reason why: it was because this time I trusted in Jesus who gave me salvation, instead of trusting in AA or NA that had previously been the case.

"My" year didn't look anything like what I had formerly believed to be the way to get clean. Along the course of the year, I invested less and less time in the traditional "12- step" groups and "working the steps" and instead worked full on towards becoming a disciple of Christ. My "meetings" became church services, Bible studies, courses offered at churches, and worship sessions. Every answer I needed was in the Bible and I had been proven over and over again that there was no doubt as to its ability to be right. The Bible and my personal relationship with Jesus had enriched me beyond belief and I was growing more and more mature in my walk with every passing day.

I remained pretty consistent towards my learning. The more I learned about biblical content, interpretation, scholarly viewpoints, and the era in which the Bible was written, the more I grew. I was becoming a new creation, day by day.

It wasn't that I didn't like the 12-step programs. They were an invaluable resource towards recovery, a system with proven results over long periods of time. But to me they were overpopulated with very sick people who conversed mainly on the topic of what happened, a subject I personally found depressing and, once it was established we were not alone in our stories, fairly unhelpful. 12-step was supposed to be about the spiritual awakening which happens at the end of the steps, at which point recovery happens, but so often it was focused on the stories of unmanageability which were in the first steps. There also seemed to be something of a butchery of the AA term "Higher Power" which to me meant God but so often seemed to mean "make up whoever one chooses to be their god." Now that I was in the know about God, it was hard for me to listen appreciatively to people talk about their made up gods working for them. It didn't make sense as to how that could possibly work. And I think the stats showed that it didn't.

But AA had something that most of the church didn't – a forum for one addict to help another. Addicts are a strange breed and the only people who could actually relate to what they had been through are other people who had also gone through it. And there was something very healing in one person sharing their story with someone else who might have felt very alone in their struggles. There is tremendous shame in addiction, and conventional circles just don't get how an addict can possibly have stooped as low as they did.

So I kept one foot in the rooms of AA solely to give back, give some time to newcomers, and, if God would have it, allow me to lead them to Christ. And I had dreamed for years about maybe taking a one year "cake" so I wasn't about to miss it.

My cake was at the Sunday night NA group I most often attended in a church basement in the West End. I kept it pretty low key and didn't invite a bunch of people I knew and when it was time for me to tell my story I gave the credit to God for lifting me from the ashes and restoring me to life, but tried not to sound too preachy as I knew it would turn people off. There was still some time on the clock after I had finished talking and before we would eat some of the cake, so the chair person opened the meeting up to anyone who felt they needed to share. A young guy in the back of the room put his hand up and said simply:

"Hi, my name is Sheldon and I'm an addict." Everyone replied together, "Hi Sheldon!" And then he said, "I don't really have anything to say," and his head was down and his voice low in typical fashion of someone just fresh in from their addiction. "I just wanted to introduce myself and, you know, like get over my fears of speaking in front of other people, cause, like, you know......
I'm........I'm........" He started to well up. "I'm just...really hurting here and I need help...," and he just trailed off.

After a moment of time passed and it seemed clear he wasn't going to go on, people started to clap and yell out, "Thanks Sheldon. Keep coming back!" Then the chair person closed the meeting and invited everyone to have some cake to celebrate my getting a year clean.

I had been watching Sheldon. It's always touching and a good reminder to hear someone fresh off the street, full of raw pain, and lost beyond measure. He was with a bunch of other young guys all keeping a low profile in the back and clearly a part of a recovery centre on a group outing to the meeting. He was young. Younger than me. And he was.......wait a second.......Sheldon? Younger than me? I had a flashback to the restaurant at the base of the mountain. Before the climb. The guy from the truck. Danny. The last thing he said to me was, "His name is Sheldon. Sheldon."

I headed right over to where he was just starting to stand up. "Hey man, is your dad like some kind of mechanic type guy? Fixes stuff?"

He was a little startled but not overly so. He had, after all, just come from active addiction. "Uh, yeah, he does all kinds of stuff."

"Lives in the back of North Van somewhere? Drives some kind of converted pickup with wood paneled sides? Eats giant Yukon breakfasts at some country cabin restaurant?" I said.

He smiled. "Yeah that's him. Yukon breakfast. Biggest and best around. He eats there like four times a week. You know him?"

"I stowed away in the back of his truck off Hastings," I said. "Jumped in the back when he was at a light running from trouble and didn't get out till he kicked me out in the parking lot of that restaurant."

"Really? Wow. You stowed away on his truck? Did he kick your ass?" he said.

"I thought he was going to at first. Then, believe it or not, he bought me breakfast. A Yukon. And we talked and he told me about you and he told me to tell you to call him if I ever saw you. Called the both of us a couple of dumb asses. And you know what else?" I said. "That was exactly one year ago, because that day was my first day clean." I hadn't told that part of the story during the sharing I had just done during the meeting. "How many days clean do you have?" I asked.

"I'm on day six. Five days in detox and I transferred to the Joshua House Recovery today."

"Were you on Hastings?" I asked.

"Yeah, for like two years off and on now."

"Yeah, I was too. Joshua House, eh? That's a Christian based recovery house isn't?" I asked. "That's awesome. Definitely the way to freedom," I said.

"Yeah, well, I don't know about the Christian part, but I needed a bed and really want to get clean, so here I am."

"Well, I gotta go cut some cake. I guess it's my duty and all, so, like, call your dad, okay? And come grab a piece of cake."

That was it for that day. But I saw him again the next week and he sought me out and we had another talk and then had coffee together a week or two later, once he was off "restrictions" and allowed to leave his recovery house on his own. He was using me as a part of his support system but we were also developing something of a friendship. We had a lot in common. Both of us grew up on the North Shore, me from West Van, him from North Van. Both of us grew up in functional homes, went to decent public schools, played sports, graduated high school, and had pretty normal childhoods. His journey down started after his mother died from cancer when he was thirteen, but he didn't use drugs until he was eighteen.

I would pick him up from the Joshua House on occasion. I had to become an approved visitor so I met the owners who were a tireless couple named Rich and Angie. They had overcome their own problems with drugs, started up this Christian based recovery house and housed and ran groups for about ten guys at a time. The house was alive with Jesus as the model of recovery they used. Jesus was the centre of recovery and it occurred to me I wished I had been open minded enough to have come to a place like this during my years of failing at residential treatment. The sacrifice this couple seemed to make continually bringing in broken men who invariably would fail at recovery was also inspiring and they made me want to be a part of it.

Meeting Sheldon, spending some time at the Joshua House, and seeing again some front line recovery from addiction in action reminded me of how difficult the journey was. Recovery from drugs was not easy. And even though I could not have come this far without God, there were still action steps that needed to take place day in and day out. Long forming habits needed to be broken, the power of the drug diminished, new habits formed, and new belief systems incorporated, and it all took 100% abstinence from drugs 100% of the time. One fall, one slip, one weak moment which turned into a bad decision, and all the work would have been lost. I had experienced this before. I could stay clean for sixty straight days, but that one weak moment would wipe it out completely, and mean nothing after the fact. What they said in AA was so true: one is too many, 1000 never enough. It was the first one that took you down.

Learning to live on my own, developing the relationships I now had in my life, finding and succeeding in a new job, living life on life's terms day in day out, and starting most of these things from ground zero was a slow and tedious process. There were moments where it would feel overwhelming, stressful, frustrating, depressing, lonely, or impossible. There were also moments of joy, happiness, and fulfillment. In the past, whether it had been to celebrate something good or medicate something bad, the impulse was to get high.

Perhaps the biggest obstacle was the inability to recognize just how sick I was. I thought I was doing pretty well until I hit six months clean and was able to look back from a place of moderate stability and recognize just how unwell I was in the first few months. When I hit nine months clean I realized how sick I had been at six months clean.

And now at around the year mark, I felt mature enough in my walk to be able to admit there was still more work to be done before I could become the man I would have been had the drugs not taken hold. But I felt like I was well on my way to reconciling old relationships, mending self inflicted wounds, overcoming the traumas of the street, breaking down false belief systems, reinstating confidence of identity, realizing my sense of self, establishing a position in community, securing my finances, and getting under way with my purpose for life.

During that process of breaking down the old and becoming the new, things had been very difficult. It was a constant feeling of being confused as to who I was, a feeling of being uncomfortable. My new peers did not seem to be like me. The peers I was in school with had gone on to start careers, were in real relationships, and were conducting their lives with youthful maturity. The young people I worked with now were just having fun, earning money, hitting the town, shopping, laughing and hanging out. Everyone seemed established and secure. Of course that was a lie, but it seemed that way to me at the time. Whereas with me, I was having a re-birth, and was not yet comfortable in the new me and had to learn everything from the ground up. There were things I couldn't do and had to accept: I couldn't carry money on me, couldn't go out for a beer, couldn't hang around people that like to party, and couldn't wander around certain parts of the city. And there was certain things I had to do which I didn't always want to: I had to stay accountable to stable people, had to do a devotional every day, had to attend meetings, had to get real with my defects of character and be bold enough to change them. I had to call myself on honesty and integrity, had to live by the letter of the law, had learn to be giving and selfless, had be open minded as to what real truths were about myself, had to clean up the wreckage I caused, and stand up and face the music where necessary.

Not easy.

And this is where the faith came in. I would pray, "Lord help me to learn who I am. Help me step into the calling You have for me. Keep me close, Lord; guide me, help me, show me, teach me." And slowly, day by day, He did that for me. And day by day I stayed clean. Perfectly clean, because in this game there was no such thing as a compromise. And three months became six, and six became nine, and nine became a year. And so on.

Chapter 26

$\mathcal{T}$ ime itself seemed to pick up speed into my second year. The early days and months often felt like they were gutted out literally day by day or hour by hour and advancing a week farther in the journey seemed like a month. But when the first year had passed, time seemed to start flowing in the same sort of pace as normal people seemed to experience it and I would catch myself saying things like, "Wow. I can't believe it's summer again already," or something like that.

I was well established with my job during this time. With Torsi having okayed the Dish Dept. as being included with his other departments, I was now invited to all management staff meetings. I would step things up at these meetings by way of dress and professionalism. I found some good clothes back at my parent's house and I would carry myself as a department manager as opposed to a dishwasher attending a meeting. Torsi's restaurant group was one of the more recognizable and premier establishments of the city; his company was significant and there were lots of meetings. My role was virtually non-existent beyond just being an attendee. But I used these meetings as a way to politic for the dishwashers rights whenever I could. I wasn't overly vocal, oppressive, or bullish. But I did do what I could to make sure the dishwashers were considered as a department of equal standing in the restaurants. And I did look for ways in which we could improve their lives. At one point, I got Torsi to okay sponsoring any dishwasher who wanted to take English classes, talking him into the notion that it would improve communication in the kitchen. And lately I had been dropping seeds about a potential scholarship program where a dishwasher of certain longevity of employment and having gone through an English class (if relevant) could apply for a scholarship to attend a culinary apprenticeship program.

Torsi was always very tolerant of my desire to improve the lives of the dishwashers. In fact he seemed somewhat amused and intrigued by my journey and usually went out of his way to see if I wanted to have a voice at any of the meetings. He told me once in the dish pit during one of his visits that he had never seen or heard of any dishwasher being so comfortable and competent as a spokesperson and business minded person. And that I should consider myself something rare. It was a flattering statement and one that I cherished. It gave me a boost of confidence that things were going in a positive direction.

I had been spending considerable time with Sheldon as well. He had grown immensely in the months we spent together. I couldn't believe the change in him that I could see even from one week to the next. The shell shocked, distrustful, skeptical, and angry youth was being replaced by someone slowly coming alive. He stood a little straighter, carried himself with a little more confidence, and became more engaged with what he was doing with every passing week. While the men he was in the Joshua House with were falling left and right and turning over in rapid succession, he seemed to become more determined with every passing day.

My "master plan" was to bring him to the Lord. And even though he was in a Christian recovery house, he wasn't fully on board with the faith. After many coffees and conversations, it seemed pretty clear he was angry at God for the loss of his mother and I had to respect something as deeply rooted as that. I myself had never experienced any sort of loss other than the losing of myself.

But I did manage to get him to come with me when I went to church and I introduced him to some of the people I had met along the way who had inspired me with their stories of faith. In my early days of recovery I feasted on amazing stories of faith that I either heard from people I met, or in reading about missionaries or historical events that occurred. It never ceases to amaze me the acts of faith that people were capable of and the more I heard them the more my mountain experience seemed to line up with the way God seemed to work.

So I brought Sheldon with me and sought out the people I had met who had inspired me. There was the older husband and wife who had joined the Salvation Army and spent their lives in and out of Africa working with children and helping people since their early twenties. These two had been married at like eighteen years old, and were now well into their eighties and still doing what they believe they were called to do and passionately talked of the miracles along the way.

I met another couple who were of Indian descent. They felt God had called them to come to Canada and here they were, despite having had to give up so much of what they had going for themselves over there. Another man I met had gone to China with smuggled Bibles in his suitcase so he could hand them out, and he did this despite the very real chance he could have been arrested and persecuted for his beliefs. Another friend was a Christian counselor who had never formally charged anyone for a counseling session. It was "if you can pay, then pay, if not, it's free." And he had been doing it for over thirty years without hardship.

There was Tony and Annie who literally lived their lives being led by the Lord. Every day they would wake up and ask God what they should do, and often they would leave town, move, spend months on the road or make midnight visits to people depending on what God had told them. I had never, and I mean never met anyone as alive in spirit as these two.

But my favorite new friend was a guy named Angus, a 6'8" giant of a man who God had told to walk across Canada with a gigantic cross when he was in his early twenties. The cross was like 20' long and 8' feet wide and had a wheel on the base so he could sling it over one shoulder and have the rest of it sort of wheel behind him. He did this walk over the course of three summers and even met his wife along the way. He took only the clothes on his back and was completely reliant on God for the entire journey. He would tell me the stories and show me the news print articles that followed him right across the country. He would tell me about how unbelievable this calling from God seemed to him because it was just so "not him" to do something like that. Yet he did it. And he told so many stories of miracles that happened along the way, without ever, not even once, being mocked or ridiculed.

I would drag Sheldon along to meet all these people and we would listen to them light up as they talked about God and what He can do. And later Sheldon and I would go for coffee.

"I can't believe those people," he would say. "It is all just so far away from anything I've ever seen. Those people aren't living for themselves. Those people have all the time in the world for other people and acts of kindness," he would say.

"I hear you man," I would respond. "And the crazy thing is they all are so darned happy and content. They're alive in the spirit."

But it wasn't those stories of faith that ended up bringing Sheldon to the Lord. No, it was my story and how it involved his father. He knew me by now and felt comfortable and trusted me. I had only really told him the entire story, from start to finish, after we had known each other some six months. So by that time he listened to it and believed the whole thing. We revisited it many times. I knew he was trying to wrap his head around its significance. He tried to understand the role his father played directly and how he was now involved indirectly.

"Yeah Sheldon," I would say to him. "Your dad made a point of telling me your name and for me to keep an eye out for you, and I did remember your name and did run into you. So if God's leading me to the mountain was a part of His plan for me, then why wouldn't your father's involvement and my running into you also have been orchestrated by God? Perhaps you and I are to work towards the vision God gave me, or maybe for you it's all about you and your dad finding your way through your loss." And I laughed when I could see his brain trying so hard to get it. "Hey brother, I've been trying to figure this out since I first saw that Bible on the mountain. But I don't go there anymore. I've just accepted that God is real, God is great, and God can do anything. I just do my best to go along with it and hold up my end."

So Sheldon became a Christian, dedicated his life to Jesus, and got baptized by Angus in the freezing cold ocean at English Bay and then we ate hot dogs and drank root beers and Sheldon huddled in a blanket and grinned from ear to ear and it was one of the best days ever.

Chapter 27

As the months moved along my thinking had been shifting towards many thoughts as to how I was to become of service to society. The specific vision God spoke to me on the mountain was still seemingly farfetched and unattainable, but the essence of it, along with all things I had learned so far, supported a calling of being selfless. I had made significant strides to change from the self-absorbed person I had been before, but I was convinced it was God who had made this transformation within me. Left to myself, I doubt very much I could have been capable of it. I had done some service work since coming down from the mountain, namely I volunteered for cleanup (dishes if you can believe it) at the church I was going to, set up at an NA meeting I frequented for about six months, and anything else that happened to come along that was within reason for my schedule and finances.

Any thoughts I had towards service were heavily influenced by what God had spoken to me on the mountain. But I didn't actually start to see any real definitions as to what I would do until I matured in my sobriety. It was Torsi who breathed confidence in me along with a gradual building belief into some of my God given abilities that I was able to see that maybe my ability to serve extended beyond just set up and cleanup of church and recovery functions. Perhaps I had some gifts in organizing, being a spokesperson, and maybe, just maybe, even some leadership.

The confidence I was slowly entering into was helped along by all the other areas of my life as I continued along on my journey. The relationship with my parents had gone from a place where issues of trust, anger from my actions, and tension existed at least on some levels, to a place now where a full reconciliation existed. I had been reinstated as a son, was conducting myself in the ways I thought a son should, and the relationship had become easy and fulfilling. It had been a journey that was only attainable through consistency, dependability, and sustained actions. The rewards had been immense and as a result of this new relationship we were all able to communicate with more ease, transparency, and freedom. I learned about my mother's childhood and her journey with God, and we went to a local West Van church together on a number of Sunday mornings. My dad and I went fishing and while we never talked too much, we did spend easy and rewarding time together doing things we both enjoyed. There was no price tag on being accepted again back into my family and I found the confidence I was gaining was in a large part because of that acceptance and encouragement I got from them.

I spent increasing amounts of time at the Joshua House as a result of my relationship with Sheldon. Certainly I could relate to the men, had a powerful testimony that the men would benefit hearing, and Rich and Angie needed any help they could get. I wouldn't necessarily call it rewarding work, as the constant relapsing of the men back into addiction was hard to watch, and the entitled, self-absorbed attitudes they often resurfaced with were equally unappealing. I recognized just how sacrificing working with addicts was and had a newfound respect for people like Rich and Angie.

On a rare Saturday I didn't have to work, Sheldon and I took the Seabus to North Van to meet up with Danny, Sheldon's dad.

"How are you guys getting along," I asked Sheldon as we made the short sea crossing.

"Better all the time," he said. "I mean, at first, I think he was glad I was around, but he was also pretty angry and mean. He doesn't understand the 'processing feelings' bullshit we learn in rehab so we don't actually talk about anything. But in his own way he cares, and it's starting to feel like maybe he trusts me again and things are feeling like they aren't too far off being really good."

"Giving any thought to the future?" I asked.

"Yeah, lots," he said. "I'm almost a year clean now and I'm still having trouble knowing when to do stuff. Know what I mean? Like when do I leave the recovery house? What do I do with myself? What can I take on and what can't I? I'm waiting on God, but the answers don't always seem clear."

I just nodded and he carried on. "But the reoccurring thought is to go back to school and maybe get a mechanics ticket or become a millwright. The old man has like ten acres and a huge shop. He already gets tons of work because he can do bits of anything, repairs, welding, fab work, whatever. I'm thinking I can come alongside and bring it up to the next level you know? Like a full on machine shop, mechanical drive design, stuff like that. Then I can sort of help the old man out, you know? Stay close, work together and I can look after him later in life."

"I like it Sheldon. I think it's a plan that not only honours God, but helps the both of you out too."

We chatted some more idly as we walked off the Seabus and up the ramp. I could already see the distinguishable junk truck and Danny waiting near the busses at the top of the ramp and off to my right was the place I had laid out my sleeping bag and eaten sandwiches with the Swedish travelers when I first came down. "Wow." I muttered to myself as I was flooded with memories from the mountain.

To my knowledge nobody had discussed any plans for the visit but it certainly didn't surprise me when we parked in the gravel parking lot of Momma's Country Cabin restaurant, settled into a booth, waved away menus and were served three Yukon breakfasts by a waitress with a nametag that said Momma.

I looked across the booth at father and son. Danny was still massive with a huge chest and forearms. His son was a younger version of him and it was easy to see what Sheldon would look like in thirty years. But there was a sensitivity to Sheldon I didn't see in his dad.

"Well what have you two troublemakers been up to?" Danny said while he stirred his coffee.

"Only good stuff Danny," I said. "You know: work, rehab, church, that kind of stuff."

"Uh huh," he grunted and shoved in a huge bite. I wasn't keeping up to Danny bite for bite like I did the first time we ate together with the key reason being I wasn't a malnourished skeleton. But I did hold my own as I had grown to like food very much, even though I still felt like a twig compared to these two.

The conversation actually flowed quite easily. Behind Danny's gruff exterior was a man who was bright and interested. I could see him look at his son and I could see that it mattered to him a great deal what he was going through and what the future held for him.

As we left the restaurant, Danny let Sheldon walk ahead and he fell in beside me a little farther back. "Listen Sam," he said, "I think you done good, okay? I don't know about the religious side of it or nothing, but I do know the kind of shape you were in that day, and, well, it's hard to believe you're the same man now."

"Thanks Danny," I said. "I appreciate it very much. You were my ride out of hell. If you weren't there that day I have no idea how this story would have gone. I would probably be dead or still on the street. You could have kicked me out of the truck. You *should* have kicked me out of the truck," and I smiled. "But you didn't and here I am. So thanks Danny. I'll never forget the role you played."

"One more thing," he said. "Thanks for helping my boy. I can see whatever it is you guys are doing, it's working."

Sheldon had already jumped into the middle seat of the truck. Danny was at the driver's door and I was at the passenger's door and he leaned his head so he was speaking over the roof of the cab and said in a voice only I could hear, "You stay close to him, okay? You stay close."

Chapter 28

$\mathscr{S}$ometime after my second anniversary of being on the mountain I took a bus out to Richmond to see Amy Harley. I still hadn't bothered buying a car. I could have as my lifestyle was humble with no real debt so saving money even at my meager wage wasn't difficult. But with all of Torsi's restaurants being such close vicinity to each other and all within walking distance from home, the only real time I left downtown was to go to my parent's house in West Van. And I didn't mind taking the West Van buses for those trips.

I called her before I made the trip out to see if she would be willing to talk to me. I told her that it was me who was the anonymous hiker who had found her husband's plane and that there were a couple of things about the discovery that I thought she might want to know. And that if she didn't find it too difficult emotionally, would she mind terribly if I made the trip out to Richmond to talk to her. She had responded in a very friendly manner and had invited me out the following Sunday afternoon at around 2:00 p.m. and gave me her address.

So I jumped on the bus and headed out to Richmond which was another community in the Lower Mainland of Vancouver. It was south of Vancouver in flat land where the airport was. I didn't know Richmond very well and struggled a little with the buses and direction. But eventually I found her place, a fifteen minute walk from the nearest bus stop. Her house turned out to be a charming sprawling rancher on about a half acre of land.

Amy Harley turned out to be a youthful late forties woman, elegant of feature, very pretty, and with an easy and charming smile. She invited me straight in and sat me down in a nicely decorated living room. After some pleasantries I got into what I had wanted to say.

I told her that I had come through an amazing set of circumstances to arrive at the wreckage, that I had been a drug addict on the verge of death in many different ways, that I had somehow been "called" to the mountain where I found the plane, and that the plane had offered me salvation from the elements and had saved my life. I went on to tell her I had found his Bible on his lap open to Ephesians 4 and that because I saw that, I read the Bible for the first time and stayed on the mountain for forty days.

I told her that as a result of finding him reading the Bible, I had become a Christian, and have never used drugs since. I told her that her husband's plane, his fishing gear, and his food supplies had saved my life while on the mountain. I told her that his Bible had saved my life for eternity. I told her that I was sorry I had violated his space and used his items, that I knew they belonged to him, but that I had to and that I tried to preserve it all as best I could when I left.

She listened intently. She hung on every word with her mouth slightly open and one hand near her face as if she was afraid she might have to cry into her hands. After a period of time which seemed very long she said, "Thank you Sam. Thank you for sharing this with me." She paused to catch her breath. "He.....he....he just so loved the Lord. He would have been so pleased to know he had helped you. He would have been so happy for you to have used his stuff."

She went on to tell me all about him as a father, a husband, and a man of God. She told me about his business successes and how he tried to follow Biblical instruction in all his affairs. He loved to fish, loved to fly and fix airplanes, but most of all, he loved his family and did everything for them.

I asked her if nobody told her that he was found with a Bible on his lap. She said that no, nobody had told her that until today, but that she found it not surprising at all that he would want to spend his last moments reading the Bible.

I went on to tell her about what I thought God said to me on my final night on the mountain and what had happened to me since I got back. And I told her I was sorry it took me so long to get here. I just didn't want to be the shaky drug addict in early recovery with crazy tales that could upset her and her family. I wanted to be sure it was a good idea and backed with some stability. I didn't want to add to any heartache.

She assured me that what I brought today filled her with joy albeit also with sadness. But that the sadness was not a bad thing; that it was okay to love and miss people and cry over them and love God and His great gift of life and marvel at how it all connects. And I agreed with her and we mourned him together for a while in our own ways.

As I was leaving I asked her if she knew whether or not Ephesians 4 was of specific importance to him or whether or not that just happened to be the page he was on. She smiled at me with warmth. "Sam, he loved the book of Ephesians, and in particular Ephesians 4. He felt that living up to the calling of God was the greatest objective that we should have in life. Take a look over your shoulder."

I turned my head and right there on the wall was one of those fake rock plaques with slogans on it. It said, "Be completely humble and gentle; be patient bearing with one another in love. Ephesians 4."

"It was no mistake he was reading that page Sam. In fact, it makes perfect sense."

Chapter 29

Not long after my visit out to see Amy I got a call from Richard at the Joshua House asking me if I had seen Sheldon that day. I told him that I hadn't spoken to Sheldon in a couple of weeks. Sheldon had taken his first year cake a month or so ago at the same time I had passed my second year of sobriety. I didn't take a cake for year two as I had all but stopped going to AA or NA entirely, instead "working my program" in the Church.

"Why?" I said. "Is he missing?" Had this call come in six months ago I would have immediately assumed Sheldon had relapsed, but I had grown so accustomed to his stability that my first thought was there had to be an explanation.

"Well, yes and no," Richard said. "He normally eats dinner at the house and if he doesn't, he calls. And he isn't here and he didn't call," he said. "He was on a weekend pass to his dad's house but should have been back by dinner today."

"Hmm," I said. "Well, let's hope he just got held up somehow. I gotta go to work, so I'll give you a call in the morning and check in and let you know if I hear from him." I did call in the morning and confirmed the worst. Sheldon had not come home.

Perhaps in any other world any number of scenarios might run through people's minds, but in the world of addiction all roads led to the same explanation: Sheldon had relapsed. It was just so commonplace that anyone involved in addiction was very familiar with the scene. Someone who appeared to have been doing well just disappears and when they resurfaced was anyone's guess. Nobody calls the cops. Seldom are families notified and there is really very little that can be done other than to wait and see if he turns up. And if he does, would he want to try and build back the foundation of sobriety again. In Sheldon's case, with over thirteen months clean he would be devastated beyond words and rebuilding himself back up would be just as difficult as the first time around, no matter if he was only out for even a day. Sadly, a person relapsing soon after achieving a milestone was not unheard of.

I had seen hundreds of relapses over the years from my various stints in recovery and had contributed dozens of my own as well. But rarely had I been as close to anyone as I was to Sheldon and for the first time felt like I knew what family members of addicts had to go through. I was worried for Sheldon and hoped beyond measure that he would surface soon and be willing to start his recovery over again as challenging as that might be.

I went to work that night as usual. Around 7:00 pm, in the heart of dinner service, the hostess came to see me in the dish area and told me I had an urgent phone call. I had never had a call at work before, urgent or otherwise, and my first thought was concern about my parents. But it was Richard on the phone sounding frazzled.

"Sheldon OD'ed Sam," he immediately said. "He's dead." I wasn't sure I heard correctly. I wasn't computing. "What do you mean?" was all I could muster.

"He's dead Sam," he said again. "I got a call from the police. They found him in a hotel room on Granville Street. They found his wallet and all his identification on him. It's him Sam. He OD'ed. The cops told me. He's gone Sam and I figured you needed to know as soon as I found out."

I just stood there with the phone in my hand. I didn't put it back in its cradle and I no longer had it to my ear. I just stood there until I realized I was standing amongst diners waiting to be seated and walked in a daze back to the dish pit. I finished my shift, although I don't know how or remember anything about it. And then I went home, numb beyond measure.

Chapter 30

The days following were something of a blur. I just put one foot in front of the other and made it through the days. Sheldon's story was one we in the world of addiction had all heard before. Guy gets clean, guy gets his first year cake, guy relapses, and guy dies on his first night using. But I had never experienced it so close to home. I was having trouble processing it. Of course I asked why? And it made me question God. Why would God have taken him? How could this have happened after having come so far? Wasn't there supposed to have been a plan in place? Wasn't Sheldon and his dad supposed to have worked together? What purpose could there be in taking him so young?

I went down to Granville Street and found the hotel his body was discovered in. I don't know why exactly. I just wanted to see where it happened. It was a hotel called *The Hotel Arizona*, one of the last buildings on Granville before the Granville Street bridge took you out of the downtown core. Granville Street, while something of an entertainment district a few blocks north seemed to deteriorate in the last couple blocks before the bridge.

I stood on the sidewalk across the street, stared up at the hotel and tried to imagine how the whole thing played itself out. Sheldon had been on a weekend pass to his dad's. He was supposed to have come home Sunday for dinner to the recovery house. Maybe something happened at his dad's house. An argument?

Or maybe he had the plan in place for ages, fantasizing about it, plotting, and planning. Tells his dad he is leaving on the Saturday, tells the recovery house he is coming back on the Sunday, thus buying himself a free day when nobody is watching. Probably thought, "I'll use *just one more time*, then stop, go back to the recovery house and get away with it."

I looked at the hotel. A dump. But not a Hastings Street dump. One rung up the ladder maybe. Sheldon would have been looking for something close to where you could get drugs, the type of place on a budget, the type of place that looks the other way, but not something right back in the heart of the war zone. I didn't know where to score drugs on Granville but one look around would tell me they were here somewhere and maybe Sheldon knew this area.

I could picture him checking in late on the Saturday. Scoring his drugs with the anticipation being almost more than he could bear. Getting into his room. Maybe with someone else. Who knew? Using into the night. Maybe drinking and taking heroin, a deadly combination of downers. Maybe he didn't factor in his lowered tolerance for drugs with his clean time. Or maybe he bought a bad batch. Or maybe he was smoking crack and just over amped his heart. Again, who knew?

And then he died at some stage. Maybe someone was with him and they just left without saying anything. Maybe that person could have saved his life by just calling for help but was afraid of being caught with dope. That kind of stuff happened all the time. Or maybe he was alone. In any event he dies. In that hotel room, one rung above skid row. And then his body just sits there until someone discovers it. I was told he was found early Monday afternoon, so if the timelines were right he was up there for a day before discovery. No maid service perhaps. Of course that was only if my theory of his intending to go back to the Joshua House undetected held true. Maybe he rented the place for a week and had no intention of ever returning. Who knew?

But then I could picture them bringing his body down on a gurney. Another stat. Another ho hum set of circumstances for the attendants. Another cold body of a young man whose life was cut short, way too young. Then the police half-heartedly investigate, only to determine it was just another overdose. Then someone makes some difficult phone calls to the people who care.

I looked around the street. There was a porno theatre two doors up and I could see an old man paying his way inside. I could see at least three stores advertising sex toys, magazines, and x-rated videos. There was a beer parlour with a sign bragging about how early in the day it opened and when the dancing girls started. I could see a homeless man with a shopping cart crouched in an alley entrance. Two girls, no more than fifteen years old were sitting in a doorway with a sign asking for money. I looked up and saw a billboard showing young looking beautiful people drinking beer and lying about the great times to be had beside another billboard showing impossibly thin girls wearing "this year's stylish jeans." I could see a bus stop advertising a hot line for people with depression. A "woman" was walking down the opposite side of the street who was clearly a man and another group of people lined up at the bus stop doing everything possible to keep to themselves.

I looked down and saw an unmistakable orange cap of a syringe in the gutter. Unmistakable, that is, to people in the know. People who had been lost down that road. People like me.

Then I looked back at the Hotel Arizona. A dump. A festering dump where the lifeless body of a good and decent young man had to sit and wait for discovery. A dump that held my friend taken so needlessly and without a shred of dignity.

And I raged inside. I hated for a moment. I hated the world. I hated the drugs. I hated the perversions. I hated the sin. I hated how distorted it all had become and I hated how the world seemed to co-sign the disintegrating moral structure of our society.

But today, I hated addiction more than anything.

"I fucking hate it," I said out loud and turned and walked away.

Chapter 31

Sheldon was buried about a week later. There was a "celebration of life" for Sheldon put on by the Joshua House at one of the churches who did work with the Joshua House, attended by the guys in the Joshua House, the staff, Richard and Angie, and an aunt of Sheldon's, but not Danny. From what I heard, his family had something of a private gathering on the North Shore but did not want anyone from the recovery community attending.

I tried calling Danny a week or so after the funerals. I just thought it best to check in on some level. I spoke to him briefly on the phone but he was distant, vacant, and sounding very old. That would be the last time I would speak to Danny. And I feared for him that things in his life would forever not be right.

The months following Sheldon's death were difficult. Not only did I mourn the loss, but it also shook my foundational beliefs and I struggled to find answers that made sense from God. I slowed down a little. I stopped helping out at the Joshua House. It wasn't so much that I was disillusioned or felt helping addicts to be hopeless; it was more that I needed to get back to basics, spend time in the church, and seek God and His wisdom. But also, truth be told, I wasn't so sure I wanted to work exclusively with addicts over say, the impoverished in general.

I had lots of conversations with my mature Christian mentors, asking them the big "why?" and questions about how God works. And I spent a lot of time thinking about how best to live today in order to eventually arrive at God's vision for me. I may not ever understand why Sheldon was taken, but I needed to remember how vivid the plan God gave to me on the mountain was and commit myself towards moving towards it. It was a soul searching period of time where I took a long look at all aspects of my life and by the time I hit the three year anniversary of having been on the mountain, I became convinced that personal change was necessary.

I had to concede that I may not have been utilizing many of the gifts God had given to me by washing dishes. And even though I had continued to have success as the department head, was considered management, had actually become something of a friend to Torsi, I was, in fact, primarily a dishwasher.

I was quite certain I was ready for change. The most difficult thing to leave would be the relationships I had formed with some of the other dishwashers. I had become quite involved with some of them towards bettering their lives. Torsi had okayed the scholarship idea and our first recipient was washing dishes for us twice a week and going to culinary school four days per week. I had two others in English classes and there were three of them who I would spend time actually visiting with at their homes to talk about Canada and how best to advance. But I figured even if I left the job, I might be able to continue helping some of them.

I had become friends with a guy named Ralph Jessop at the church I was going to. We talked a fair bit at various functions and I discovered he was a realtor. I had always found real estate quite fascinating as I like to look at architecture, liked design and layouts, and was interested in gardens. I found myself looking around all the time when going for walks and identifying the different styles of architecture, ages of homes, size, landscaped gardens, location, views, and value. My formal education had been in business admin, so real estate seemed like it would at least compliment what my original interests had been.

Still, from what I was told, I would have to take a course in order to get a license and that might take up to six months. I thought long and hard about this. I had to weigh out so many factors, like whether or not it would compliment or influence my recovery which had to come first, whether or not it would compliment my faith and/or influence God's calling on my life, and whether or not it was something I could be good at, enjoy, and be fulfilled.

God's calling on my life still seemed impossible, at least in the way it was presented to me. But the seeds of that calling were to be found in service work, helping the poor, and volunteering my time. I didn't really see a correlation between a career and service to the poor. Even Jesus was a carpenter and Paul was a tent maker. Neither occupation took away from their callings. So why couldn't I be a realtor and still help the poor? Breaking it down that way, I could see little wrong with making a career move. Godly people still needed help buying houses, after all.

After a long period of deliberation, I finally went to talk to Torsi himself to see what his thoughts were. I waited on him to make an appearance in the dish pit and dropped it on him.

"Torsi, I'm thinking of making a move out of dishes and into real estate. It would be a six month course to get my license that I would like to do while I worked here. Then I would like to ask you to, well, bless my departure. What do you think?"

It took Torsi by surprise. I could see it in his eyes and I could see it upset him. "Of course Sam. We'll support you any way we can. I guess we always knew you wouldn't be here forever. But, well, it wouldn't be the same here without you. Did you not ever consider advancement here? I mean, more so than you have done? Like, out of the dish pit completely and into something else here?"

I smiled. "Torsi, I've been washing dishes here for nearly three years, which is the equivalent to probably, like, fifteen years at any real job and I turned down every opportunity to get into the kitchen. This job was one of the primary reasons I could get off drugs. It was all I could do, really, and I owe you so much. But this industry isn't for me. I'm no restaurant guy. But thanks though. And believe me, this isn't easy for me. You've been like this major player in my life."

He smiled back. "You've taught me more than I gave you Sam. You taught me about patience, about hanging in there and just waiting on yourself. And you did it without complaining. And you taught me to care more for other people. The other dishwashers owe you a lot. And you taught me about God. You have faith Sam and it's served you well. But real estate? Really, Sam?"

"I gotta do something Torsi. I'm over thirty now, you know," I said. 'What do you think?"

"I think it's a tough racket, real estate. Lots of people in it, lots of competition. But if you are good at it you can make some money. But what I really think is you are a smart, loyal, creative, and hard working young man and that your abilities are vastly underutilized here washing dishes. Whatever struggles you had in the past, I think you are over them now. So, Sam, I think you would be a fool for not going for whatever it is you want to do, and whatever you want to do I think you will succeed at. So, go take your course."

"Wow, thanks Torsi. That means a lot to me. And hey, I'll be here six months at least to finish the course, so plenty of time still. And, you know, I gotta get a few of those future scholarship things in place with you before I take off, eh?" and I laughed. "Got to look after those dishwashers you know Torsi."

"Yeah, I know Sam, I know. God likes dishwashers, right?"

So I committed myself to the course towards getting my real estate license. It amused me that the first step in the process was that I had to pass a criteria test of "being of good reputation." This made me laugh, but only because I knew that all had been clear with me for a number of years now. I had experienced a few times where the past caught up to me that wasn't so funny. That's all part of having lived such a destructive lifestyle for so long.

But I was deemed of good reputation and accepted to take the course and after a period of figuring it all out launched into the world of real estate. I took courses in things like land ownership, real estate property law, land titles, liability law, strata concepts, financial statements and so on and so on and so on. Most of it pretty boring. Some of it difficult, some of it kind of cool, and all of it passed successfully.

I burned the candle pretty hard at both ends, taking courses by day, washing dishes by night and studying whenever I could. The life of a student came back to me though, which felt nice, like after many years, I was now really back on track. And I felt equal amongst my peers for a change as there were many people around my age, changing careers or taking new directions or finally getting serious about life.

As the course was finishing up I gave my formal notice at work and on a Saturday night, I worked my last shift in the Trattoria. Halfway through my shift Torsi came into the dish pit and told me to take my apron off and "try to make yourself at least somewhat presentable, if possible," he said lightheartedly. I wasn't sure what was happening, but he led me out into the restaurant and sat me down at a table and said, "Last night, let's eat."

And we ate. Right off the menu, anything I wanted amidst looks from the wait staff who just weren't computing that the dishwasher was eating with Torsi. I had this amazing steak and prawns and enjoyed myself immensely. I was mildly concerned about the dishes piling up in the back but cast the thoughts from my mind. Whatever, this was just too fun. He assured me he would keep the scholarship program going. In fact he shared with me that he was very proud of the scholarship program, to be able to hire from within, and giving opportunity to those less fortunate. In turn, I told him I would like to stay in touch, check in on the dishwashers, blah, blah, blah. He had a glass of wine. I had a sparkling water and it was very, very nice.

Chapter 32

$\mathcal{I}$ was now a proud, card carrying, licensed real estate agent. I was ready to roll. My friend Ralph was the owner of a small franchise of Sunrise Realty and he told me before he would hire me on. Of course, in the world of real estate, being hired on didn't exactly mean I got a wage, as the world of realty was a world all about commissions.

The best path to getting commissions was to actually have listings. A listing is when someone agrees to let you be their realtor of choice to sell their home. Most realtors got off the ground by soliciting pre-existing connections asking everyone they knew whether or not they were planning on buying or selling a house.

I had no listings and I had no connections. I guess I had some old friends and neighbours from my West Van days who I could have potentially hit up, but that world all knew about my collapse into drugs and I think there would have been some red flags in their minds about letting me sell their house for them. I decided to leave that market alone.

So I was literally starting this from the ground up. No leads, no connections, no contacts, and no advertising fund I could draw on. Plus, I had to step it up for a wardrobe and I had to buy a car, which together, was a pretty good blow to the savings. I bought a modest used Dodge Neon, green. Good on gas, reliable, and presentable enough for my low end entry into the business world. Mrs. Byrnes let me keep the car in her garage as she had stopped driving years before, so that part was nice.

Even though I knew the early days were going to be challenging, and had saved like mad coming into the switch, I was still shocked at the immediate impact of having no real dependable salary coming in. While the dishwashing was really a pretty crappy job, no doubt about it, it was at least stress free, dependable, consistent, and the cheques rolled in every two weeks in the same amount.

Now all of a sudden, I had to look presentable, had to maintain a car, the work was all over the place, erratic, stressful because it was all so new, and the pay was inconsistent. I had been educated to expect all this but it was still a difficult transition. On the other hand, it was nice to be out of the "pit" and into some decent clothes and feeling like I was in a form of mainstream life amongst my peers. I felt like a business man even though I was being paid less than a dishwasher.

I gutted it out the best I could. The bottom rung of the real estate industry was being sent out to hang out at open houses, or at new apartment/condo complexes in the show suites waiting on prospective buyers to show up. The name of the game was selling, so for everyone who showed up I would try to sell them the house, or unit, or whatever it was where I was that day. Ralph's realty office had the rights to this massive new condo complex that was about a third built in South Vancouver that had a show suite elegantly appointed and on display for the general public. There were over 150 units that would eventually be finished in three different designs. I would hang out in the display suite, usually with one other realtor and we would wait on people to come in. We would try to sell them one of the units first and foremost. But many of them (seemed like all of them) were "just looking" so the next step would be to see if they would like me to accompany them on their search, which would be leading them to accept me as their buyer's agent. And the last pitch would be to give them a card and the line, "and if you're looking to sell your existing home, I would be happy to come out and help you determine its worth and sell it for you."

It was the realtor who had the listing to sell a home that made the most commission. Next would be the realtor who brought the buyer to the home. Next would be the one who "assisted" towards the sale of someone else's listing which was what I was doing at the condo complex. If I sold one of those condos, it was Ralph who got the commission, of which he would give me a commission out of, less a percentage that would go towards the display suite, etc., etc. A commission on a commission less expenses. It was in these waters where I was currently swimming.

My first sale came at the condo complex in my second month. The units I was selling would be have been considered lower end starter condos with keyword advertising that focused on slogans like "why rent when you can own" and "starter condos starting at $129,900" as opposed to the more elegant condos and town-houses that used slogans like "well appointed executive town-houses" or "you've arrived at the top."

I sold my first unit to a young couple who had just been married. It was their first purchase and I helped them negotiate for blinds and appliances. I sold the unit for $132,700. The couple didn't come in with a realtor of their own to act as a buyer's realtor, so the full commission went to Ralph less what he paid me. I ended up getting $1400 for my end.

Really, I was pretty ecstatic. I'm not sure I had ever had a cheque for $1400 in my life and it was my first sale, so I was pretty pleased. I tried not to think about the fact that my total earnings for two months was also $1400 making it not so good and quite a bit less than my former job and that I had no guarantee as to when the next sale would be. I just looked at the size of the cheque and thought about how great it would be if I could just sell another one right away! And if I could just land one listing of my own, I might be able to really turn it into something!

So I settled in, and showed up at the open houses and at the display suites and gave out cards and talked to people and had a few hits, and a few misses and learned and figured out some stuff while I went. And slowly some minor successes came and I sold the odd unit, and landed the odd buyer who agreed to let me be their buyer's agent and so on.

Chapter 33

I did still check in on the dishwashers from time to time. And if Torsi happened to be around we would hang out for a bit, chat and catch up on news. I was surprised to discover just how much of a void not being involved with the dishwashers had left. Not the job description part. I mean the time I spent with them, at their houses, chatting with them about their lives and helping them transition into Canadian life easier, all of which I did in my free time.

And with deciding not to carry on with volunteer work at the Joshua House after Sheldon's death, it seemed to me I felt like I needed to tweak how I served the Kingdom of God. I certainly didn't want to get complacent on my work for God or my recovery, and I had to admit with first the schooling, and then focusing on my new career, I hadn't done much work towards volunteering. The last thing I wanted to do was fall back into my addiction, and even at almost four years clean, I had to guard against complacency and keep at the forefront of my mind what got me this far.

The church I had been a part of for the past couple of years was involved in a street ministry partnering with a bunch of other churches and taking one shift a week running this east side drop-in that served breakfast and lunch every day. I had deliberately stayed away from helping there because it wasn't a wise idea for me to be anywhere near street life while I was in early recovery, but with significant clean time under my belt I felt

189

like I could now debate whether or not this was an area I should help out at. No question about it, my own testimony and experience would serve me well at a place like that, but there was certainly some fear around getting too close to the fire. This wasn't the same as the front lines of the Joshua House where everyone there was trying to get clean off drugs. At a place like this, there were all kinds of people still acting out their dysfunction in their environment, and some (or most) with little desire for change. However, I always knew I would want to give back in this area at some stage, so it seemed the door was opening now.

I talked to the church leaders who are always more than happy to accommodate anyone who wants to volunteer for anything and got myself on the rotation. Our church was responsible for running the place every Saturday from 7:00 in the morning until about 1:00 in the afternoon and anyone on the rotation was asked to do one shift per month.

The name of the place was Street Hope and it was located off of the corner of Cordova and Carrall Street. Really it was only a couple blocks away from Torsi's Gastown restaurant but only about the same distance away from the epicenter of Hastings life, the corner of Main and Hastings. Things changed drastically over a few blocks down there, from the trendy, tourist area of Gastown which bordered the war zone of the Hastings area. I'm sure many a tourist would find the scenery quickly starting to change if they wandered too far down the street and would quickly turn around. I was familiar enough with the area for both having been a local and from my drug days. There wasn't a back alley down here that I hadn't done drugs in. But for the most part my usage and lifestyle happened a number of blocks east in the Oppenheimer area.

My first shift was strange. Familiar yet far off. While my past was never far from memory, it was surreal to see the reality of it play out in front of me in the forms of other people. The ones who came in high or in a state of paranoia or looking to find dope were pathetic beyond belief and I found myself wondering how in the world I had ever dropped to such depths. Did I really look like that? Did I really behave that way? Did I really think I was fooling anyone? And now with four years clean I couldn't figure out why in the world it took me so long to get clean. Why didn't I just recognize how bad of shape I was in, and go to all lengths to get the hell out of there?

And then I remembered. I got to that level because the addiction was *that* strong. I *did* try to get out and didn't have the strength. I *did* go to all lengths and it wasn't good enough. I *was* that bad and I knew it at the time. And I *did* care, but was completely powerless over my addiction. And the addiction took me to those depths; I didn't volunteer for it nor want it.

But with the clarity of sobriety, my eyes now saw lots of sights I did not remember seeing before. The addict only saw what was drug related – an existence fueled by the singular necessity to feed the addiction. So I would look for dealers, people who could help to facilitate the next high, opportunities for money which often meant opportunities for low level crime, or for drugs themselves. Searching for drugs was part of the psychosis, this psychotic belief that maybe you would just find some drugs on the sidewalk if you looked hard enough. Drive through skid row sometime and you'll see someone scouring the sidewalk as if they lost something. They're looking for drugs.

But with the freedom I now had from the addiction, my vision for seeing what was down here was much broader. Sure I could see the "plays" like the guy shuffling up and down the same section of the street who was undoubtedly selling drugs, and his partner who was more inconspicuous across the street who would have been handling the actual drugs or keeping the cash separate from the drugs. I could see the people whose eyes were scanning all over the place, the guys who were looking for opportunity to hurt, steal, rob, or whatever it took.

But there were others who came into the shelter: single mothers carrying young children, middle aged men who didn't look at all like they were on drugs, women who were carrying shopping bags from food banks or dollar stores, older people who seemed to know one another, and even adolescent boys and girls who did not fit the drug addict look I knew so well. There was definitely a community here of people who lived in this area who had little, but not necessarily because of addiction. It was just poverty. Or perhaps they had other issues, or maybe they were like my dishwasher buddies only without dishwashing jobs. They were trapped in the worst part of the city, cohabitating amongst crime, prostitution, drug addiction, and slum hotels. Trapped with little way out. The scope of Hastings just got a whole lot broader in my eyes, and I felt a little tingle inside of me that told me perhaps this is where God was telling me to be.

The shelter itself was more or less one medium-sized room at the base of a building that had who knows what else in it. The entrance was off the street, and there were windows running the length of the street so you could get a good idea as to what was happening all up and down the block, which was seldom boring. There was a counter where the food preparation took place, some portable griddles for pancakes, grilled sandwiches, etc., a self serve coffee station, a dishwashing area with pot sinks and a decent machine (because I knew), and some storage areas. In the public area were a tattered old couch, some tables and chairs, and a couple of recliners that seemed popular. There were bulletin boards, pictures of people at the shelter enjoying Christmas dinners and the like, various cheap art works of Jesus and other Christian themes. All of it clean, none of it new or terribly nice, and all in all a place I was enjoying more with every passing minute.

Chapter 34

Sometime before my fifth anniversary of being on the mountain my father died. He was seventy-eight years old and had been deteriorating quickly from emphysema. Trouble breathing led to hospital visits, which led to in and out hospital stays, which led to weakness which led to a fall at home and a broken hip, which led to the last hospital stay, pneumonia, and finally his passing. It was a process that took about six months from start to finish, although the signs of breathing problems were visible beforehand.

The reality of the severity of the problem grew the further into the process it went. At first I had dismissed it as something that would pass. Dad had been pretty stoic and minimized everything and both my parents spared me any real details as to how the struggle played out in their home. The first hospital stay, which lasted about four days made him frail and it showed. He changed from a vibrant older man who didn't come off to me as limited in many ways, who still maintained his home and fished with his son, to a frail old man after a four day stay in the hospital.

I became increasingly worried and found myself going out to the house on a more frequent basis. I found myself very grateful for having the car. Mom and dad needed the help and I wanted to be there. Things started to seriously deteriorate about three months in. He started to lose weight, his breathing became noticeably strained, and he was unable to do much of anything. I filled in on chores, did plenty of store runs, hung out with him as much as possible, and went through many hours sitting at the kitchen table with my mom talking quietly while he slept.

The ordeal was taking its toll on my mother too. She kept much of it in and never spent a moment falling apart, but the toll was showing on her. But we were more transparent with each other than we had been prior to my becoming a Christian, so we were able to have real and meaningful conversations about how we were doing.

I went fishing with my dad the last time about six weeks before he died. It wasn't much of a fishing trip given how weak he was, but we packed up and I drove him down to Fisherman's Cove, the biggest local marina that was joined with the West Van Yacht Club a few kilometers away and we walked to the end of the closest pier. We dropped our lines in. Nothing fancy, just lines allowed to drop straight down about ten feet.

This wasn't a fishing area anymore really. Yes, kids who's dads had boats here still dropped lines and kids who lived nearby would still get their first initiation into fishing here, but really, people didn't fish here that were avid about fishing. But this wasn't really a fishing trip; this was more about a father and a son just bonding again when both knew the days were numbered. We lasted about forty-five minutes and it was the best day of fishing of my life even though we caught nothing.

He broke his hip puttering around the garden. He was weak and seriously ill by this time and the fall was nothing significant. A step forward, a loss of balance, a leg that didn't support the weight, and a drop to one knee. That was about it. Another trip to the hospital, the diagnosis and the realization that time was now running out. Still, the doctors were still talking about physical therapy, and there was still this hope that somehow he would recover and be able to come home. But really, all this thinking was just reaching.

He was in Lion's Gate Hospital in North Van, just off Lonsdale and about seventeen blocks farther up the street than where I was first dropped off back into civilization from having been up the mountain and from where Sheldon and I met his dad off the Seabus. Fortunately, real estate was an industry that allowed you to make your own schedule, which made sense given the fact nobody actually paid me any kind of salary unless I sold something.

Dad had been moved up to ICU and we were finally given the news in no uncertain terms that he would not ever be coming out of the hospital and that we were now day to day for him living.

So I would pick mom up, take her to the hospital, stay there with her, drive her home, go back to the hospital myself, go home to get some sleep, and do it all over again in one form or another. It was on such a night that I had taken her home and come back that he passed away. I was alone with him in the room when some beeps and blips from the various machines he was hooked up to sounded off. He had been unconscious for a couple of days by this time. The on duty nurse came in, a very nice, caring and competent woman who I had grown to admire. She leaned down close to me and said in a very quiet and sure voice, "It's time now Sam. It's happening so you should say what you need to say if you haven't already." I looked up at her face, reassured by her and grateful for her.

"Okay," I said. "Thank you."

I leaned into my dad, held his arm which was exposed outside of the sheets and whispered into his ear.

"Dad, I love you. I'm here with you right now and I'm not leaving your side. I'm praying for you dad. I'm telling God you are ready to come home. I'm asking him to take you and comfort you. I'm right here dad with you and I'm not leaving you."

The nurse, who never left the bedside and just looked at the machines, and fiddled with this and that, leaned down on my shoulder and gently put her mouth right beside my ear and said, "He's gone now Sam."

Despite the knowledge the day was coming and despite having held it together throughout the process so far, I completely lost it the moment she spoke those words. I convulsed uncontrollably and heaved and gasped and cried deeply for a long time, right there with my head buried into his side. Not since my moment with God on my last night on the mountain had I experienced anything so powerful.

I had spent a great deal of time with my father in the months leading up to this. I saw many things along the way: pain, hurt, fear, confusion, discomfort, unease, resiliency, stubbornness, bravery, stoicism, and defeat. Not all visible, or spoken or acknowledged, but at one time or another, during this process I had picked up on the nuances of any or all of those things. But I never saw a sense of comfort. Not on a real or sustained level. I never saw a peace, a wholehearted acceptance, a resignation that included acceptance or peace. There was a part of his soul that resisted, that fought, that was scared and wanted to live.

That is, until the last moments. It was unmistakable, it was clear, and it was as obvious as anything I had ever witnessed in my life: he had that peace in the final moments and at the time of his passing. He was in a state of acceptance, a state of peaceful resignation. He was no longer scared, no longer fighting, and was in a state of bliss. I had never seen anything like it and I knew one thing then beyond any measure of doubt:

God was there for him.

The nurse asked me if I wanted to spend more time with him after she removed all the tubes and stuff. I just said no thanks, that I was done. But I asked her if it was okay to give her a hug and she smiled and said sure. Then I left the room to go and call my mom.

His death had a profound effect on me. For the first few days I was practically paralyzed and would often be flooded with emotions I could no longer seem to control. It was almost as if all the traumas of life, with the street life, the losses and violence I had seen, and stresses of losing it to addiction, the pain I knew I had put so many people through all came to an emotional head. But it was more. It was joy as well. I realized how fortunate I had been that I had recovered from the drugs in time to have reconciled my relationship with him. It all became so clear how precious it all was, how time *was* of the essence and how treasured a gift it had been to be in good standing with my dad once again. If I hadn't gotten clean I would never have known this moment. I would have been high, numb, and mourning in ways that would have been unnatural and I never would have gotten another chance to get it right.

It was so painfully obvious the importance of the period of time. It was so clear there was a design behind our existence. That God was my Father, that my dad was my earthly father, that my rightful place was here, now, sober, and positioned in proper standing. This is the way it should have been; me by his side at the end, ready to help my mother, knowing my dad has gone on to be with God, and knowing I still have work to do.

I was mourning as God designed it. I was feeling the feelings that I was supposed to, without medication, and I was in awe of the cycle of life, the sadness of loss, the happiness knowing it all had purpose, and gratitude for my own rebirth. Yes, I was grateful for God, and determined never to go back to my old ways.

Chapter 35

Mourning ran its course and we adapted into life without dad. At first, I just got slowly back into the routine of work and life and spent lots of time with my mom. She decided she wanted to stay in the house despite the fact it would be heavy on maintenance without my dad there. She just didn't want to leave "her home." It was fine with me. My mom was a hard working resilient woman who would find a way to make it work, and I was going to be helping out too. Roles changed, we adapted, we carried on, and we settled in.

I continued volunteering at Street Hope on an increasing basis. At first it was strictly to the schedule of one Saturday a month, but as I was learning about volunteer work, if interest was expressed, pressure was put on to do more. I found I was being called on more and more by people in my church who asked me to fill in for their shift for various reasons: kid's soccer tournament, they were sick, they had an opportunity to go away for the weekend, or whatever. Some months I was there every Saturday and my passion was increasingly growing for helping with the poor. I started to develop relationships with individual people who regularly came in and I became familiar with their stories and why they were there.

Unlike myself who grew up in a functional home, had an education, and had prospects and potential to tap into if I came out of addiction, many or most of these people were given little chance to begin with. There was Manny, a nineteen year old aboriginal boy who grew up with no father and a prostitute mother right off Hastings. In and out of foster care, back with his mother when she had periods of sobriety, out of school at twelve years old, every person he knew was on welfare and addicted to drugs or an alcoholic. Yet he would come to Street Hope every day on his own and share his hopes and dreams for the future.

There was Sheri who was twenty-two but looked thirty-five, who was bi-polar, abandoned by her parents as a child, was tossed about from foster home to foster home where she was raped in every one of them, had somehow fallen through the cracks and been on the street since the age of eleven, forced into prostitution to survive and though now off drugs, she was battling mental illness and living on welfare in a flea ridden slum hotel.

There was Linda, a thirty-something single mom of four kids who lived on a welfare existence. All her kids were under the age of seven and she would come in every day, hauling her kids with her doing everything she could to provide but in a constant position of being overwhelmed and ill equipped to cope well enough. She tried so hard, but everything was always just a little beyond her, and her four kids were becoming educated early on street and welfare existence.

And there were so many more, with so many more stories. And yes, some were rude, ungrateful, mean, mentally ill, and the like. But many were grateful, friendly, kind, and amazingly resilient given their lot in life. It made helping them, listening to them, and being there for them seem, well, purposeful.

At two years into real estate it seemed I had peaked. Starting from nothing I had worked hard to land that first sale of the condo, then worked hard to build on it. And I did. I could pat myself on the back for being moderately successful and could see I was running middle of the pack with many of the realtors I would associate with. I developed contacts, talked to many people, pursued leads and had my victories. I sat in countless open houses, show suites and landed my share of people who used me as their buyer's agent. I also got some of my own seller's listings, which were, of course, the most desired from my perspective. Sometimes things snowballed along. I would land a listing and then the same people would have me also represent them when looking for the place they would move into.

But the real estate office I worked out of with Ralph was in a more South Vancouver location and I found myself in the niche of low end condos, less expensive townhouses, and older homes. I hardly ever landed a newer or large or expensive house, although I did get the odd one which seemed a higher class than where I seemed to get most of my business.

So while, yes, I guess I could be considered still fairly new to the industry at two years, I thought I could see the future and it looked like it wouldn't change much from the way it was now. More cheap apartments, first time buyers, lots of hanging out, the odd decent listing to keep me enthused, some dry periods followed by a flurry of business, and at the end of the day a decent if not mediocre career.

It was around this period of time when things started to slip away from me.

Chapter 36

I guess it was complacency. Maybe life was just boring me a little after the thrill ride of addiction. I read about that – pleasure centers of the brain maxing out because of the drugs, and life seeming stale or ordinary as a result. My faith was diminishing. Not because I was doubting my beliefs, but because things were stale. In the beginning days/years it seemed like God himself was walking me through the Bible and the words seemed to come alive. Life was new, exciting, and revelations were constantly being made. I was on fire for Jesus and had the life altering mountain experience to keep me energetic towards my life. Plus I had a personal calling from God himself as to what my future held.

But weeks turned into months and months turned into years. I had long since acclimatized myself to "normal living," my addiction was a thing of the past, the vividness of the mountain faded, morning devotionals were often feeling like a chore, I was on the treadmill of life towards career, I felt no closer to God's vision than the day I came down the mountain, and the repetition of life was lulling me into complacency. It was a slow drip. I didn't just wake up one day and find myself in a bad place. I just compromised myself by just a little at a time.

I went from rising every morning early to read the Bible to only a couple days a week. My Bible reading was, at best, not searching or deep or even retained. I missed some Street Hope shifts. I started to "see" more of the seedy side of the street life when I did attend. I started to date some women and hang out with some non-Christian people, found myself coveting material things more, spent less time with the people who had influenced me, worried about money more, and things like that.

I started to think about getting high. They were just casual thoughts at first; passing thoughts I would dismiss as crazy, but then more serious, longer lasting fantasies would take place. I started planning a relapse and factoring in when, how, and where I would "use" and how I would get away with it. My brain started lying to me, telling me I *could* get away with it, telling me I could use *just once*, and then go back to life as normal. I started to fixate on how much I wanted this, how insignificant a "one time" session would be in the big picture. On a smaller scale, I thought about drinking beer. I thought about watching hockey games in the pub, going to clubs with other young people, and tried to convince myself *drinking* wasn't a problem, only drugs.

Of course they were all lies. If I used drugs once, I would use again, and before a month was up I would be a full time, twenty-four hour a day crack addict again. If I drank it would inevitably lead to getting drugs. But my brain was telling me otherwise. It was justifying bad behaviour.

In the end I got lost in the thoughts, depressed in my lifestyle, feeling lost from God, unsatisfied in every area, disillusioned about life and on a dangerous path that would ultimately end in my death. And then, just in time, one single event changed the direction of this path.

Chapter 37

$\mathcal{S}$unset Realty, the realty franchise owned by Ralph that I worked out of, had a home office in South Vancouver. The life of a realtor seemed to take place mainly on the road, in open houses, at show suites, at the homes of potential clients, or even at my own home desk and computer. But the franchise office also served a purpose as home base. This is where Ralph spent most of his time managing his business, and there were about six realtors working through him, including myself. There were a number of generic offices any realtor could use when wanting to spend time at an office, there was a board room of sorts for meetings, and there was always at least a minor buzz of activity going on. If it was convenient I would meet clients there before heading out to see a house, have meetings with clients, use the office to run a course of negotiations with clients, or attempt to close deals.

But today I was just sitting there. I had spent the morning going through the show suite of a new townhouse complex going up off Southeast Marine Drive in Vancouver that I thought maybe I could take some prospective buyers through, but nothing really more on the calendar for the day. I was unenthused, bored, and distracted and not really being all that self motivated to make things happen. I took the next softest option other than just going home for a nap, and that was to sit in the office and scour listings and review some of the potential leads I had. In other words, I was just passing time.

Ralph came out of his office to chat with me. Ralph was a great guy and I admired him greatly. He was always so calm, had an outstanding faith and was the kind of guy whose faith you could see at church, at work, or in-between. He was older, probably late sixties and had been in the realty game a long time with moderate success. He wasn't one of the high flyers, but he owned the branch, had income coming in from a number of realtors, and still generated his own listings. But he often talked about his days being numbered, how all what he wanted for his wife and himself was to become full time missionaries as a way to retire and move to some far off place for a simple life of helping others.

Today, he and I were just idly chatting as we did from time to time and he was asking me where I was with my day and what I had on my plate. I filled him in but told him today was pretty clear. Well, completely clear. He told me he was heading out to West Van with a client that wanted to see this 1.4 million dollar house. The client was a friend of a friend and wanted someone from a trusted source to accompany them while they toured houses. Apparently they had toured a number of houses with a number of realtors acting as buyer's agent in the past but for one reason or another, things didn't work out.

"Maybe they're difficult people," Ralph said. "You know the kind? Impossible to please, maybe? I don't know as I have never met them and won't until we get to the house. They just want someone there to represent them on the tour, that's all."

"Wow, sounds good," I said. "Should be interesting if nothing else."

Ralph looked deep in thought for a moment. "You're from West Van, aren't you? Didn't you grow up there or something?" I nodded and he carried on. "Well why don't you come with me? I don't know anything about the area. Hardly ever go out there. You never know, I might need some local knowledge."

I thought about it for a minute. "Okay Ralph, why not? It might be fun."

So off we went in his car and made the drive northbound and into the core of the city, over the Lion's Gate Bridge, and then west into West Van. I didn't know whereabouts we were going, but as we continued farther and farther west and closer and closer to where I grew up, it occurred to me to ask where exactly we were going.

Ralph dug around for the address he had written down and passed it to me. "Maybe you could even tell me how to get there as I have no idea once we leave the highway," he said.

I looked at the address and realized I knew exactly where it was. It had to be within five minutes of where I grew up. "As a matter of fact, I do know where it is. I know it well, in fact. Take the Caulfeild/Woodgreen Drive exit off the highway. I'll guide you down towards the ocean."

Ralph smiled. "See you're helping me out already! Lead on!"

So we took the exit, wound down Caulfield Drive all the way past Caulfeild Elementary, hung a left on Keith Road and found the address. It wasn't "my neighbourhood" per say, but close enough that I knew the area intimately, had spent plenty of time at various friends' houses while growing up, and felt totally at ease with the easy knowledge one is at home.

The house was unremarkable from the front really. I had seen the house many times in the past but had never been inside it. But it was probably high enough on the hill to have an ocean view once inside which is probably why the place was listed in the millions. Of course, it was getting hard to find a home anywhere in West Van now for under one million. West Van had become the most expensive community in all of Canada for its stunning views, proximity to mountains, oceans, and city and homes were being bought up from people from all over the world.

Ralph parked in the driveway and there were already two other cars there. Both of them were BMW's leading me to believe one was the listing agent's car, and the other was the people looking to buy. We got out of the car and headed up to the house where we saw three people talking just outside the front door. It was clear who they were. The realtor was standing on his own, dressed in a modern and expensive style and was carrying a folder that no doubt held all the home information. Standing across from him was a couple standing closely together with nothing in their hands at all: the potential buyers.

"She" was a very beautiful, tall, long haired, middle-eastern looking woman, dressed in casual elegance in expensive designer jeans, new looking boots, and a long flowing sweater. "He" was older, but not ridiculously so. Maybe ten years her senior, making him maybe forty. He was also dressed nicely in a casual suit, stylish shoes, expensive looking belt, and sport coat. He looked like he took care of himself, was well groomed and stood in a confident fashion.

Introductions were made all around. Then the listing agent excused himself into the house with a key he had gotten from a lockbox and said, "I'll give you guys a minute or two to get acquainted because I know you all are just meeting for the first time, and I'll just make sure the dog is in the garage. Just come on in when you're ready for the tour."

So we did just that. We all chatted for a few minutes with small talk, about wants and needs, initial thoughts, and the weather. She came off very friendly and excited about seeing the house. She immediately embraced us as all being on the same team, didn't question my being there at all, and was all smiles.

He, on the other hand, immediately came off like a pompous ass. He came off as arrogant, superior, and condescending. He acted like he needed to set the tone of being in charge, that he wasn't going to be a man who could be taken advantage of, that he was a wealthy and powerful man who knew what was going on, that he would ultimately be the decision maker, and that his expectations were high. At least those were my initial thoughts on how he came off. Maybe I was wrong, I don't know. I guess we would soon see.

But I considered myself something of an expert on the wealthy given the fact I grew up here and had seen a lot of families with money up close and personal. My perspective and insight had developed even more as a result of having seen the complete other side of the spectrum on the street. Having been so exposed to the two extremes of wealth, it made the characteristics of each side more pronounced and I had become fascinated with the make up of each. I became even more rounded in personality evaluations after my entry into Christianity where the poor, the rich, and the in-between cohabitated under a different set of rules.

Many of the rich I knew were no different than anyone else. They just had more money. And of course there were degrees of richness. Many were just upper middle class, still concerned about spending, saving, retirement and all the same things everyone else was. They just had bigger houses, nicer cars, and took more vacations. But it was really only a pretty small percentage that had so much money they could do whatever they wanted however they wanted and never worry about a thing.

But it seemed clear that if a class of people were going to be overly concerned about power, entitlement, deservedness, control, and a sense of being "better than" it was going to be the wealthy. While the poor had their own set of dysfunctional pitfalls and characteristics, so did the rich. Seeing over and over again how the rich could be so susceptible to dysfunctional lives, depression, broken marriages, adultery, or alcoholism was just reinforced evidence that the key to life was a life lived through Jesus.

From my perspective in the here and now, being among wealthy people doing things wealthy people did, like buying million dollar homes, I knew that my role was to conduct myself in a confident fashion, like I belonged and was familiar with the goings on. And even though my role was really nothing more than observer, I carried myself in that capacity. This wasn't a stretch for me. After all, I was no more than a few kilometers away from the house I grew up in and lived here most of my life. I carried myself with a sense of belonging because I did belong – this was home to me and I felt comfortable and sure of myself.

The tour was conducted in a very professional manner. The listing realtor was a man named Jim Jennings of Jim Jennings Realty, who wasn't much older than me, maybe late thirties. He was polished, had easy mannerisms, knew everything he should have about the house, was well prepared, and had an appropriate balance of involvement versus allowing the clients space to take in the home on their own. I was very impressed and had done many tours from which I could have compared, even though tours of $110,000 condos for first time buyers were not the same as million dollar houses in wealthy suburbs.

The house was very nice indeed. While somewhat unremarkable from the front, the inside was gorgeous after a very tasteful full renovation two years before. The house itself was probably twenty-five years old, was two floors with the bedrooms on the main with an open living space, and one more bedroom and rec room downstairs which opened up into a charming backyard with partial ocean views.

The clients were Mr. and Mrs. Adams who were from Ontario and were relocating out to BC. Mrs. Adams seemed very impressed with the house. She asked many questions and went into every new room with wide eyed enthusiasm and excitement. It was obvious that her main concerns were all child related and it came out they had two young boys. She was interested in the location of the bedrooms in proximity to each other, the rec room, play areas, visibility from the kitchen into the main room, etc. And she wanted to know about schools, bus stops, and hospitals. Everything.

Mr. Adams, on the other hand, seemed to be looking for faults in the house and said at least four times something along the lines of, "Well, it's nice I suppose, but I would think for 1.4 million dollars you could get a lot more..." He found some fault in just about every room and seemed very difficult to please. To me it seemed like he had expectations that he should be getting a lot more for his money.

Jim, the realtor, handled him well but as the tour was winding down and we were outside on the back patio off the kitchen level where the view was really very nice, his complaining was becoming tiresome. He was either just difficult to please or he was trying to set some preliminary tone to drive the price down on negotiations later. Either way, he was behaving badly.

Things really started to go badly when his wife started to show her exasperation with her husband. We knew they had already been through a few buyers' agents and had toured many places. It was starting to look like the wife was breaking down from the process.

"Honey," she said, "we can't keep doing this. What is it going to take for you to like a house? I mean come on Jeff, what is wrong with this place."

"What's wrong with this place is that it isn't good enough for 1.4 million dollars. We can do a lot better, I'm sure of it, and I don't like the way all these places in this area are so overpriced. These people are trying to rip us off!" he said.

They went back and forth. At first Jim was attempting some gentle mediation while Ralph and I just stood there. But it was one of those intimate discussions between husband and wife that should not have been public and it was becoming increasingly awkward. Jim, who I am sure, had the feeling this was going nowhere backed off into the kitchen to organize some paperwork. Ralph also backed away. I gave them some space but remained on the patio, moving closer to the edge and looking out over the ocean.

I had an opinion on the matter. I just wasn't sure it was my place to say it and I wasn't sure if it would be welcome or serve a purpose. So I just gave it a minute. I took in a deep breath and smelled the ocean air. Man I loved it, and that, as it happened was the deciding factor and I spoke:

"Can I tell you guys something?" I asked. Neither said anything but both looked at me. "Can you smell the ocean? It's the salt in the air, and even though we are probably half a kilometer from the ocean you can tell it's in the air. Any closer and we might smell some low tide which can be stronger, but from here, it just smells salty and fresh. I grew up here you know? And I can tell you for a fact that if you lived here and then left? You would miss the smell of the ocean. It becomes a part of you whether you know it or not. It seems to, well, contribute towards health, vibrancy, being alive and fresh. I grew up not far from here, right on the other side of Lighthouse Park. Have you been there?" Both shook their heads no. "It's one of the nicest parks in the world; fabulous trails, ocean side cliffs showcasing the rugged coastline of British Columbia. The West Van coastline is so full of adventure. You have boys? It's so awesome around here. Tucked away coves with gentle slopes into the ocean, swimming in the summer at little known beaches a short walk away, trails, creeks to play in, lots of forest. Truly amazing. Do you know most people who even grew up in Vancouver or the suburbs have no idea many of these tucked away coves are even here because they are completely hidden from the roads and you can't see them. Cypress beach, Caulfield Cove, Lighthouse Park, Eagle Harbour, Fisherman's Wharf, Sandy Cove. Some of them walking distance, none of them far. Do you like boating?" I didn't wait for a response. "Because you can moor a boat at marinas located not ten minutes from here with only thirty minutes boating out of the harbor before you are in the gulf islands where there are endless places to anchor, picnic or whatever. Do you ski? Well there are three local mountains and every one of them has lights so you can ski at night. Drive to the closest in fifteen minutes. Imagine your boys can go skiing *after school* and it won't take you any time at all to drive them there.

"And all of this, and get this now, you're only a twenty-five minute or so drive into the centre of the city. This isn't city living, not by a long shot, but the city, one of the best in the world, is right there. I mean literally *right there,*" and I pointed to it because we could see it across the water.

"You see Mr. Adams. In West Van you're not just buying a house. You're buying land in one of the nicest places in the entire world. It is a place that will breathe into your very being and never leave you. Believe me; I know this to be true. Property prices here are expensive because they are *desirable*. People have found out much of what I am saying and they want to live here. You could move to North Van, right next door and still on the North Shore and, yes, you will get more bang for your buck, but you lose some things along the way as well, like the coastline which is more industrial in North Van and more natural in West Van. But if you really want a spectacular house for 1.4 million, head east. Yeah, go to another suburb of Vancouver. Go to Burnaby, or New Westminster, or farther to Surry. If you want to live in a palace and be like, the richest guy in town, move even farther out, to Abbotsford, or Mission, or Chilliwack. But the farther you go, the longer the drive into the city, the farther from the ocean, the greater distance to the mountains, the less charming the shops, the more congestion of people, box stores, and strip malls, and lackluster views. Here, part of the house price is like an admission price into one of the nicest areas you will ever see, and until you consider that, you will always be disappointed if you think you are just buying a house. This house is in West Van. It's a very nice house with an ocean view. It's selling for 1.4 million because that's what it's worth, so get used to it." The last line was a little harsh perhaps, but I thought he might respect some pushback from all his arrogance.

"And for you Mrs. Adams," I carried on without missing a beat. Heck, I was rolling now and even Ralph and Jim had come back into the fray to listen. "You're all about your boys. And let me say, that having grown up here, and gone to school here, and known many people from here, I can tell you there are good people around here. Good people with good moral values, people who care about their communities. West Van has their own bus system and their own police department because, well, there are perks with living among the wealthy and the systems are good. The teachers are top of the line for public schools, the sports are great with great facilities, and when you throw in the beaches, skiing, boating, forests, and everything else, I can't imagine a better place for a boy to grow up. Plus, most families move here and stay. In fact, I could rattle off ten family names of people who I know for a fact still live in this very neighbourhood. So you get to know them which promotes community and your boys will develop relationships and friendships with kids who they will know for their entire childhoods until University and they will never forget having grown up here and who they grew up with."

I was done. I just stopped and paused for a moment and smiled at them. "But hey, that's just one man's opinion who's probably pretty biased. God will tell you the right home at the right time and it's a tough decision – a huge decision – so please don't worry about getting stressed by it. We all understand that. It makes total sense. I'm sure the right house will come to you at the right time and you'll get into it and be very happy. We can't ask for more than that."

Mr. Adams didn't say anything at all. He just looked away from me and looked out over the view. Mrs. Adams thanked me for the wonderful insight into the area and asked me some more questions. Jim stepped in at that time too and joined in with some answers and finally things broke up. We said some good-byes and we went on our way.

The drive back was quiet. In fact Ralph really only said one thing: "Well you certainly sold *me* on West Van, Sam. If I had the cash I'd buy that house right now," he smiled. I smiled back and he went on to say, "That guy was something, wasn't he?"

And so the day ended and I went back to concentrating on low end condos and my leads and living in my denial that I was sliding down the road toward relapse when about a week later Ralph called me up and asked me to come into his office.

"Two things Sam," he said as I settled into a chair in his office. He was a man who got straight to the point. "Remember the Adams family from that West Van house? Of course you do. Well they bought the house. We had to grind out a negotiation which was no real surprise given *that* hard ass. He advised me to play hardball and I went through all the motions and in the end the house sold for 1.28 million. I went back and forth with Jim who represented the owners of the house many times through the process and we talked quite a bit." He paused, leaned back in his chair and put his hands behind his head. "Listen Sam, it was a good sale to some tough customers and both the Adams told me their decision was based on what you told them. Mrs. Adams told me that first. She was very impressed and is pretty excited about her boys growing up in that community. Mr. Adams admitted, in his own sort of way, after the close, that he needed the education on how to view house values in West Van that you gave him."

"Well, hey Ralph, only too happy to lend an assist. Glad whatever I said might have helped," I said.

"I feel like I should be giving you a percentage of the buyer's agent commission. I mean I only just met them that day too."

"Oh, come on Ralph. Don't even go there. You've done more for me than anyone else I can remember. I'm only in real estate because of you. And I just tagged along for fun. And anything I said was only because I grew up out there, loved it, and was biased. I would have said the same thing if I had just struck up conversation with someone on the street. So, please don't worry about it. Seriously."

Ralph rocked back and forth in his chair for a moment. "Well, okay Sam, if that's the way you see it. But there's something else. I said two things, remember?"

"Okay, then, what have you got. Throw it at me," I said.

"That Jim Jennings guy? Well, he's like this real up and comer in West Van real estate. He has lots of listings, enough that he has his own company and isn't affiliated with a brand real estate firm. He heard most of what you said that day and he knew that the sale ended up happening mostly because of what you said as well." He paused and I didn't say anything. "Sam, he asked me if I minded if he offered you a job to go work for him."

Chapter 38

That ended up being the event that brought me back onto the right track. Not at first, but it propelled me out of a rut and into an exciting new direction that reinvigorated me on every level. I knew that leaving one job and entering another would be a challenging time, so I really pressed into my devotional time with God. And for the first time since my dad died, I really felt His presence. I felt as if He was with me and I loved the feeling of being close to Him again and this in turn propelled me into deeper relationship with God.

Ralph had been exceptionally graceful in encouraging me towards making the move. He said, "It looks like you're a mediocre, low-end realtor with promise to be an achieving, high-end realtor, so go." I took it as a compliment, although it could have gone either way.

I met with Jim and we got on well from the start. He was really making it happen in West Van realty and just becoming a member of his team was like making it to the major leagues. He had five people working directly for him, all polished, all professional, and all very bright. This was nothing like Ralph's realty office in South Vancouver; everything was a few notches up. He had a very well appointed office a block up from the ocean in the small shopping village of Dundarave. His office had a full time receptionist who also served coffee in bone china mugs in an elegant seating area, and there were spacious offices in the back to conduct private meetings. Jim's office was bigger with a custom made enormous desk and tasteful art done by local artists.

Jim had a staff of five realtors who looked after his listings, viewed with potential buyers, followed on leads, and did all the usual stuff. Plus, he had the full time receptionist who, on top of greeting and serving coffee, was very competent in helping with all the paperwork, filing, or whatever. Then he had another full time person whose sole job was to maintain and develop all the production, advertising, and high tech issues. He would maintain and keep current the cutting edge web site, would be in charge of all the professional home photography and videos for new listings, would authorize and provide the formats and pictures for all magazine, on-line, billboard, and signage advertising, would be in charge of organizing interior decorators for showing advice, staging furniture purchases or rentals, pre-listing renovations and all of those creative, high tech, or "showing" related issued. Quite the job!

I was never the kind of guy to try and B.S. my way through anything. I was in over my head and wasn't about to pretend I wasn't and told Jim as much.

"Listen Jim, I really appreciate this job and the opportunity and I'm willing to do anything in any capacity to learn but I'm feeling I'm in over my head and I'm not sure I'll be able to live up to this."

He smiled, leaned back in his leather chair and said, "Sam, let me tell you lesson number one in selling real estate: You can't teach it. I saw enough of you that day to know you have the natural skill. If you have that, everything else can be taught. Don't worry about it. We'll bring you along slowly, help you where you need help, and I'm sure you'll be great. And if not, I'll just fire you and send you back to low end apartments," he smiled again. He carried on, "Listen now, you just show up, work hard, and give it everything you have. Up front there are only two things you need to change. Are you ready? You need to get a new wardrobe. Seriously Sam, we're not selling to the Thrifty Food crowd. Image is very important and we need to represent professional quality. And what is that *thing* in the parking lot? Is that like a Neon? Domestic? Seriously?" He was completely tongue in cheek. Giving me a gentle needling with a serious undertone and I took it well. "Hey, seriously," he carried on, "I've got nothing against Neon's or any form of transport. Personally if I had it my way I would be driving a truck, but again, how we are viewed needs to compliment what we are selling. It might not make sense, it might be shallow and pretentious, but if we consider clothes and cars and such as tools of the trade to better our craft, then it's easier to justify. I'm not expecting you to leave right now and go buy a Mercedes or anything, but there are some affordable leases for some of the lower high-end cars that you might consider for down the road. In the meantime your car will be fine for errands and the like, and if we're seeing some bigger players, we can go together in my car or you can borrow one of mine. Sound good? Just don't let anyone see that Neon."

"Sure Jim, sounds okay to me." I wondered just how many cars he had.

I liked him. He was one of those guys who had something special. He was driven, charming, funny, energetic, professional, and exceptionally bright. I wondered if he was acting out his calling from God. He had a natural talent for this; that much was clear. A natural talent plus a relentless work ethic as it turned out as everyone who worked for him worked tirelessly for long hours any day of the week with Jim always working one step harder.

So I launched into my new career with excitement and passion. Everything was different in this job. I was working in the community I knew like the back of my hand, I could see the ocean with every glance, the scenery was spectacular, the home architectures always interesting and unique with gorgeous landscapes, properties, gardens, etc. I was able to promote and sell in a community I loved and respected. I worked long, ridiculous hours as the clients' needs were all over the map – weekends, late nights, early mornings, it didn't matter. We catered to their needs and many of these people were flying in from all over the world, only in town for a few days, had erratic schedules, changed plans on a dime, cancelled, were in a hurry, expected long lunches after a viewing, or had unusual or borderline eccentric requests. Jim would work with around thirty listings at any given time. Virtually all of them were in West Van, although sometimes we would get listings on the west side of Vancouver out near UBC which was another very expensive area. Or sometimes they were in North Vancouver and we even got a few on Bowen Island which was a fifteen minute or so ferry ride from Horseshoe Bay at the most western end of West Van. Most listings were for over $1,000,000. There would seldom be any listing for less than $800,000. We currently had two listings for houses for over $7,000,000 each.

I soaked it all up and learned everything I could. Often I would accompany Jim on viewings, and would observe how he conducted himself. He was only about five years older than me, but he acted older and I considered him a mentor. Ralph showed me how a Christian man sells real estate and Jim was showing me how to be successful at selling real estate, and my goal was to find my balance between the two.

I learned everything I could in all aspects. I wasn't just interested in the sales aspect, but also found the advertising, technology aspect, and the staging/interior decorating parts fascinating as well. A house could show "as is" and be listed for one price, but take out their furniture, stage it professionally, minimize the clutter and perhaps make a few inexpensive cosmetic changes, and all of a sudden a home can list for considerably more. When you're dealing with houses worth millions, proper staging and changing how the house is viewed when showing can make the difference of hundreds of thousands of dollars in selling price. To convince a client to get rid of their own personal items, invest, say $50,000 of their own money, cash out of pocket, towards staging and furniture and trust the realtor will get significantly more on the sale was challenging and risky. But if it paid off. It really paid off. But you could have access to the best tools, the most effective advertising, and great listings and it could all mean very little if you lacked the ability to sell.

I took what I thought was a scriptural approach to the whole thing. I was aware of the fact that West Van realty involved big bucks. Big bucks making big commissions, making people potentially driven by money. Idolizing money. Jesus said the love of money is the root of all evil. I took that to mean money itself wasn't evil. It was *loving* money and putting it before God that was evil. My approach was not "how do I sell so I can earn." My approach was "what can I do to serve these people who are looking to buy or sell a house." There was a difference. I treated my job the same way I treated washing dishes; to do the best I could to serve and honour God, to give glory to God in my job, and to treat my role as an act of service.

And it seemed to work. My objective was to serve the clients in the best possible way and not to sell a house at any cost. If a house sold, great. If not, well, as long as I did my part, that was okay too. God had elevated me this far and He could elevate me farther if that's what He wanted.

But it also turned out I had something of a knack for dealing with this level of client. My passion and local knowledge of West Van helped me tremendously, which was limitless for conversation of familiarity with sellers and education for buyers not from West Van. I was also naturally interested in architecture and landscaping so it made me interested in the properties. I had a local's insight that could only be from someone who had been born and raised here. But more than this, and more than anything, was this seemingly God-given talent I had for being able to talk to people on the level they needed to be talked to on. Rich, poor, or in-between, relationships were developed by caring, listening, and being humble. People had a need to be heard and have their needs met. By tuning into that, people responded. And in the world of real estate, it meant they often responded by buying or selling through me.

Jim started me on only a salary, which was good money in itself and probably equaled a good year of slogging it out at the old job. At a certain point, when he deemed me ready to be responsible for one of his listings, I moved into a commission structure. This came about six months into my mentorship when I was given responsibility for a waterfront townhouse on Belleview Avenue, just one block below Marine Drive, and within walking distance to the office. The townhouse was located right on the water, with only the Seawall, a scenic public walk, between it and the ocean. It was stunning at $1,200,000 for a 1200 square foot townhouse. The owners had retired into it five years ago, but now wanted to move closer to their grandchildren in Ontario. I drank tea with them on their patio and regaled them with stories about the history of the restaurant a few doors down where they ate once a week. I told them it used to be called Peppe's and had been locally owned by a family with scads of kids, some of whom I went to school with.

The eventual buyers wandered in by themselves without a realtor to a Saturday open house I hosted immediately after listing it on the market. It turned out they wanted to downsize from the family home they owned near Lighthouse Park now that their kids had moved out. It turned out I knew their kids from school. In the end I sold the townhouse to them and acted as both seller's agent and buyer's agent. And then, if that wasn't enough, I got the listing for the Lighthouse Park home. Jim was pleased. And I was pleased. My end of the townhouse sale ended up at $19,800. And I had the Lighthouse Park house as a listing which, when sold, my cut would be higher because I also brought in the listing.

And for the very first time the vision God spoke into me on the mountain had the first glimpse of seeming possible.

Chapter 39

ealing with the rich made me crave working even more with the poor. Perhaps, in part, it was the injustice there seemed to be over distribution of wealth, or perhaps it was just the extreme differences in lifestyle I found fascinating. But I doubt it was either one of those reasons. Firstly, I interpreted the Bible to call us to help the poor. It seemed pretty clear. I felt a certain affinity for the poor because I had been on Hastings myself. I felt an obligation to give back, share my story, and give of myself. And of course, it had been well ingrained into me by now that the primary success of my life since the mountain had been derived through being as unselfish as possible. But there was something else. It was being able to see through both classes of people, to see the actual person separate from their environment, and I was amazed to discover so many similarities. Both could hurt, mourn, grieve, protect, anguish, laugh, or cry. Both were of the extremes of society and their respective struggles with living in a broken world represented proof that God created us all equal.

The hours working for Jim were obscene. But because I was in West Van all the time anyway, it was easy to pop in to see my mom and help her out with her needs. I kept spare clothes there so I wouldn't trash my now expensive wardrobe, and did chores for her, or just hung out.

The shift at Street Hope just wasn't working for me as Saturday mornings were prime realtor hours. But I discovered nobody objected to me just dropping in there whenever I wanted to help out, and this became my primary function in my off hours, an hour here, a couple hours there.

Sunday mornings rarely worked for attending church as well. So my church just sort of became Street Hope. I would get my spiritual nourishment through other resources to keep my own growth and education stimulated and the rest of the time I tried to be of service at Street Hope. I developed relationships with the main organizers there and started to tithe directly to them to help with any number of needs they had. And there was always something needed: short on pancake mix one day, the portable griddle packed it in, no money for dishwashing solution, no bread delivery happened, and so on, and so on. I was happy to give, honoured in fact to the point that I was surprised at how the formerly self-serving me seemed to have been replaced with someone only too happy to give.

The more time I spend there the more I got to know the regulars and the more I found out about some of their personal needs. I found myself branching out of Street Hope into the community at times to help individuals who had specific needs. Manny, the nineteen year old aboriginal boy I had befriended needed help to move into a new place as the place he was living had turned into a crack shack of sorts. So I helped him find a place and got him some decent used items of furniture and kitchen ware. I helped someone else deal with some creditors by talking to them and organizing some solutions on their behalf, and I bought someone else a bike after theirs had been stolen. The more involved I became, the more needs I became aware of.

Of course, I had been schooled in street level cons from first-hand experience. I knew many of these people were manipulative con artists, and knew how to deliver good sales pitches to organizations that helped to get what they wanted. I never gave cash and I just used my own level of discernment to determine the validity on a case by case basis. For the most part, I think most of the needs were genuine, at least with the people who I had known as regulars. Legitimate needs for people who either lacked the resources or the ability to get them met on their own.

I had been doing this for several months when over the course of about two weeks, I ran into two people I knew. The first person was Mrs. Adams, the wife of the couple who I had influenced towards the purchase of the West Van home that led to my new job. I recognized her right away, although was perplexed at first as she seemed so out of the context I had met her in. She was talking to an older street lady when I approached her and said hello. It also took her a moment to process it, but she caught on quickly.

"Ah yes, Sam," she said, "I remember you well and I have you to thank for my beautiful home."

We exchanged pleasantries and she told me to call her Gretchen. She said she had found a West Van church who took a shift at Street Hope once a week and she loved doing this sort of volunteer work. I told her my story was much the same with the church I had been going to being affiliated with Street Hope. I think we both found it somewhat comforting to see a familiar face. I asked her if her husband also came here, and she said that no, sadly, Jeff didn't like going to church and generally watched a lot of sports. I told her I was really happy to see her there.

The next person I knew took me a lot longer to figure out who she was. There was a hint of familiarity but I couldn't place it. I think she must have been going through something similar because she kept staring at me until finally I just asked her who she was and if I knew her.

"I'm Minnie, Sam," she said. "The last time I saw you was when we got shot at. I thought you were dead. I never forget a face."

"Holy smokes! Minnie! I can't believe it!" I was genuinely gob smacked. It was no wonder I didn't recognize her. She was at least thirty pounds heavier; she had aged but looked way better. She was healthy looking. "How are you? You look totally different. But then again, it's been like almost seven years. But you look great!"

"I'm clean Sam. Going on two years. Things changed for me after that day. I never got that fear out of me. I used for a few more years on and off. But I really wanted to get off the street so bad. I just couldn't do it though until I finally put it together a couple years ago."

It was all so incredible. In the past I had tried to find out about what happened in the hotel that day but couldn't find any archived news reports except a couple of vague newspaper articles about a suspected gun going off in the downtown East Side. But there was also a side of me that just didn't want to know either. Minnie had been duly traumatized by the events that day. We shared our stories and she couldn't believe I hadn't used since that day and my journey up the mountain. She was amazed and happy for me.

We shared about what we remembered and about what happened after we fled the room. I told her my version and she told me she heard all the shooting but never looked over her shoulder. She just ran and got out and kept on running. She had sensed the gunman had followed me instead of them and thought for sure I had been shot; a thought that seemed to be reinforced after she never saw me again. She lived in fear for many days and months, sure someone was going to "off" her on the street. And she heard street talk of gang hits, a major drug rip off, rival gangs killing each other with escalating violence leading into and for a long time after that day. But such as street stories went, we didn't know the real truth, and neither of us knew if anyone died that day.

She told me the event of that day had changed her. That her fears became too great and she went in and out of treatment facilities until she finally landed some real sobriety. She was on her own, but was on anti-depressants, other medications, and was still on welfare. She got into some shared accommodations a few blocks west of here. Off the street, but not far off. She came here sometimes for the meals because she couldn't generally stretch her money out without the free food.

I in turn shared my story but minimized some of the recent success for fear of making her feel bad. I told her how it was Jesus that saved me that day and led me into a new life and that a miracle had happened. I told her it was like a miracle had happened for her too, and finally I asked her if she would mind terribly if I shared a little more with her about Jesus and what He is capable of.

She told me she would like that very much.

Chapter 40

The more time that went on with Jim, the more proficient I was becoming as a realtor. Starting at being the junior in every aspect of the company I eventually surpassed every one of the other realtors in sales and commissions. Jim and I had become quite close over time as well. We would do a lot of joint listings where we would collaborate on strategy and take turns with open houses or showings and as a result, we spent quite a bit of time together.

Not long after my first big commission cheque, I leased myself a new car. I got myself a brand new Audi A4. I struggled somewhat with being able to justify a high-end car when the people at Street Hope were going meal to meal. I had to do some serious work looking at scripture and checking my motives. In the end, I decided if my personal road contained riches, it was okay as long as God came first and the poor got their fair share.

And I have to admit, it was a fun car to drive.

Jim was the epitome of success. Not only was he very good at what he did, but he looked great doing it. He made his tireless work ethic look easy, he treated people fairly, he was rich, handsome, loyal to his wife, true to his word, and lived a lifestyle that only few achieve and most want. So when he told me about his son being autistic I was very surprised.

We were on Rockridge Crescent. A 6000 square foot home built in the late 1970's. It had a pool, a jacuzzi that seated twelve, an indoor koi pond running the length of an enormous front entry, seven bedrooms, eight and a half bathrooms, a 360 degree panoramic view of oceans and mountains, and an intercom and stereo system wired through every room. When it was built it was the start of a generation of magnificent homes for the super wealthy. Twenty years ago this house was a jaw dropping, eye catching world of only the super rich. Today it was a little dated, smaller that the real monster houses of today, and one amongst many of similar stature in the area. Listing at just over $4,000,000, it was an impressive listing, but there were bigger and more expensive in West Van.

We were alone in the house walking through it and making some decisions about staging and how to best show the home and had just settled into a couple of expensive leather chairs in the library talking idly. For the most part our conversations were work related. I had shared enough with him for him to know I was a Christian and did lots of volunteer work. He also knew I had gone through some periods of adversity, but without any real detail. I knew he lived in West Van himself, was married with three kids and I had met his wife a couple of times.

Today was not really any different and we were talking about work and showings, and whatever, when his voice just started to drop off. He kept talking but he wasn't there anymore. He was incoherent and started to ramble and then he just stopped talking and looked out a window at nothing.

I was speechless. The whole scene was just so out of character that I could do nothing more than just wait on him to come back. He did after a moment or two, and refocused, and looked over at me as if just discovering he wasn't alone.

"I'm sorry Sam," he said. "Wow, I just, well, I just....I just don't even know sometimes. It's just.....my son.....gosh it's all so hard sometimes. It's just so easy to sell houses and so hard to live life sometimes. Do you know at all what I mean?"

"Well, no, I don't know what you mean specifically about your son, but do I know about hard living. Uh, yeah Jim, I think

I would probably horrify you with some of the truths from my past."

He told me his son, who was now eight years old, had been born autistic and how challenging it all was. How his wife had to learn to cope with it all and how much she sacrificed. How each and every day was filled with so much pain, how the other kids were affected, and how his marriage was affected. And he told me how he escapes his responsibilities as a father by going to work so much. And that was what broke him: he saw himself as a failed father.

I listened and we talked, and eventually I shared with him my failings as a son, my adversity and where I drew my strength. And we just chatted for a long time in that house on Rockridge Crescent until the owners came home and we went on our way. It was a humbling experience for me and brought depth to our relationship. I went from seeing him as a model of perfection to a brother in life, and it was better as the latter.

Chapter 41

$\mathcal{R}$eal estate in West Van was booming in the early to mid 2000s and the landscape of West Van had been changing. The older generations were moving on, dying off, or retiring to somewhere else. Their older homes, mostly built in the 1950s through the 1970s were being torn down and new houses put up. Often, two houses next door to each other were bought, torn down and one giant house on one bigger lot was put up. Some of the prestigious lots on the waterfront, or high on the hills, became enormous "monster" houses of jaw dropping designs. Houses right on the water, private and seldom seen, were being constructed for money in the tens of millions of dollars.

While West Van used to have plenty of families living there of modest incomes and modest houses, their children were having to move to other parts of the lower mainland when they moved out unless they had become very rich, as nobody was coming into West Van anymore without at least a million dollars in their pockets.

This also meant the dynamic of who lived in West Van also changed. The super rich Asians with more money than could be spent were coming to West Van for second homes, or looking for ways to invest. Americans were coming too, as were rich Iranians and people from other parts of the world, along with the noteworthy and famous. West Van was becoming more of a cultural melting pot, and the entire community seemed changed, yet familiar because, well, it was the same place.

I had been with Jim two and a half years and was now thirty-six years old and over eight years since the mountain. My life as a drug addict now seemed like a distant blip on the radar and I had developed into a confident self assured man. I had established myself firmly into place as the number two guy at Jim Jennings Realty and had generated a strong following with a steady stream of personal listings.

One day Jim asked me to lunch to go over some things. After we had eaten, he said to me "Sam, I've been doing some thinking. A lot of thinking for a long time actually. And I think it's time to expand the company."

He went on to tell me he thought we should change the scope of how we looked at the firm. We needed to be more concentrated on the international buyers coming into West Van, that we needed to advertise overseas and in America, and be in place as their agents before they set foot in Canada. We should consider it an expansion of the company and perhaps set it up as a separate division working out of a separate location.

We sipped coffee and discussed the trends of the market for a while. Then he put his coffee mug down slowly on the table and said, "Sam, I want to make some changes. I want to expand and grow the company, and I think it would be wise of us to recognize that the changing conditions in the marketplace means we need to change too. But I want to change too. Personally, I mean." He paused again and his voice quieted with a softer tone. "I want to be a better father Sam. I want to dedicate my life to my wife and children in a way that is more substantial than just being a provider. Yes, I can provide, and can do it better than most. But what they want from me, money can't buy. They want my time; they want my love, my patience, my guidance, my commitment, and my loyalty. They want to be before company. And my son Sam, my only boy, who struggles with his autism so much, well I need to be by his side. I need to walk this out with him Sam. I need to. And now, I *want* to."

I didn't say anything. I got the impression he wasn't done, so I just sat there and looked at him. And he went on: "So I want to grow the company because it's the smart move business wise. But I want to work less and be at home more. I'm into my forties now and my perspective has changed. Heck Sam, I might even want to go to church with you one day," and he smiled. "Maybe your Jesus could give me the strength to make these changes. God knows I'm scared out of my mind. But here's the deal Sam. Here's the pitch or the close or whatever you want to call it. I can't do this alone and you're the only one I really trust. So I want to offer you a partnership. We can go over the details, but we become partners, share the work load, start up an international division. The company grows. Hopefully. There are more than enough profits that I don't take a big hit, you become a partner and reap the rewards that come with that, and we both work a little less. Well, *I* work a little less and you probably work a little more until you get your end settled and into a routine."

He stopped again. And again I didn't speak. He just didn't look quite done. "I've thought about this a lot Sam. I've gone over it and over it. I'm pretty well off you know. I've done pretty well. It's worked for me. But I can't continue on the same way. I need to look after the area that keeps burning at me to look after. There's something about you Sam. A part of you that shines. And I think this is a deal that works. I wouldn't offer it to you if I didn't see it working and I think if it comes off as planned it will help us both. And I think you should take the deal"

Chapter 42

And I did take the deal. It took about six months to get through. Jim and I talked for many hours and days about how it should look. Then we went to lawyers and accountants and I entered into the world of corporate structures. It was a complicated, expensive, and lengthy process. At the end, I felt like I was a complete businessman, knowledgeable in many areas of business and corporate structures. And on top of all that, I was now a bona fide partner in a successful real estate company with the title of president. *Jim Jennings Realty* had now become *Jennings & Wyatt Realty* and it was surreal to see my name on the backs of magazines.

Jim and I agreed we would open a second office. This one would be downtown that would be convenient for people coming in from overseas and staying in the downtown hotels. I took considerable time to find the right location and finally found one just outside of Yaletown, a warehouse district of upscale shops, restaurants, and converted condos. I found a very nice office that had been converted from a warehouse with high ceilings, exposed ducting, and a modern feel. But the primary reason I selected it was that it was on the sixth floor with a northeastern view. I was high enough that I could see in a direction that would go right over Hastings Street and see the North Shore mountains. And yes, it had a very nice view of "my" mountain.

I had spent the better part of the last eight years looking up to it any chance I could. I would stare at it, remember my journey, think about my transformation, re-dedicate myself through remembering and pray to Jesus. If I was going to own a company, call myself president, and find a location for a new office, well, it was dang well going to have a view of the mountain.

I hired a receptionist (and coffee server) who did a variety of tasks and spoke two Asian dialects. I hired one realtor to be dedicated to work out of this downtown office exclusively for international clients and Jim and I co-managed the existing affairs of the West Van office. He in turn was true to his word and backed off on his work load. He took a dedicated two days off per week that he would not compromise under any circumstance and worked shorter days on the other days.

My income took a hit in the early days as I adjusted to life as owner, and became acutely aware of the expenses of the business as much as I was aware of the income generated. The expenses took the lead in the early days of the new office. But because I was also involved in the West Van office business, income came in steadily, and in time, the downtown office started to hold its own.

I pioneered an advertising campaign overseas in places like Hong Kong, Singapore, Europe as well as in the States, primarily California and New York. And it paid off with establishing relationships before clients or clients' buyers came to town looking. I would meet people at the airport, set them up in hotels, act as tour guide and cultural guide and take them on tours of West Van or the West Side of Vancouver. It was a fascinating insight into culture, accepted rituals of business, and buying tendencies. I adapted quickly and became successful at it. It was also intriguing to see how bold some other cultures were in their religious beliefs. Not all of them were Christian, but many were bold and upfront on how their lives, decisions, and outlooks were directly related to their belief system. I would respectfully accept any religious belief any of them had without judgment, but when I found out a customer was a Christian, I would try to engage them in conversation about their journey with God, how God was influencing their homeland or whatever they wanted to talk about. And I met some very interesting people who walked with the Lord.

Chapter 43

I took Minnie out for lunch to the *Trattoria*. Torsi was there and he sat down with us for a few minutes and charmed Minnie and was terribly friendly and interested in our lives and any updates there were. I had never strayed too far from Torsi over the years. I still came in from time to time to say hello and there were still two of my old dishwashers on staff, one being Sulyman who was now line cook, and the other was the first recipient of the culinary scholarship who was now a very well respected sous chef at one of Torsi's other restaurants.

Minnie had continued to come into Street Hope regularly and we spent considerable time talking. I told her all about Jesus and the Bible and she expressed interest and started going to a church that was near where she lived. I introduced her to the Christian counselor friend of mine who never charged for his fees to help her work through her issues. She had grown up mainly on the street and had lots of baggage she needed freedom from. She spent six months working with him once a week and I gave him $100 an hour for the time he spent with her, only I didn't tell Minnie that.

Minnie started to show some real growth. She got officially "saved" by saying the Lord's Prayer, got baptized at her local church, and did so well across the board she was able to give up all her meds.

I was able to throw her some work cleaning houses for show-ings and moving furniture in and out for staging jobs and she was

233

able to afford a few things she needed. We talked at length about being of sacrifice to Christ and she started to help at Street Hope. She was the only one who both needed the service and helped out for the service. And we would work many hours together sharing our testimonies, washing dishes, serving food, and investing in people's lives.

Over time it was easy to see the light start to shine off of her. She was becoming an obedient servant, grateful for what she had, alive in Jesus, thinking about her future, and very clearly a miracle in her own right.

Chapter 44

Mrs. Adams, who I now called Gretchen, also ended up being something of a regular. She had an amazing heart for helping the poor. She would bring her two boys with her often who were no more than five or six, and she would get them to help wash dishes, help serve, and wash down tables. The boys were learning about serving, and the locals all loved seeing children in their joyous, non judgmental state be in the building. Sometimes she would come alone, but she rarely missed a week and was often there more than once a week. She would talk with the women who came in, and always seemed to have all the time in the world for them to talk to her. Every once in a while I would see her husband Jeff drop her off or pop in to see her for a few minutes. I talked to him once or twice and despite his prickly and arrogant nature, it almost, just almost, looked like he envied what was going on just a little. Perhaps there was hope for him after all.

One day Gretchen brought with her another woman from her church who she introduced to me as Marina. Marina had natural good looks, a great smile, easy disposition, easy charm, and had that unique quality of looking like she would be comfortable in the trenches or at the ballroom. Gretchen got pulled away to talk to a street woman that she knew so I took it upon myself to show Marina around and how things worked. We ended up washing dishes together for a while side by side while we talked easily back and forth.

Marina shared with me a little about herself, that she grew up in North Vancouver, got a job with the Ocean and Fisheries department of the Canadian government not long after high school and worked at an outlet in West Van near Cypress Park, not far from the house Gretchen bought. She led a simple and non spectacular life where she did little wrong, got into no trouble whatsoever, and was a good daughter to her ageing parents. She never went to church as a child, but always felt the desire. So, within the last year, she just decided she was going to start going to church and get involved. She picked a church in West Van, immediately met Gretchen who immediately brought her here.

We talked easily and laughed a lot and it was a fun shift at the ol' Street Hope. And when it was over I found myself thinking about her.

Quite a bit in fact.

Chapter 45

Things were starting to unravel a little at Street Hope though. Just rumblings of change and some flare ups of issues that seem to be fairly common in the world of volunteer work for the poor. Churches that would be involved at one time would go through internal changes that would affect their relationship with Street Hope, so staffing was an ongoing issue and there were many days when nobody was there to open the doors at all. The organizations who would contribute food, clothing, bread, or finances to help the place stay running would change, bail, forget, or circumstances would prevent them from helping. One week there would be lots of bread. The next week none. For two weeks in a row there would be hot, cooked breakfasts supplied, then cold cereal only for the next month. One day there would be three portable griddles that could be used, then one would break, one would go back to a church that loaned it, and having only one wouldn't cope with the demand. These were the sorts of obstacles that seemed pretty common.

Of more critical concern was the building itself. Street Hope consisted of the ground floor of a six story building near Gastown. It was old, run down, and falling apart. It was close enough to Gastown that it wasn't a stretch to think it could be considered valuable real estate one day if the tourism that flocked to Gastown somehow fuelled business growth that had nowhere to grow except into the fringes of skid row.

It seemed the landlords may have sensed that they could get more out of their building than essentially renting out their bottom floor to churches for negligible rent and some write offs. And the rumblings of change were persistent to the extent that the future of Street Hope seemed uncertain.

Chapter 46

*T*he biggest, most complicated real estate arrangement I ever got involved with originated from an unlikely source. I had advertised in an upscale California travel magazine on a trial basis. I took out a half page ad and ran it three times. Advertising cost a fortune. It was a necessary evil of the real estate game, but one that you at least wanted to believe generated some leads.

A call came in one day from the San Jose area of California by this young woman who told me she and her husband wanted to inquire about waterfront properties in West Van and had seen my ad, checked me out on line, and were wondering if I could come out and interview for the job.

"The job?" I said.

"Yes, the job of looking for a house for us," she answered.

"You want me to come out there? To San Jose?" I asked. I had never actually been asked anything like that before.

"Yes, that's right," she answered. "We want to interview you, and if we hire you, we would like you to find us a property or house and property and then we would pay you a commission. That's how it all works, isn't it?"

"Well, yes, that's about how it all works," I said.

So, in the end I flew down to San Jose, was picked up at the airport in a limo, transported to an upscale neighbourhood called Cherry Acres and was deposited on the doorstep of a very nice home where I was greeted by a *high school girl*.

She introduced herself to me as Mary Lou Brock, the same person who had called me and arranged for me to come down. It took me a moment for my brain to catch up to the fact that nothing appeared as I thought it would until I started to piece it together the more she chatted. And she chatted *a lot*. She was an overly energetic, spunky, bright eyed, enthusiastic, and contagious young lady.

And she wasn't in high school. She was twenty-two. I got the entire story as she invited me into the house and brought me into a living room. In between she asked how my flight was, if I wanted an iced tea, told me what the big plan was, and brought it all back to more family history. I got it *all* in the first thirty minutes.

Mary Lou was twenty-two and married to her husband Don. They got married when they were both nineteen. They grew up in Washington State, in a city called Everett, between Seattle and Vancouver. I knew it and had been through it once years ago and passed it many times on trips down the I-5 to Seattle or beyond.

Don was one of those whiz kids at computers and developed a car racing video game when still in grade ten. He founded his own company called Avalanche Software by seventeen and distributed the game through it. He negotiated with Ferrari to use their cars in his game, of which they gave him a Ferrari to drive in exchange. When he was eighteen and just graduating high school his company was acquired by Technoship Inc, made Don the president and gave him $12,000,000.

The focus continued to be racing games of which they put out a part two and three of the original game and a landslide of more cash came in. Technoship was then, in turn acquired and became Technoship USA Inc. and development branched into smart phones. And of course, more millions transferred hands.

Mary Lou had been one of those energetic, bright go-getters in high school. Not one of those cheerleader kind of gals, but with natural good looks that when added to her great personality made her a vibrant and beautiful girl. Don, on the other hand, had been a dork. They grew up three doors down from one another and had been friends since kindergarten. She had always looked out for Don and always respected his mind and unique gifts. They started dating six months before Don finished his first game despite coming off as an awkward looking couple.

Not so awkward though, when Don pulled into the school parking lot a year later in a Ferrari. They lasted as long as they could in Everett, but had to move to San Jose after the first acquisition. Both of their parents were Christian and didn't want them living together in San Jose. So they got married in Everett and moved down to start their lives together. They eventually rented this home fully furnished and drove down in the Ferrari to start their married lives.

But their hearts weren't in San Jose and with the continuing technology allowing remote working options they felt they wanted to live somewhere else and commute to San Jose several times a year. Their hearts were in the Pacific Northwest, but they didn't want to live in Everett. And they didn't want to live in Seattle either for whatever reason. But they did want to be close to their parents.

Mary Lou had been to Vancouver several times as a child as she had an aunt who lived there and had fond and vivid memories. In particular, she had memories of taking the ferry from Horseshoe Bay in West Van to the gulf islands and standing on the deck and watching the coastline as the ferry pulled away. So after much discussion her heart decided on West Van waterfront and his brain agreed.

By this time we were sitting in the informal family room when Don made his first appearance. And *he was* a dork. Pretty stereotypical, with a button up shirt done up one button too many, glasses and an awkward presence. He also looked like he should still be in high school. But he was pleasant and the longer we chatted the more evidence of his brilliance came out. These two may have been young, but they were on the ball and had a plan in place. We talked at length about what they were looking for and how they wanted to go about achieving it. I talked at length about West Van, the geography of the area, the climate of real estate and value of land, and real estate as an investment.

At some stage, they seemed satisfied and switched gears away from business. She insisted on barbequing some hamburgers for dinner and he wanted to show me around. The more time I spent with him, the more comfortable he was becoming, and I was able to witness a small piece of how his brain worked. He showed me some of his gadgets and toys and spoke in terms I had no hope of understanding. He showed me his Ferrari and made me sit in it and fire it up. Are you kidding me? I loved it.

At thirty-seven I still felt fairly young, and I think the addiction had stumped some of my maturity, so I loved the youthful exuberance of this brilliant man and the tour of basically, games. We ate and we all talked some more. Then they told me I should forget about a hotel and stay there, because they had like five spare rooms. We played a board game and then I kicked Don's ass at fuse ball, because, well, he was a bit of a dork.

At about midnight we ordered pizza, they showed me pictures of their parents and where they grew up, and then finally, about 2:00 am we all went to bed. All this and they never touched a drop of alcohol. While she was pretty, easy to be around and exuberant, he was brilliant, socially awkward, and slightly eccentric. Together they were infectious and I liked them both immensely.

I landed the deal officially the next morning over coffee. They wanted me to find them waterfront property in West Van, gave me permission to speak to people on their behalf, and sent me on my way back to the airport.

Chapter 47

At the end of the third time Marina came to volunteer at Street Hope with Gretchen, I asked her out on a date. It was a clumsy, awkward, and red-faced moment. One of the best pieces of advice I had received in early recovery was to stay out of relationships. This is a piece of advice I would have normally dismissed as inapplicable to me, but the mountain experience gave me a newfound determination to accept new ways of thinking that I didn't have in my previous attempts at recovery. And now, having long since rounded into the man God had intended me to be had my addiction not taken root, it was easy to look back and recognize just how sick I had been leading into, during, and for a long time after the addiction ended. The bottom line was I was not well enough or mature enough to have been able to act like the type of husband God calls us to be. And while, certainly, I have been well a long time now, the maturity I had developed as a result of my spiritual growth gave me the wisdom and patience to wait on the woman God chose me to be with, and well, she just hadn't come along.

But Marina was a different business all together. She was just so wholesome and kind. She had never tried alcohol or drugs in her entire life, a feat I found remarkable in this day and age in this culture. "Didn't want to," she would say. Just that easy. She was the youngest of four kids but nine years separated her from the next oldest, so essentially she was raised as a single child and we shared the fact we were both products of older parents. At seven years my junior, Marina was humble, generous, grateful for what she had, energetic towards life, loved the outdoors, was loyal, kind, fun to be around, a great cook, had a great work ethic, and was progressive towards new ideas and concepts. She embraced her relationship with Jesus, believed every aspect of it with all of her heart, and soaked up everything she could to enhance it.

I found her to be exceptionally beautiful.

We went out for dinner the first time to a North Vancouver restaurant she enjoyed. The conversation flowed easily and it was an amazing night. Afterwards, we drove up Mt. Seymour and parked in one of the pullouts and looked at the stunning view over the North Shore, Burrard Inlet, the city and beyond. It reminded me of the view I had from the summit of "my mountain" and I felt comfortable and at ease. Everything felt very right. I took her home and dropped her off around midnight and drove home with all kinds of wonderful feelings stirring around inside.

In the next days and weeks we were virtually inseparable making time for each other amongst busy schedules. I shared with her my entire testimony from start to finish and minimized and omitted nothing: the good, the bad, the ugly, the discoveries, the revelations, the successes, and progression. She was fascinated, accepting, and grateful for the honesty. It was scary to confess so many things that I thought might turn her away, but there was a need for transparency and honesty.

We had a great time together. I would take her to see some of the houses I had listings for, took her to dinner at *The Trattoira*, showed her the dish pit, and introduced her to Torsi who was beaming in delight at my being with a woman. I pointed out Crown Mountain and described to her what it was like. I introduced her to Jim and his wife and she took me to meet her parents and we sat in their garden for many hours. I took her to meet my mom in West Van and we went with each other for tours of the neighbourhoods we grew up in.

Neither of us had been married. Both of us believed that marriage was a spiritual gift created by God, that He picked the person that we were be united with, the person we were to join into one with, and we both believed in the guidelines He set forth for the courting process as impossible as they seemed to be to uphold at times.

We both believed that God had put us together.

We had known each other for six weeks when we both decided we wanted to get married.

Chapter 48

*F*inding West Vancouver waterfront wasn't easy. At least not with the guidelines Don and Mary Lou had given me. Ideally, they wanted to tear down and build unless by some miracle a house was on the market that met their desires, which were specific and lengthy. We all agreed the odds were slim of that happening.

The biggest challenge was going to be lot size. They wanted something big. Really big. And really private. They did not want their house to be seen from the road, wanted direct waterfront, as well as trees and a natural surrounding. They did not want to be able to see any neighbour's house, wanted to be able to have exposure west and east, and wanted a lot that was not treacherously steep or rugged as some of the lots in West Van are. And that was just the lot! West Van essentially sat at the base of the mountain range sloping down into the ocean, which was what made for so many view properties. But the slope into the ocean could be steep, overly rugged, and always rocky. It was a rocky coast with the odd small pockets of beach.

The tricky part was that to meet their size, privacy, and all around grandness criteria, it was more than likely going to take two lots minimum. Maybe more. And if there was a house for sale that already was on multiple lots, chances were it was on the newish and incredibly expensive side. It couldn't possibly be good financial sense to tear down what would already be considered a deluxe home in order to immediately build another massive and expensive home. But these were very wealthy people, so who knew the extent they would go to get what they wanted.

There was nothing at all that I thought met the criteria, but I kept my eye open for new listings and networked among my peers to let me know any inside information. I looked at whatever came close, sent details of whatever I thought was in the ballpark down to San Jose where they were immediately rejected. I learned quickly that Don and Mary Lou were not the kind of people to compromise on what they wanted. First time buyers or not, they held firm that I was going to get them what they wanted.

My break came about three months into the search. A fifty year-old house on a gorgeous piece of waterfront was coming on the market for $6,000,000. Any prospective buyer would be looking at a tear down and rebuild. The lot was stunning, with a long medium grade slope down from Seaside Place in the 5000 block of Marine Drive. The land nearest the ocean was relatively flat with raised rock bluffs. It was ideal for an imaginative architect to come up with a design involving the flatter parts with the elevation and come up with a house that both had elevated views and immediate water access. It met all of the waterfront criteria to a tee. Except it wasn't big enough. Not nearly so.

I had been given a head's up by the realtor who was getting the listing before it came onto the marker and I knew I would have to immediately look into neighbouring properties to see how they would compliment each other if morphed together and then try to approach the owners to see if they would be willing to sell.

In the meantime, I sent all the information to the Brocks so they could see there was a potential lead developing. They immediately responded and expressed interest. "Get on those neighbours Sam and get us some land!" Don had said.

I was moving quickly. I knew time was of the essence as, even though the West Van market had slid into flatter times the immediate waterfront would always raise eyebrows for people looking for that specifically, and this was a nice lot.

I went down and checked out the property first hand. I knew the place as once again, it was very close to where I grew up. I knew the area and many of the families in the area, but it was a very private lot so I had never seen it up close except for a few times from swimming out as a kid off the nearby rocks and looking back to shore.

The lot in person was as advertised and perfect if it could somehow be made larger. I nosed around the neighbouring properties as best as I could without being overly intrusive and discovered the house on the western side was less practical than the house on the eastern side.

The house on the western side was on the other side of a rather steep rock. Ideal for privacy but not ideal to try and make one seamless lot out of the two. Plus the house on the other side was big and new. Again, ideal as a neighbour, not ideal to rip down and rebuild.

But the house on the eastern side had promise and lots of it. It was separated from the house that was for sale by some trees and an outcropping of rock that jutted into the ocean, but the actual land between the two houses would compliment any future build. In fact, I could see in my mind's eye a spectacular finished product using the jutting out of rock as the feature point of the house creating a separate sort of view looking southeast and southwest, towards the city.

And to boot, the house on it was old and the lot size seemed to be very big. I would have to check with the zoning and find out for sure how much land they owned, but it all looked very promising. I did check with the land titles office and found all the relevant land information on both lots. Both lots were almost identical in size at about 18,000 square feet each, give or take. Combined, over three-fourths of an acre of prime West Van real estate. Enough for any multi millionaire software genius first time buyer.

I called Don and he gave me the okay to approach the neighbour which I immediately did. I called them and told them I had a prospective buyer who was interested in their property. I was met with the usual skepticism, distrust, and reluctance to speak that I was accustomed to hearing from people who are cold called from strangers. But I held their attention long enough to explain a little about my clients while keeping their anonymity to get myself an appointment at the house.

They turned out to be a mid sixties couple who were recent empty nesters. I told them all I could about my clients, told them their neighbours were about to list for $6,000,000 which would be a good guideline to estimate what they could receive for their property.

The dollar figures had their interest, I could tell. And why wouldn't they? They bought the property some thirty-five years ago for way less than a million, and given what I could see of their house, cars, and furnishings, these weren't millionaire lifestyles.

In the end they told me that they were still attached to the property, still felt young enough to maintain it, and believed that if they held out until they were ready to sell in maybe ten years, that they could get even more. They told me that the offer was very nice, just a few years premature. I thanked them and left for the day. But I knew it wasn't over.

I talked it over with Don and Mary Lou, with all three of us on the phone. In his youthful exuberance Don had expected the entire process to move faster and he wanted to jump all over the neighbour. "How about we offer him more than what his neighbor is listing for?"

Surely money talked and I agreed with his logic. That is if he really wanted the property. There were just lines that needed to be respected, like the line between generous and stupid or the line between having the neighbour agree, and paying way too much for the lot. Don and I agreed on the amount to offer would be $6,500,000, about half a million more than what we thought it was worth. I waited a few days to allow the last conversation with the neighbouring house to settle in, and then called again.

"I have been instructed to tell you that my clients are willing to offer you $6,500,000 for your property, of which they have the funds in cash." I thought it was a good opening line and I knew right away I had interest. I learned to really listen to how people spoke and watched for body language, or pauses in conversation, tuned into breathing, etc. When I introduced who I was on the call, I first detected an intake of breath like he was hoping I would call back.

The conversation went back and forth. At no time did he just flat out say, "No." He was guarded and evasive. I recognized this to be a form of negotiating where he was essentially interested if he could run the price up. And up. But for today, he just ended the call with a grumble about the timing not being right, their emotional attachment being too strong, but he grudgingly accepted to "think about it."

A couple of days later I got a call from an agent on their behalf. I knew this agent and respected him. He was another player in West Van. About the same time, coincidentally perhaps, the neighbouring house was officially listed on the market.

The agent, a man by the name of Slabin rounded into the reason behind the call. He told me his clients, the Ford's, were willing to negotiate, but because of their age, reluctance to move, their existing plan for staying another decade and their emotional attachment to the property, they would only consider selling for quite a bit over the previous offer. He told me if my clients were willing to talk numbers in the $9,000,000 range, there could be some conversations.

The word "range" was ambiguous. If he really thought he could get $9,000,000, he would have given a figure. I made all the right noises about the soft market, the glut of high-end houses on the market, my clients not being prepared to be bent over the fence, many other areas they could live, blah, blah, blah, and I finished with the perfunctory, "I'll talk it over with my clients."

Which I did. Don thought things were serious enough that they should fly out and see the property. He felt convinced if it was right he could "buy" this guy out of his house. They flew out on a Lear Jet (did they own this thing I wondered?) the next day and I picked them up at the airport. Mary Lou was like an excited child, absolutely thrilled to be in Vancouver and actually looking at houses. Don was tough to read. He was one part caught up in the excitement and one part all business. He had done big dollar ventures before. More than I could even comprehend.

We ended up having a terrific day. I showed them the two properties (with permission) and then I toured them around the area. Afterwards, I showed them where I grew up, toured them up and down Marine Drive, then took them for lunch at *Troll's Fish & Chips* in Horseshoe Bay, a landmark restaurant with great views of the ferries coming in and out that Mary Lou had such fond memories of. We chatted over coffee and walked around Horseshoe Bay, and then I drove them back downtown to my office where we went over some things.

Finally we had dinner at *The Trattoria* where Marina joined us and the four of us had a fabulous evening of pasta and orange juices. I took them back to the airport when we were done and on the way reviewed how we felt. The day had done nothing but increase their desire to live here, and they both absolutely drooled over the properties and the possibilities of what could be done on it. "I want to offer them like 8.5 mil and be done with it," he said.

To me it seemed overly generous. "Let's not throw money away Don. I think we can get this property *and* not have to fall to their demands too. Will you trust some of my strategies?" I replied. I could see the familiar look of people who desperately didn't want to lose something they really wanted. They looked worried.

I reassured them. "Listen, I think we have some time here and I think we can negotiate and work on the price. I don't think we have to just go in with top dollar. We can play it out a little and still get what we want. I feel good about it."

"Okay Sam," Don said. "We'll trust you on this. Go get us our lots."

And with that, they boarded the Lear Jet for the trip home.

The next day I deliberated with Jim on the entire matter and we both agreed on a strategy. I made a call to the listing agent of the house that was officially on the market and told him I had a prospective buyer and to let me know immediately if there was any legitimate interest in the house from another source.

Then I called Slabin and told him I was instructed to increase the offer to $6,800,000, but that would be the highest it would go. I told him my clients told me they would walk before they went higher. He waited two days and called me back. "The Ford's have requested I go in at 8.3 million. And they have informed me to tell you that they never wanted to sell and will only do so if the price is that high. If not, forget the whole thing, they'll just stay put."

I called him back two days later and said, "Sorry Slabin, the deal's dead. My clients just couldn't justify going so much higher than the real value of the property. They live in San Jose and could move anywhere they want. They are now looking in the Bay area of San Francisco." I could hear the disappointment in his silence and continued, "I know, it's a tough one. I really thought we could bring the two parties together, but it's just done. Sorry to say," and we said goodbye.

Then I waited. This was the hardest part. I was bluffing. And they had been bluffing. And now it was time for someone to either call, fold, or to prove they weren't bluffing. But it wasn't without stress. I knew the Brocks desperately wanted these lots. I knew that with every passing day the house that was on the market could sell to someone else and sink all possibilities. I knew that I could go higher on price, close the deal, and get a bigger commission. The higher the price, the bigger the commission.

But I didn't think anything over $6,500,000 was a fair price. And I could see in the eyes of the Ford's that they wanted this deal and were just trying to get as much out of the Brocks as possible. The risks were tremendous. If the deal fell apart, I would blame myself. But I thought I knew how this was going to go.

I sweated it out for two days before they called back. It was Slabin: "My clients have reconsidered. They felt like maybe *it was* a good time to move on, and they would like to accept the offer of $6.8 million."

I said, "Give me an hour," and hung up.

I sat at my desk for an hour and looked out the window at the mountain, then called back. "Sorry Slabin. My clients were pretty insulted over the 8.3 business. They just got soured over the whole thing. They felt like they had been very generous offering $500,000 over what their neighbours are listing for at six million, and felt like your clients wanting over eight million just showed greed and lacked goodwill. They found a house in the Bay area they like and are negotiating as we speak. But they said if you guys accept the original offer which they feel they delivered with goodwill and a heart of generosity because they absolutely loved the lot, then they would take it. But that they are done negotiating. So 6.5...take it or leave it."

There was a long pause. "Hold the line Sam," and he was gone for several minutes.

When he came back on the line he said, "Okay Sam, they have accepted the offer."

After we hung up I waited a few minutes for my heart to calm down, then called Don. "We got lot number two for 6.5 million Don."

I then had to call the listing agent for the house that was on the market. Twenty four hours later we closed that deal for $5,750,000. Two houses with lots sold for a combined $12,250,000. Commission payable to Jennings & Wyatt: $145,000. And Don and Mary Lou were absolutely ecstatic. It was a tremendous victory surrounded by a one-of-a-kind set of circumstances. And if that were to be the end of it, I would have classified it as my greatest work moment ever. But little did I know, Don and Mary Lou were not done with me yet.

Chapter 49

Marina and I got married in the spring, some six months after meeting and some ten years after I hiked down the mountain. Neither of us was interested in anything overly lavish, but we did want to do justice to the occasion and honour God in the process.

We were married in front of about fifty people, mainly family and some close friends, at the church Marina went to in West Van in the 2800 block of Marine Drive. The pastor was a kindly man named Dean Peters who had led us through some marriage preparation in the weeks leading up to the big day.

From my side my mom came along with a few of her close friends from the neighbourhood, Jim Jennings, my landlady Mrs. Byrnes, Torsi, Minnie, Sulyman the dishwasher-come-line-cook, Gretchen and grumpy Jeff Adams, and a couple of the Christian mentors from along the way. I also invited Amy Harley, the wife of Gordon, the pilot from the plane, as we had stayed loosely connected. She ended up crying harder than anyone else during the wedding service.

It was a remarkable day; the weather was nice, everyone looked so fabulous, people were excited and genuinely happy for the occasion, my mom was an emotional wreck which was fascinating to see, the service was elegant and formal, and my bride was simply the most beautiful sight I had ever seen. But it was more than the magnificence of the day; it was coming before God and participating in this unity that was designed by God.

It was my spirit being joined to Marina's spirit, and the two of us becoming one.

I was so grateful on that day that Marina and I had waited to connect on the highest level, and even though neither of us was raised in the church and neither even knew any of the "rules" we had honoured them as best we could from the time we met. And now that we were brought closer to God, together as one spirit, we could feel His presence and approval of our marriage. Later, when Marina and I were alone, we consummated our relationship to the deepest level and felt the intimacy of God's design.

After the wedding service, we went to a reception at a local banquet hall we rented and had appetizers and did a cake ceremony, got lots of pictures taken, and all the usual stuff. But we had asked our guests to forego giving us gifts and instead asked them to bring food items and money for Street Hope, and we raised over $2000 and got tons of non-perishable foods.

My mom, however, and Marina's parents had collaborated on a gift for us and presented to us a trip for two to Hawaii leaving the very next day. Our original plan had been to go to Vancouver Island for a week, but we readily agreed to change plans! When the reception was over we went to the Four Seasons Hotel in downtown Vancouver and had the rest of the evening to ourselves. In the end it was a fabulous day to mark the start of a lifetime I would spend with Marina.

When a fabulous week in Hawaii was done, we came home and I packed up my things and moved out of Mrs. Byrnes and into Marina's. It was an emotional moment for Mrs. Byrnes and me, as I had spent ten years living in her house. She was into her eighties now and would miss my company and the help I did around the house. But she had good children who were always looking out for her and I promised I would stay in touch.

Moving out had taken me all of about two hours, one of the joys of living in a small space and not being much of a collector of anything, except maybe fishing flies. Marina owned a condo in North Van. It was very nice, had a nice view and was pretty roomy. It would work well for us for the discernible future.

So we settled into married life. We were both active in our careers; Marina liked to decorate and cook and stuff like that in her free time and I liked to fish. But for the both of us, our hearts remained closely tied to Street Hope and we spent quite a bit of time there, together and on our own. Sadly, Street Hope was on a slow downward trend. There were still rumblings about the building being sold, church involvement was erratic and unreliable, volunteers were always cancelling or dropping out, and some of the organizations who supplied food were undependable. It didn't look good for the future of Street Hope.

Chapter 50

$\mathcal{A}$ few months had gone by since the closing dates had arrived and possession of the two houses had become Don's and Mary Lou's and it had been about the same period of time that I had been married when Mary Lou gave me a call.

"We're having a hard time Sam," she started. "For one, we don't know what we're doing!" and she laughed in her easy contagious way. "We're like all this way away from Vancouver, we're trying to figure out zoning for the lots, permits, find architects, builders, general contractors, figure out designs, and find out what the heck all those government regulations on houses and lots mean. I mean, like how do you figure this stuff out? Don has all these high tech 'house concept things' he wants to do, but is always so busy with his work he never gets to them. So I'm left with a bunch of the responsibility and, well, here's the bottom line Sam; we just don't trust anyone out there we've never met, and well, we don't know any house designers here either. So, well, we need you to help us," and she finally took a breath.

I thought about what she was asking me and said, "Mary Lou, hey, I have no doubt that none of that is easy, but you guys are like zillionaires and can afford the very best architects, planners, general contractors and any and/or all of them could guide you along and take care of all the details for you. All you need to do is approve things, basically. I could give you some names of people I know who do work in this area, and they can help you with all of this stuff. But, you know, I would help supply you with names, contacts, or you could run stuff by me any time you want. You know I'm here to help, right?"

"Yeah, Sam. And yeah, I get all that what you are saying. I know we can afford whoever and do this and that, but we don't *want to*. What we *want* is to work with someone we trust, who has a good head on his shoulders, who *gets* us, who will look out for our best interests, and who shares the same vision as us. Not everybody *gets* us, you know Sam."

"Okay, Mary Lou," I responded, "I'm hearing you. But I'm a realtor. Not a builder. I always leave the minute the deal closes. I have no idea what goes on beyond that. Well, maybe I have some ideas, but it's not what I do or anything. Really, I'm sure you and Don could do equally as well as me. We would all be blindly going about it."

"But you're out there Sam. And you know people. And you know West Van. And you know us. And you just said it yourself; you *do* have *some* idea as to how to do it. We're not asking you to *build* the house, or be the contractor, or the architect. We are asking that you be the guy that they all report to. And then you report to us. You'll be like the general contractor to the general contractor," she laughed again and carried on. "*Please* Sam. We need someone out there to be our guy. We need eyes and ears on the ground," and laughed again. "*Pleeeeaaaasse* Sam?!"

Of course she talked me into it. And I spoke more about it later with Don who gave me his version, equally compelling, as to why they wanted me on board. And I talked to Jim about how in the world we bill for something like this, and we both sort of shrugged our shoulders and he said, "Bill them by the hour I guess. I dunno. Or treat it like a hobby and do it off the books. Not sure, really."

So it was all pretty loose and informal, and I really had no idea as to what to do. But I agreed to be the "whatever you want to call it." And I went about looking into zoning for the two lots.

Chapter 51

The house, their house that is, ended up consuming me for the next two years. From the initial zoning and approval issues, site surveys, applications for permits, tear down of the existing houses, to the drawing up of plans for the new house, finding the right architect, and collaborating with the Brocks until a final plan was decided on. From there, it was finding a good general contractor, and dealing with the unlimited number of issues that came up on a daily basis. This house was being built mostly on rock, which included blasting and grading of the slope as part of the design and it also included a new driveway cut through rock. Weather, salt air, terrain, difficult access points, ever changing ideas, strategies, and an endless stream of challenges made for an issue of some sort on a daily basis.

The design was creative, unusual, and challenging to pull off. It involved elevation changes, slopes, rounded corners, and was all designed to utilize the latest in technology of construction materials with an eye towards environmentally friendly and "green" products.

I soon discovered that despite the unconventional system of using a realtor as site manager of a home construction, it was actually wise of the Brocks to have someone who acted as "GM" of the show. It didn't take long for me to realize that general contractors, architects, and designers were all just people as well, susceptible to mistakes, confusion, ignorance of the latest technology, miscommunications, and the like. They all needed someone above them to make final decisions, consult with over the issues of the day, and keep them on track towards achieving the finished product. There also seemed to be something of a universal attitude where the thinking went something along the lines of "Oh well, they're rich so who cares how long it takes or how often we have to redo something..." and I didn't agree with this sort of abuse of money.

The more involved I became the more I embraced it. It was a fascinating project in an area I loved, doing something I had interest in but had never done, with an unlimited budget of someone else's money. I found myself taking it on like a new-found hobby, and went to the site almost every night after my "real" job was done. Marina also became involved, often accompanying me to site visits after hours where we would roam around and brainstorm ideas the Brocks might benefit from. Marina was gifted in design ideas and often it was her suggestions and ideas that the Brocks ended up going with.

It wasn't that Don and Mary Lou weren't involved, because they were. They made all ultimate decisions, gave direction on what they wanted, picked the top people from lists I provided, and gave me instructions on a weekly if not daily basis, and flew out about once a month. But the more involved I got, the more people who came to know me as the boss on site, the longer the project went on, and the more involved I got, the more it seemed people came to me directly with every question.

But it wasn't really the house construction, decision making, curveballs, the massiveness of the project, the uniqueness of the project, or the steady stream of people that became dependant on my involvement that caused me to be as involved as I was. No. It was Don who single handedly created that for me.

Don was a genius. And his mind worked outside the box. And he was one step ahead of everyone. And he was a techie. He wanted everything state of the art or he wanted things not yet even invented. He changed his mind constantly. He discovered new things he wanted, or thought up new ideas he wanted to test out, and I would get a steady stream of phone calls with questions or statements like, "Sam, let's look into thermodynamic heating," or "Sam, what do you think about a heated driveway?" or "Sam, I'm creating a software that will run the entire house, irrigation system, alarm, lighting, heat, generator, hot tub temperature and I need you to find me someone who can wire all the systems for compatibility," or "Sam, we need to consider rainwater runoff tanks to regenerate for irrigation," or "Sam, I'm thinking of tapping into the seawater and sending it through a purification process for fresh water usability," or "Sam, we need to consider I might want to run oversized or multiple servers and we need back up and redundant power sources," or "Sam, I just had this idea for a self sterilizing door handle. Can you hold off on ordering the other ones while I configure it?" or "Sam, what do you think about Star Trek doors and 3D walls? Over the top perhaps?" or "Sam. I've been reading about submersible wharfs. SUBMERSIBLE WHARFS Sam! Think about it!"

Yes, Don was forever increasing my level of involvement to try and keep up with his relentless mind and vision. But he wasn't overbearing, entitled, or difficult. And the combination of Don's eccentric brains and Mary Lou's wholesome charm was magnetic. If anything, what they brought to the table personality wise, just made my involvement all the more fun. Plus I got to learn about things like submersible wharfs. Stuff like that just brings out the boy in me.

Things really started to bog down once the detail work on the inside commenced. There were decisions on moldings, hardwood, tile, fixtures, windows, paint colors, decking, and just about every other item going into the house. Marina was very helpful during this part of the process. Coming around the final stretch were decisions on appliances, countertops, landscaping, outdoor lighting, railings, and finally, furniture, art, and the like.

Finally, it was done. Or at least move-in ready. And if I do say so myself, the house was a masterpiece. Don and Mary Lou may have had buckets of money, but they weren't the kind of people to have, say, gold shower curtains. They wanted quality products in the latest technological advances to complement their earthy, simple tastes. While extravagant, nothing was gaudy. While big, there were plenty bigger. They took the natural surroundings and complimented them. The house was fluid with the rock, the slope and the ocean.

The driveway wound down a private, forested path to a courtyard that could park eight cars with a pond beside it separating trees from the cement. The house was 6300 square feet over two floors, a main level with the courtyard and a lower level that had a massive computer area for Don, panoramic views, and had a wing that came within a stone's throw of the ocean. But it was the great room that you came immediately into from the massive front door that was the crown jewel. It had an eighteen foot ceiling with huge wooden beams crisscrossing the top and a rounded roof giving the impression you were staring up into the inside of a hull of a wooden ship. With recessed lighting, an enormous rock fireplace with rich dark hardwood and floor to ceiling windows that gave immediate panoramic ocean views, the room gave the impression of being warm, rustic, and comfortable. It was an absolutely stunning room. From room to room, the house was immaculately designed, beautifully furnished, had cutting edge features, high tech gadgets, and amazing views from every angle. The outside was landscaped to compliment the rock bluffs and trees that were natural to the property and would take minimal maintenance. They had paths to the ocean, paths to outdoor vantage points, and sitting areas with benches at three different parts of the property showing different views from each.

And yes, they had a submersible wharf – a submersible wharf I had better be allowed to fish off of!

It had only been a few weeks since they last saw the house, but even then there were crews all over the place busy with last minute details. So the move in day was the first time they saw the house in its completed form and empty of people. Marina and I went with them that day but waited outside so they could go in through the front door on their own. They came out about half an hour later. Mary Lou was crying tears of joy and immediately fell into Marina's arms. Don did this dorky and incredibly awkward sort of two step dance of joy. Then all of us went inside and walked through the house and marveled at the fact it was ready to move in. Then we had a toast of sparking apple juice over the kitchen bar. And it was one of the best days ever.

Don asked to see me about two weeks later after they had been back to San Jose and moved out of their rental completely. He said he wanted to come by my office with Mary Lou later that day. After they both sat down at my desk, Don started talking.

"I've developed a new software Sam."

"Why do I not find that surprising Don," I replied, smiling.

"You might find it surprising that it's about you," he said. And Mary piped in, "Yeah Sam, you got your own software. What do you think about that?" and she laughed.

"Uh, I'm not sure what I should be thinking," I said.

"Actually, interestingly enough," Don carried on, "is the fact that I came up with the concept because of the way you were billing me for the time you spent working on our house construction. While you invoiced for your time, it seemed to me as if you didn't really bill to the extent of what you invested." He sat back in his chair a little. "Does that make sense to you?"

"Well, I just sort of billed by the hour as I didn't know how else to do it, and yeah, maybe I wasn't all that concerned about nailing it down to the minute or anything," I responded. The truth was I had no idea how to bill, so just sent some lame invoices once in a while with guestimates of what I thought might have been appropriate, but essentially, I almost treated the work like a hobby.

"It got me thinking," he carried on, "about, well, the worth of a job. So I created software that would factor in all relevant data and come up with a method of putting a value on work done. For instance I would come up with input criteria: What was the job being done? Was it being done well? How long did it take? What was the skill level of the person doing it? What was the importance of the task to the employer? What was the level of trust involved? Were there savings created as a result of the employee's diligence? What was the emotional value of the job done? Was the end result satisfactory? Did the employee uphold moral and ethical responsibilities? How much money was at stake? How much was the employer freed up to do his own business? And I would input all this relevant data which would be cross referenced against the employee profile and it would spit out a figure – a figure of actual work for the specific job done. I found it an interesting concept to compare against, say an hourly wage, or a pre-determined figure. And you know what Sam?"

"What?"

"The figure that the software came up with showed that you undercharged for your services. By quite a lot actually."

"Well, better than over charging, I guess," I said.

"Sam," Mary Lou cut in, "What Don is trying to tell you, in his own 'software' sort of way, is that we feel tremendously grateful to you for helping us wind up with the house and property of our dreams. We simply couldn't have done it without you, and we know you barely charged us anything for all that time you and Marina put in." She leaned over to Don and pulled an envelope out of his breast pocket. "And we want you to have this bonus in appreciation for what you have done. Oh Sam, we just love you so much so please just accept this and know how much we appreciate you." And she placed the envelope on the desk and slid it over to me.

"I'm doing away with the software Sam," Don said. "Damn thing wanted to give away all my money. Way better for me to try and get away with underpaying," and he laughed hard at his own joke. "Seriously Sam, thanks for everything. Don't be a stranger, okay?"

It had been an uncomfortable moment for me. I didn't want to accept anything from them, but could see that it was important to them and that they had gone to a lot of effort to make sure they gave it to me. So I had gracefully accepted the envelope but didn't look at it until they had gone. Once alone, I opened it up and took a look. The amount on the cheque was $547,000 made out to me personally. Over a half million dollars. I felt a little sick to my stomach. Sort of like when I used to get on a ride at the PNE that I found scarier than I let on.

I thought about things long and hard. It all seemed too surreal to me to comprehend. The successes were too great, the dollars more than I could wrap my head around, the ascent up from nothing to where I currently was hard to accept as reality. I put the cheque in a drawer. I couldn't even look at it. It was too distracting and I didn't know what to do. I needed to get back to basics so I could process correctly. I swung my chair so I could see out the window. I just stared for a while, lost in thought, and then, as what usually happened when I looked out my window I lifted my eyes to the mountain and prayed to God.

"Lord, you are the King of Kings. I owe my life to you and give you credit for all things. Without You, I would have nothing and I know that. I know that beyond any shadow of doubt. I deserve no credit. Lord Jesus, it all belongs to You."

At first I felt like I was just starting to drift into a daydream as my thoughts seemed to shift. Then a familiar feeling washed over me. One so great and with such enormity on every level that I knew without any doubt whatsoever I was now in the presence of God. My soul was channeled to Him, the light of my being lit by God himself. I had not felt this since the last night on the mountain, and it was so obvious and so magnificent that it could not be mistaken or misinterpreted.

For the second time in my life God spoke to me. I became engulfed in His almighty Glory. His closeness enveloped me and the majesty was beyond description. Visions came and went, flashes of brilliance, and unspeakable glory. While there were snapshots of images, pictures in my mind, and a clear vision, only one word seemed to come through: **NOW!**

PART FOUR

BACK

"So Christ himself gave the apostles, the prophets, the evangelists, the pastors and teachers, to equip his people for works of service, so that the body of Christ may be built up..."

Chapter 52

*S*tanly Wu was a slumlord. I knew all about him because I hired an investigator to check into him. He owned four of the worst hotels in the Lower Mainland, all of them of the skid row variety, and had garnered a reputation as a ruthless and uncaring landlord. He would continually be up on tenancy complaints, have hearings with the Tenancy Board, and was accused of many things from double renting rooms, charging cash that was never claimed as income, not keeping his units to any kind of standard, and to general abuse of tenants. On top of that he seemed to be at least loosely affiliated with the Asian underworld and either participated in, or ran illegal gambling rooms in the alleys of Chinatown. Stanley Wu, it seemed, was not a nice man.

He was also a man who was heavily in debt. Perhaps it was the gambling. Or perhaps he spent so much time dodging tenant complaints he rarely had time to run his businesses. But he had leans against properties, was in foreclosure on a home he owned, had significant credit card debt, and more than likely, he had some "personal loans" among the unsavory of the Chinese underworld.

But it wasn't Stanly Wu personally that I was interested in. I was interested in the fact that one of the hotels he owned was none other than The Sunshine Hotel, and it was my intention to buy it from him. I called him and told him I had a prospective buyer for one of his hotels, specifically, The Sunshine Hotel. His response was similar to the West Van clients I had dealt with in the past with cold calls and offers to buy their homes: wary, suspicious, and guardedly interested. Only, the responses from Wu were a lot rougher around the edges and laden with expletives. I had experience as a low end realtor, high end realty, but this was to be my first entry into skid row realty. But the way I figured it, his greed and debt would put me in a position to negotiate hard, and that was what I did.

I baited him along with long gaps between communications, let him believe I had abandoned the negotiations altogether on two occasions but made sure I stayed clear of offending his "face." I knew enough of Chinese culture from West Van buyers to know if I somehow embarrassed him he would not go through with any deal.

There was miles between my offer and what he wanted. He seemed to be relying on the fact that seeing as how I called him, it must mean I would pay anything for the building. Of course he was correct in thinking he *was* in the negotiating driver's seat, because I *did* only want that building and *he* was the one who owned it.

But the more I let him believe I would walk away, the more I showed him how disinterested I was, and the more I allowed him to think his building was only one of many "my client" was interested in, the more I turned the tables into him believing it was "my client" who was in the driver's seat.

In the end I waited a full two weeks between communications. When I finally did call him I said to him, "Listen, my client represents an enormous corporation and they aren't fools. Between you and me, they know all about your cash problems, the people you owe money to, the house you have in foreclosure, the legal problems you are facing, and even your marriage problems. And they know all about this hotel of yours and where it's located. Sure, you could try to convince some people to believe the value is in the land, but not my clients who know all about city planning, neighborhood enhancement plans, future zoning changes, future transit routes, and everything else about the area around your hotel. And hear this: your hotel is on skid row. It will always be on skid row and new business, commercial, or residential growth will never hit this area. Sure, if this was four blocks west, or even six blocks east, but it isn't and nothing will ever change.

"Add to that the fact that the government is at a loss on how to handle the poor, have implemented standards for low income rooming houses, and you're going to be looking at a forced renovation that will suck any remaining resources you might have dry. And you know why? Because your place is a dump, that's why. And rodent and pest control alone will break you not to mention things like, oh I don't know, proper running water? Toilets that flush maybe?"

I paused and he said nothing. And I continued for the kill: "My client will make you a final offer and your choice is to accept it or forget it. But they want you to be very clear on one thing here: they will not go another round of negotiations. This is it. End game. Final deal. You have twenty-four hours to accept it. It would seem, Mr Wu, that you would have little choice but to play nice from here on lest you risk complete financial collapse. The final offer is 1.1 million dollars. Take it or leave it."

"But that's under your last offer," he immediately said.

"Twenty-four hours Mr. Wu. The talk is done."

And twenty-four hours later, almost to the minute, he called back and accepted the offer. I had formed a holding company called Crown Mt. Ltd. at the time I became a partner in Jennings and Wyatt Realty, and it was my holding company that bought the hotel. Wu signed the final documents in my office never knowing it was me who bought it from him. At the end of the day, you could see the relief on his face at closing the deal. He may have thought it was worth more, but he was going to be out of the financial hole soon. Unless of course, he decided to go gambling instead of paying off his debt.

As for me, I was now the proud owner of a glorious skid row hotel, the very same hotel I had at one time jumped out the window of while being shot at by drug dealers.

Chapter 53

innie and I sat in my car on the opposite side of Oppenheimer Park and looked at the hotel I would soon take possession of. We both had Vente Starbucks coffees and were chatting about the hotel and our connection to it. We talked about that day and how it had changed both of our lives. Our stories varied on the events to some degree but the essence remained the same. We talked about the power the drugs had over us and how difficult it was to do anything about it while we slid further and further down the drain.

Minnie had gone on to become a certified trauma counselor with a little help in tuition from me, and she had grown into a woman of tremendous insight with a heart for helping the poor. While much of my time had been spent amongst the richest of the rich in West Van, she had never gone far from the street and currently worked as a counselor in a woman's drop-in clinic three blocks to our west, very near the corner of Main and Hastings, in the heart of the war zone.

Every few minutes Minnie would say something like, "I can't believe you actually bought that hotel." It was news she just couldn't seem to wrap her head around. And I had to agree with her. I was having a hard time grasping it myself.

"And what exactly were God's instructions to you?" she said.

And so I told her. I told her that it wasn't so much what He said, over what He showed me through visions, pictures, and just, sort of planting stuff inside my head. I told her it wasn't easy to explain and that I had certainly doubted myself over the years. The vision God had given me was that I was going to transform the Sunshine Hotel into a place of refuge for the poor; feed them, teach them, lead them to Christ, love them, and help them advance in their lives. He showed me that I would be the owner of the hotel and that I would gut it completely and renovate it into the shining star of Oppenheimer Park, that it would be the first piece of a puzzle to change the entire block surrounding the Park into a park that glorifies Jesus, that the poor will come for salvation, that people will rise up to their callings, that businesses around the park will join in, that the park will be filled with joy, that miracles will happen, and God will be praised for His glorious work. And I told her that it was twelve years ago that God spoke to me about my calling, when I was broke and living out of an airplane on top of a mountain. And that I had found the vision completely unrealistic for years until I started bringing in huge commissions from the West Van realty and learned about acquisitions, loans, and corporate structures. Piece by piece it seemed to come together over an impossibly long period of time.

"So, when God said 'NOW,' you just jumped on it? Just like that?" she asked.

"To be honest Minnie, when I got that cheque from the Brocks all I could think about was a new house for Marina and me, a luxury vacation, the latest Audi, and how far that money would go towards investing towards retirement. And even when God spoke to me I wanted to doubt it. I tried to talk myself out of believing. I tried to look at things as a 'realist,' but in the end I just couldn't."

"What changed?" she asked.

I told her nothing had changed. I took my coffee cup and help it up in the air and waved it in front of me.

"Minnie, you and I used to live out there with those people. We were the walking dead. Dead on every level. Bankrupt across the board. And yet, here we are sipping Starbucks and sitting in an Audi. And for both of us, we owe all of it to God. We know this for a fact. Both of our lives changed on the same day. God got me up a mountain and down the other side. He restored me to health, reconciled my relationships, forgave me of my sins of which there were too many to count, and above all, He sent His Son to die for us on the cross.

"And while I might forget that. While I might make some major mistakes along the way, take my will back at the first sniff of trouble, I know in my heart He saved me. And I believe if He could save us, of all people, then we should believe all of it. We need to act in faith. And as hard as that might be, the right thing to do is to do it."

Minnie wanted to know what was next. I told her once we take over the hotel on the closing date, we would renovate it. And then find a way somehow to start up programs, find supporters, find people to help. I told her that I found a way between my own cash and the bank to come up with enough to purchase the building and do the renovation. After that, I had no idea how it was going to support itself. And I admitted I was pretty scared about the whole thing right across the board.

"At worst, I'll own a nice piece of property in a good area," I said and smiled meekly.

"It's different down here now isn't it Sam?" Minnie said while staring out across the park. And it was. Just as Minnie and I had both changed, so did the makeup of skid row. It had become worse. There were more people in worse shape. The homeless population seemed to have grown tenfold. One might think there was something of a demonstration going on, or a march based on the amount of people on the sidewalks, but there wasn't. It was just the way it was now. Groups of thugs, prostitutes, the disabled, the mentally challenged, the beggars, and the poorest of the poor all over the place, as if lined up for an enormous bus to come and take them away.

The drugs had changed too. While crack cocaine and heroin were still the powerhouses, there was now crystal meth which was made up of all kinds of toxic materials and was making people exhibit unpredictable and violent behaviour. And there were other "homemade" drugs I knew very little about, like Ecstasy, GHB, and others with names I didn't even know. And there were people of all ages. Way more kids on the street now. Practically children. And old people too who should have been cared for. The problem seemed to be epidemic and was rippling through other communities as well. While it was always concentrated in the Lower East Side (Hastings) in the past, there were now people begging for money on street corners throughout the city, and into the suburbs. Every community seemed to have a homeless problem, drug problems, and gang problems.

We both stared ahead. We looked at the park, people watched, looked at the hotel, talked about possibilities and our histories, but had lots of periods of silence, each of us lost in ourselves and what had happened to us on those streets.

After one such long period of silence, Minnie looked over at me and said, "I want to be involved Sam. I believe in God and I believe this vision and I believe in your calling, and I want to be a part of it. I want to be a part of it in a big way," and she smiled and radiated life, and hope, and Jesus. And I gave her a hug and thanked her.

A minute later she followed it up with, "But I hear things about the street Sam, because I never really left it. And I heard things about The Sunshine Hotel, and they aren't good."

Chapter 54

*M*innie told me that of all the skid row hotels, The Sunshine had become the worst of the worst as far as active drug dealing was concerned. There appeared to be major drug dealing done out of the hotel and all the street dealing funneled through some sort of distribution network in the hotel. Not many rooms in that hotel even had tenants anymore. It was really just a very large multi room crack shack and distribution site. Minnie told me the violence on the street now was way beyond anything we knew about, even with us actually getting shot at. She went on to tell me that the violence was incomparable to what we experienced. People were literally getting thrown off the top of buildings over $20 debts that weren't paid. Gangs were popping up all over, all needing to come off as stronger than the next, all needing to violently protect their territories, uphold their names, or muscle others out of the way. Guns were becoming more commonplace and gang members being cut down in a hail of bullets was a news story everyone was becoming familiar with hearing. Hastings might be poor, but it was a lucrative drug trade.

"I'm not sure how it's going to go over trying to throw those people out Sam," she said. "I mean, there's the law that most people abide by, and then there are these people. They could make your life miserable in a hurry."

I looked at Minnie for a long time. I was no hero in those types of situations and truth be told what she was saying was making me nervous. But I hung onto the notion that, by law, I owned that hotel, and could do with it what I wanted. And if I wanted to gut it, well what could anyone do? They would have to move their operations elsewhere.

"Hopefully they take it well," was about the only thing I could think of to say.

Chapter 55

The closing date came and went, permits were granted, a design was approved and tenants were given proper notification to move out. The business side of things went relatively smoothly, or as smoothly as any project that needed permits and approvals went. The problem was on the "street" side of things. I had made several trips on site by this point on my own or with contractors, designers, foundation specialists, and friends. Minnie was right that there was a strong drug presence in and around the site and there was a clear turf issue with them surrounding me taking over the building.

Even murderous gangsters couldn't stop the wheels of progress though and they didn't even attempt to "not" move out. Although some of the druggies were just too wasted to make it happen and were found getting high right until the final eviction. But the dealers weren't about to let it all go without letting me know their displeasure. They would posture about on the street and stare blatantly at me every time I visited. It was unnerving as I knew how very bad these guys could be, but at the same time I felt like they would eventually just move their operation somewhere else and forget about what I was doing.

There was one guy who looked to me like he was pretty messed up on drugs but associated with dealing as well. He wouldn't have any "status" in the gang, as bona fide gangsters would not be allowed to do hard drugs, and probably worked in the middle of the drug dealing somehow, perhaps bringing cash from the street to the hotel, but who knew? One thing about him was that he was super aggressive and very visible. I knew the type. Nobody liked a guy like that, but most were too afraid to tell him where to go. He would strut about with his shirt off; tattoos covered his arms and neck, waving his shirt at people, telling people he was going to kick the crap out of them at every injustice he determined which was a very low tolerance. And he would come right up into my face every time he saw me. "Oh yeah, here comes the Jesus freak," he would say, or, "You think you can make a difference down here, jerk? You think you know the street?" he would yell at me. "You don't know squat! We gonna sell our dope right inside your drop-in and you wouldn't be able to do a thing about it!"

The word was out that I was going to open a drop-in centre but he had no idea of my own personal history. I remember Hastings having one of these guys on just about every block. Always intimidating people, using fear for everything, being overly loud and obnoxious, always demonstrative with aggressive violent gestures, wildly unpredictable, and sure to rip off every customer in one way or another.

His aggression and intimidation against me personally seemed to elevate to an irrational level. Really, there was very little reason to do anything he was doing. Nobody down here was opposed to a drop-in centre that gave them all free perks. Hell, they were *for* it, not against it. The only point the heavies needed to establish was that this was *their* street and, moves aside, drugs were going to continue to be sold. So nobody else was "backing" this guy, but at the same time they weren't stopping him either. He represented "their" side, while I represented the white collar types, the people that had "everything."

The situation continued to escalate. He would go far out of his way to look for me coming. Would deliberately block my path so I would have to go around him, or would make sure his shoulder hit mine as he walked past. "Sorry about that," he would say. Then a second later, "Not!" The guy was hilarious.

On the day before the renovation was to start I was down at the site with Minnie and Marina as I got a call saying the last tenant was so drugged out they weren't leaving. It ended up being a non-issue as when we arrived she had migrated from the room to the sidewalk with all her belongings: two green garbage bags full of clothes and a lamp. But she was wasted out of her gourd and was ranting about the injustice and "*discreeemination.*"

The bad ass jerk guy used the opportunity to rally up the crowd against me. "It's that guy there who did this!" he yelled and continued, "Yeah this homo comes down here all up in his nice car and fancy clothes and thinks he's a gonna help *us* find the Lord almighty! Like he knows what the hell we's going through on THE STREET!"

It wasn't like he was rallying a riot against me. Nobody was necessarily joining him. But he was overly loud and aggressive and people were starting to sense something was going to happen. Marina sensed it too and started to back up whispering to me, "C'mon Sam, let's maybe get out of here," and even Minnie was looking like she was a bit worried.

But I went in another direction. I was tired of this guy loud mouthing his lies all over the place and I felt an easy calm of bravery. I walked right up to him and stopped right in front of his face and said calmly, "The Lord almighty brought me from this same street and set me free. And he can do the same for you if that is what you choose, but hear me now: you are either for us or against us as my God will no longer listen to your lies." And I turned around and walked back to Marina and Minnie. "Let's go," I said.

The three of us started walking back to my car which was parked on the north/south facing street beside the park. So we cut through the corner of the park. The entire walk the guy was screaming at me as if what I said set him off and he became completely unglued. There was no logic any more to his anger. It was like he was possessed. "You know the street? You know nothing about the street. You think you know me? I'll mess you up bro.

I'll eat you for lunch bro. I'll kick your Jesus' ass right across this street and smoke his ashes in my pipe. You think you know us bro? You think we want to be saved by your God. We *are* hell bro. We *are* the devil bro."

And he just went on and on not stopping for a second. When we got back to the car I "beeped" the doors to the unlocked position and opened the passenger door for Marina while Minnie got in the back from the same side. When I knew they were both in the car safely I said quietly to Marina, "I'll be back in a minute. Keep the door locked," and I closed the door on her before she could respond.

I immediately went to the trunk, opened it from my keychain, and dug under the carpet until I found the tire iron. I gripped it in my right hand from the top and started walking back towards the hotel and the commotion. The tire iron was steady against my leg as I walked. Not obvious, but not hidden either. And I walked slowly and deliberately in the direction of the guy who was yelling.

Badass came out from the sidewalk still ranting. He leaned back against a car that was parked along the street and spread his arms wide and looked back at all his cohorts on the street. "Well looky here. Looky who's coming back." Then he crossed his arms all confident and leaned back against the car waiting for me with non-stop yapping about how he was Satan himself.

I crossed over the corner of the park and was now maybe forty steps away from him, diagonally on the other side of the street. I yelled to anyone who could hear as loud as I could, "WHO IS THIS GUY THAT HE SHOULD DEFY THE ARMIES OF THE LIVING GOD?"

I started to cross the street in a diagonal fashion, heading right at him. When I was about halfway across, things started to slow down in my mind, and my "spiritual eyes" of the unseen were opened to their widest. I could see both the evil in front of me and feel the presence of the Lord's armies looking down on me and I was walking right in the middle of both. Eight steps from him and I was watching his mouth yapping but no longer heard words. I vaguely wondered why he wasn't preparing himself to fight. Why wasn't he standing up straight and taking the initiative? Why wasn't he rushing out aggressively to meet me? That's what street fighters did; they met the fight head on without fear. Never show fear on the street. Always throw the first punch. But he just continued to lean back as if confident I would do nothing or was somehow just frozen to the moment.

Four steps from him I brought the tire iron back to full extension, went two more steps, then planted my left foot, dragged my right foot and drove the tire iron forward with full extension and torque like a sidearm pitcher at the point of releasing the ball. I swung it as hard as I could, with him, unbelievably, still not having moved a muscle and connected with the full force of the tire iron onto the left side of his jaw. The connection happened in slow motion and it looked like the lower part of his jaw moved to his right about six inches while the top of his jaw remained still. I could see blood spatter and teeth flying through the air. If his jaw wasn't broken I would have been amazed. I could see the flicker of his eyes in the nano-second before impact and I could see fear and surprise as if he just couldn't comprehend what was happening.

His head snapped back into place and the backward momentum made him fall off the side of the car onto the ground. He ended up falling almost straight back in front of the car with his head resting right beside the curb.

I was now acting completely on instinct. I had no idea what I was doing but I took two quick steps forward and stepped on his neck. With one foot on his neck and the other planted beside it I pinned him to the ground even though he was barely conscious. I must have looked like Tarzan after he defeated a lion. I took the tire iron and raised it to the sky and screamed to all the onlookers:

"I TELL YOU PEOPLE, IN THIS PARK HE WILL BUILD HIS CHURCH, AND THE GATES OF HELL," and I pointed the tire iron down towards his face on the ground, "WILL NOT OVERCOME IT."

I dropped the tire iron beside his head, squished his face into the road with my heel as I turned around and slowly walked back to the car. When I got back into my car I just started it up and drove away as both Marina and Minnie did nothing but stare at me with their mouths open and eyes wide.

Chapter 56

*T*he very next day I was standing in the driveway of a $22,000,000, 12,000 square foot home in the British Properties area of West Van, waiting on a Chinese billionaire and his wife to show it. It was impossible not to acknowledge the cultural and environmental differences between what I saw last night that was not a thirty minute drive away.

While I was contemplating that, I got the call from the contractor I had hired that they had arrived on site and that the renovation had commenced. To know we were finally breaking ground was exciting news and I couldn't wait to get back to the "street" to see the day's progress later on.

The renovation ended up being a monumental task. The building was old and structurally weak. I had the bottom two floors gutted completely with every wall taken out and replaced by supporting structural beams. The end result was one open large room with a nine foot ceiling with the floor even with the street. The upper two floors we modified into four modest apartments per floor. We built two new staircases up to the apartments, one on each side of the main room. Each apartment was self contained with a small kitchen, a single bedroom, and a small living room. I also had designed a charming little rooftop garden and sitting area. It wasn't an expensive add on, but it had fantastic mountain views and would become a peaceful retreat.

In the main room, we put in a commercial kitchen and dishwasher area and broke the space down into one main gathering room with tables set up for meals, and then three smaller rooms, of which two would be offices and one would be midsized for uses to be determined later.

The renovation itself took six months with the structural issues taking the most time and expense. I watched my budget dwindle down at a furious rate and found it very stressful at every roadblock along the way. But in the end, after a six month full on renovation which completely gutted the inside and made over the exterior, we had a finished product.

In the meantime, Street Hope had continued to suffer from problems and was in trouble of shutting down completely. I had been in constant talks with the leaders and, collectively, we thought the best thing would be to move Street Hope to my building and continue it there. It seemed to be a win-win scenario and we all decided the name Street Hope would be used as the name of my building and that The Sunshine Hotel was erased completely.

The time period during the construction and as we entered into our first months of being open was also used towards brainstorming ideas and getting people involved in different capacities. For the principle players, every single one of them came to me and volunteered themselves.

Torsi not only designed the kitchen (he let me design the dish pit) but he volunteered to have his company of restaurants supply *all* the food for the first year. He organized a delivery system whereas all of his restaurants would donate their day old food/bread and leftovers to Street Hope and any other food needed that wasn't being donated from elsewhere would be paid for by Torsi.

Gretchen Adams became instrumental towards organizing and coordinating and she asked for one of the offices to be designated solely towards working with female youths from the street. She even got her cranky husband Jeff to have his law firm sponsor her "department" $1000 a month towards expenses to be used as Gretchen and I decided.

Amy Harley, widow of Gordon Harley the pilot, asked that the estate of her late husband be allowed to contribute all the furnishings for the apartments upstairs, a task she embraced herself and tastefully designed each apartment with quality second hand furniture and kitchen items. I asked her if we could dedicate one of the main floor rooms to Gordon. We could put a picture of him on the wall with a caption that read: *Gordon Harley: husband, father, pilot, and lover of the Word of God. A man whose dedication to the Word was the seed that grew into this place.* Amy was very touched and thrilled with the idea. Later she would become a constant supporter and contributor.

Jim Jennings suggested we have our realty firm donate regularly to Street Hope as a tax write off. He had made a successful turn away from working too much to be a better father and had become something of an advocate for children with autism together with his wife. Collectively, we decided to dedicate the second largest room towards helping families with autistic children, fetal alcoholism, or kids with difficulties, of which there were many, and that Jim's wife would become a leader.

Don and Mary Lou went completely off the charts and pledged to support Street Hope to the tune of $10,000 a month. Don's company had turned production of video games into a billion dollar corporation and his concept for the newly developed phenomena of social media sent his personal worth into the stratosphere. With both of them having come from Christian families, they both respected the fact I had taken their bonus money and put all of it towards this venture. In fact, they seemed to be going through something of a change themselves with the experience of going from smallish town high school sweethearts to billionaire young adults, and they desired to help the poor and be involved.

The money from Don and Mary Lou allowed me to hire two people on full time staff. One was Minnie who headed up the care aspects, did one-on-one and group counseling, and about a thousand other things. The other full time worker was a cook who managed the kitchen and doubled as building manager. While the former Street Hope did breakfast and lunch, we were only going to do breakfast. There were enough organizations doing food in the area and we knew nobody was going to starve. We wanted our focus to be on helping people with greater needs and we wanted to attempt to help people get from being stuck on the street into new lives.

And that was essentially what the apartments would be for. We left them empty at the start, confident that the use for them would become evident along the way. But the design was not so much low income apartments for just anyone, but to be able to offer temporary housing to a few select people we deemed needing it with the vision that we could work with the people towards helping them transition away from poverty and Hastings altogether. So we would be looking for people who were "stuck" on the street but had a heart for change as well as potential for change. If the apartments were full, we would charge a fair rent that could be paid through the welfare system, giving us another source of income. Minnie and I had many discussions about the apartments, and both of us were convinced that the next leaders of our ministry, the people to whom the torches will be passed to, will come out these apartments. Both of our journeys from destituteness to leadership also started from these same 'rooms' and we felt God had the same plan for others.

The former Street Hope was still connected to many churches in the community and still had a number of interested volunteers. Many of these churches and individuals went through a rejuvenation of sorts at the new life and location of Street Hope and there was tremendous interest in helping out. If there were issues, it was because too many people wanted to be involved and not too few.

As for myself and Marina, we both kept our day jobs and spent as much time as possible at Street Hope. I cut back on my work responsibilities and donated as much time as I could. I had a heart for the addicts, especially the ones who showed desire for change, and spent many hours trying to help them navigate themselves into sustained sobriety. But I was sort of CEO of the entire operation and rarely a day went by without being there. Marina had a passion for food, so she was often in the kitchen creating and showing young women how to cook. It was a busy season for both of us as the renovation was taxing on many levels and the first months of being open took a lot of settling in.

Chapter 57

The first six months of Street Hope were full of new beginnings, figuring things out, incorporating systems and schedules, putting out fires, and figuring out rules. Every day something would come up and there were constant variables in play, not only with a new building to look after, but the never ending barrage of issues that came in through the door. One day we would have to figure out how to deal with people who were too high on drugs to be able to stay, the next day would be a mental health issue, or we would learn we couldn't leave the sugar out because people would fill their pockets. There was no end.

But it was a joyous time full of people wanting to help and wanting to be a part of it. There was no trouble from the street, gangs, or dealers. Once we settled in, there seemed to be an unwritten rule that we were there to help so the dealers just set up somewhere else.

The building was a beacon around the park. With its recent renovation and fresh exterior it looked new and vibrant and its physical presence alone changed the overall look of the park. The design had made it so the main room was even with the sidewalk, and we put in lots of windows, so for anyone walking down the street it was easy to look in and see the buzz of helping hands and grateful people.

The concept ideas were coming to fruition. Gretchen was so passionate about working with young woman that they would just gravitate towards her. She primarily just listened to them, helped them with coping skills, supported them and showed them the love so many did not have. Minnie and Gretchen collaborated on a support group that met three times a week that was facilitated by Minnie and great things were happening. It was one of these young women who would become our first tenant upstairs, a nineteen year old woman alone in life and a foster care runaway from the age of thirteen, but bright, full of promise, and was eager for change. Even after only two months into her living upstairs, we were well on our way towards getting her enrolled in high school equivalency with ideas towards careers.

By the time we were four months in, we had six of the eight apartments filled. Three of them were young women with similar stories to the first one. Another was a young Honduran man who came to Canada with hopes of legitimate employment but struggled so much he fell into the Honduran drug dealing community on Hastings. He had such a heart for God and just couldn't live that way and he came to me directly with pleading in his eyes. I moved him in the next day. This was a young man who seemed to have tremendous potential.

Another apartment was a mother with two children who were living in an apartment complex that was full of prostitutes and drugs but she was too poor to move. We thought she was a good prospect to get employment and better her life.

The other main room also morphed into what the original idea was, and that was dedicated to children and children with special needs. Jim Jennings wife Macy became more and more involved and would bring her autistic son with her who was now older and had adapted nicely to living with his condition. He was good with the younger children and beamed with delight every time he came in.

With every passing week it seemed our "specialty" was becoming women and children. The young women would gravitate towards Gretchen and would get counsel from Minnie who not only was a talented counselor but had also "been there, done that." Often these women would have children and often these children would have issues. So the kids would go to the kids' room and spend time with Macy Jennings and her son, and the mother's would simultaneously go to another room and spend time with Gretchen. Minnie would go from room to room and spend time with individuals and she also ran her various groups.

The main room, of course served the breakfast which was always well attended. We always did it up as well as we could, with relatively fresh bread, hot breakfasts with all food compliments of Torsi and cooked up on our commercial equipment. After breakfast stopped, in mid morning, the main room would become something of a gathering place where people would come for coffee, sit and talk, or get out of the elements of weather or street life for a reprieve. There were always people there. And this is where the volunteers from the various churches spent their time, helping keeping the place clean and organized but mostly just sitting and talking with all the people. Rarely a day went by when someone didn't let their guard down and let their emotions show. Street life was rough and I knew this first hand, but we were all vulnerable to our emotional well being and when in places of safety you would see the people behind the facades. People would come in for coffee, start talking to a church member who might pray over them, and next thing you knew some big tough guy was crying and would accept prayer and receive Jesus.

It was in the main room during these times that I would enjoy the most. There were those on the street who had no desire for change, people so ingrained in their lifestyles, so limited in their thinking, and so closed towards change that it was hard to imagine any other life than what they were living. And I wasn't terribly interested in them beyond making sure we could offer a hot meal and a warm room for an hour or two. But there were those who came in that had fallen to this place and were trapped, unable to get out. People that arrived here the same way I did all those years ago. And I could usually spot them. There was a part of them that looked like they didn't belong. They hung their heads low, they looked sad and lost, and they looked like they never wanted to leave the room because they really had nowhere to go. But at the same time they looked anxious. And I knew what the anxiety was all about. It was all about drugs. Hooked beyond measure. Hopelessly addicted. Just the notion of, by some miracle, being able to find "just one more" good high, enough to keep them living on the streets without any hope whatsoever. And it was these young men I wanted to speak with. I would sit and talk with them, share parts of my story that I thought they were ready to hear, and try to offer hope. I would listen to their stories and do what I could to help.

If there was desire for change, we would make sure we took advantage of those situations by having developed relationships with Christian recovery houses like the Joshua House, or drug and alcohol treatment centers, and would try to get these men or woman who were ready to accept help transitioned towards help before the moment passed. It would be a great day when someone who came in for a coffee, would find himself picked up a few hours later by a recovery centre willing to take him away to start a program with just the clothes on his back. I would call Richard from the Joshua House and say, "I got one who is ready right now," and he would say, "I'll be right there to pick him up." Both of us understood that the "window of willingness" of an addict to get help is often very small and if we could get someone to check in somewhere immediately, it might be the difference between a new beginning of life or a tragic death on the street.

On occasion I would put one in a room upstairs while trying to prepare a placement for them. And I would get burned on occasion. They would skip out in the night, lie to me, use in the rooms, steal something they thought they could sell for drugs, or whatever. But it was nothing I didn't expect or think I would have been capable of doing myself in the heart of my own addiction. So it didn't deter me. It just made me remember what a powerful creature addiction was and how much I wanted to find one of these young men and be a part of their restoration towards sanity and their own personal callings.

As a general rule we shut down at 2:00 pm with some exceptions to groups that Minnie ran. The apartments upstairs had their own access doors so they weren't dependant on Street Hope itself to be open.

A few months in, when things were running relatively smoothly we decided to do a grand opening in the middle of the park. It was a decent day and we moved all the tables into the park and catered a lunch. It was a nice late spring day and the weather cooperated. Torsi insisted on taking care of the menu and preparation. He had done food shows before and had a mobile restaurant setup which he brought to the park as well as enough food to serve a hundred people. He organized an amazing spread of pasta's, fresh bread, and fish. Well beyond a hundred people came and there was fear of running out of food, and Torsi kept on sending his staff running for more. Somehow, not only was there enough food for everyone, there were leftovers that we gave to people to take with them.

The day was amazing. Everyone came and I just walked around witnessing so much love. I could see Gretchen and Macy sitting at a table with these young moms and their kids. Grouchy Jeff was sitting with Amy Hartley and some homeless men and even he was smiling easily. Don and Mary Lou were sitting with some young teenagers and Don was showing them a hand held gadget he had no doubt invented and the kids were wide eyed and amazed. Mary Lou was smiling as well. They looked nothing like the billionaires they were and appeared right at home in Oppenheimer Park chatting with teenagers. They had all the time in the world.

Torsi had an apron on and was serving people lined up for the fish. I had never seen him radiate such joy and later he would tell me that he had completely forgotten the joy he had serving people his own food himself. He told me how refreshing it was to serve the food he loved more so than running his restaurant empire. Minnie was right there with him serving up food on the line or taking plates to people who needed assistance. I saw my mom sitting with Mrs. Byrnes and another older street lady all huddled close and I imagined they were probably reminiscing about Scotland.

The local businesses surrounding the park also embraced the idea and pitched in however they could. One Afghan corner store owner actually sought me out and told me he had embraced Christ as his Savior and had gotten rid of the pornographic magazines he used to sell in his store. "After you moved in, I just couldn't do that anymore," he said. And with that I got my first glimpse at what could become an entire park radiating Jesus and decided right there and then that we would do communal meals in the park once a month, rain or shine, winter or summer.

Marina and I just walked about, saying hello to people, welcoming people who were watching from the fringes and chatting with friends. At one point I was by myself watching it all from one of the corners of the park. I just wanted to get the full scope of what was going on. Scanning across the sea of people I could see every type of person: the rich, the poor, the sick, the godly, the young, the old, the strong, the weak, the smart, the diminished, the bold, the meek. If I looked into it all, I could see the richness of West Van and the poverty of Hastings and for a moment, I got it. I could "see" as Christ saw, that this disparity of classes had blended here in this park to one end: a group of people who were compassionate towards one another, who were willing to help one another, a group of people who were all members of one body, all created to be like God in true righteousness and holiness. It was here, in Oppenheimer Park where West met East and came together. And it was a glimpse as to how an Oppenheimer Park might look once a transformation was complete and it was one of the best days ever.

As we approached the six month mark, things seemed well established. Between the corporations that had committed to fund us, the donations we received, and the churches that tithed to us, we had no problems in being self supporting. If these early days were an indication of things to come, I would not have to put more money out of my own pocket. In fact, I was able to pay down the mortgage and loans easily from the income Street Hope brought in. I had found a way to strike a balance between work, Street Hope, and personal life with Marina. I didn't work as much but Jennings & Wyatt was still a viable and thriving real estate office and even in market downturns, we did well. I gave a lot, but got back a lot, and with Marina working her job as well, we were able to have a very comfortable existence.

Street Hope was able to think about budgets and spending and were already thinking of putting Gretchen on the payroll at least part time. God had given me a vision of restoration of the east side of Vancouver, which still seemed broad and unrealistic, but any doubts I once had, had been replaced by faith from what I had seen so far. As for our little corner of Oppenheimer Park, we were off to a very good start.

Chapter 58

I had been asked to speak at a Christian conference. I think I was "set up" by the Adams who were always on me about sharing my testimony and I was pretty nervous about speaking in front of a few hundred people. I had shared my story many times, sometimes in pieces, sometimes only parts of it, but always as I felt prompted by God. I had never been asked to share it in its entirety in front of a group. It was at one of the massive congregation churches in Abbotsford, some fifty kilometers east of Vancouver. The Adams came with me as did Marina, Don, and Mary Lou. We had all become very tight as friends and I felt I needed their support for this one. Mary Lou was showing a nice little baby bump at five months pregnant and Don would hardly ever leave her side.

I got called up on the stage and went into my story. I knew there was a drug and alcohol treatment center in the crowd so for their sake didn't hold back on the severity of my addiction. And I told them the story from start to finish. I told them as I would recite facts, and I told them with as much brutal honesty as I could muster. I went through the entire story, from the depth of my addiction leading to the crack shack shooting, climbing the mountain, finding the plane, God's speaking to me on the last night, the journey back to the city, the battle for sobriety, the twelve year journey to purchase the skid row hotel and transform it into Street Hope, and concluded with a summary of where we currently stood towards a complete city transformation and the fruition of God's plan.

And then I stopped and thought about things for a minute. It was silent in the auditorium, but I had gotten over my nerves about five minutes in, and truth be told, I could barely see anyone with how they had the lights set up anyway. So from my perspective, I was just staring into an abyss of lights and darkness.

I cleared my throat and continued. "I want to make clear a few things that I feel strongly about. While God planted the vision in me and saved my life and paved the way for an incredible series of events, none of it was easy. I had times when I doubted my faith. I found myself in times of personal turmoil where I felt like I never understood anything. I thought I was going to die a lonely and pathetic death both in that hotel and on the side of the mountain. I was alone and afraid. Getting clean was the hardest thing I have ever done in my life. It wasn't a process of days or weeks or months. The struggle was hourly and took a few years to completely undo the damage and the fixation. My emotional and spiritual wellbeing was damaged immeasurably. I didn't always know what to do. I never got any blow by blow instructions beyond the Bible, and there were times reading the Bible was hard and I couldn't muster up the energy or enthusiasm.

"But there was always hope, even if at times it felt faint. Something had been ingrained in me, within me, and that was the light of Jesus. And that kept me seeking. That kept me grateful and that kept me wanting to experience love and intimacy, kept me wanting to live, to survive, to be whole, to be complete, to be a part of the Truth. So I kept going. One day at a time. And along the way God gave me one thing at a time to look after. He never gave me more than I could handle and step by step, year by year, He promoted me to new things.

"For me, God gave me a calling. He gave all of us callings. But it was that one line out of Ephesians 4 that I saw, which was the first line I ever read in the Bible that meant more to me than anything else. Ever. And then, on my last night on the mountain he gave me the vision of Oppenheimer Park, Hastings Street, and the entire east side of Vancouver. And I always thought that was my calling: that I would one day, as unlikely as it seemed, and as much as I doubted it, that I would one day fulfill this calling. And in many respects, that's exactly what happened.

"But I was wrong. My calling wasn't to own the hotel I once jumped out of. My calling wasn't to move Street Hope into it and morph it into the way it is today. My calling wasn't to transform the entire Lower East side of the entire city." I paused.

"No. I was being 'called' to Jesus. I was called to put down my self-serving indulgences, called to change my life, called to stop harming people, called to stop the wake of destruction that was me, called to become a contributor instead of a taker, called to become a son and later a husband, called to be a member of a body, called to be a son of God, called to the family of Christ who suffered for us. I was called by Jesus. I was called home.

"And why I had to suffer so much for so long, why I had to become as self-absorbed as I did, why I had to nearly die and have to climb a mountain and live on top of the mountain before I would listen is anyone's guess. I don't care why. I just care that eventually, I did listen. And that He called for me despite all the things I had done.

"And because I listened, and because I believed in God, He spoke to me. And He gave me a vision. And the vision He gave to me was a testament as to what is possible when walking in His glory. He called me to equip me for acts of service and then showed me what would be possible if I was obedient.

"And that started as soon as I came down the mountain, because when I came down off that mountain, I no longer stole. I no longer lied. I no longer operated with cunning and deceitful scheming and my heart was no longer hard. And I looked to do for others. I washed dishes to the glory of God. I served my job, I served my parents, and I served the people I lived with. I attempted to speak the truth in love and I was compassionate. Was I perfect? Hardly. But I never forgot that I was serving God.

"Oppenheimer Park, Street Hope, and anything that happens down road? Well, all of that is just a testimony as to how great God can be if we walk in our callings. All of that was God's vision as to what is possible through Jesus. And what I learned is ALL things are possible through Jesus."

Chapter 59

"I think you just paved the way for a new career as a circuit speaker," Mary Lou said once back in the van and on the highway. "Wow that was something. Makes me want to start going to church."

"That was the idea, Mary Lou" I said. "That was all to get you to come to church with us," and I smiled.

"So let me get this straight," Jeff said. "I let a former drug addict who lived on a mountain, sell me a million dollar home?" and he laughed his head off. "Man oh man, what a story! There was so much of that I didn't know. Unbelievable."

"I would do it all over again there groucho if I could hear you laugh like that again," I said. And we all laughed, even Jeff.

We all drove back into the city together. Everyone was raving at my story and how I delivered it, but I was having trouble in even remembering what I said. I didn't think I wanted to do that again anytime soon. We had been picked up at Street Hope and driven out in the Adams' minivan. It was approaching late afternoon and Marina suggested we all have dinner at *The Trattoria*, but that we should meet there in a half hour or so. So we got dropped off to collect our own vehicle and when we were alone Marina said, "Hey, it looks like sunset is about to happen. Let's go upstairs to the roof for a few minutes."

So we climbed up the stairs to the rooftop garden and stretched out in the chairs. It really was a spectacular night, not yet cooled down to any level of discomfort. Now that I had come down from the nerves and adrenaline from public speaking I was feeling tired. I looked over at Marina and for the first time noticed that something was not right with her. She was, I don't know, like glowing or something.

"Sam," she said, "Your heavenly Father has been very good to you, hasn't He? And your dad, well he was a good man too, right?"

I said yes, but I really wasn't sure what this was all about.

"Sam.......do you think you would make a good earthly father........do you want to be a dad?"

And I looked at her. It wasn't a question. She was radiating joy. She was radiating life.

"You're........you're........you're," was all I could say.

"Yes, Sam. Our God is good. We're going to have a baby."

And I felt a rush of joy. It was all I could do to hug her tightly. And we hugged and she cried tears of joy for a long time then I turned her just a little so I could see the mountain, and I looked up to the highest peak of Crown Mountain and I mouthed the words:

Thank you.

CPSIA information can be obtained at www.ICGtesting.com
Printed in the USA
LVOW06s2045290914

406416LV00007B/19/P

9 781498 412520